Dover Thrift Study Edition

The Merchant of Venice

WILLIAM SHAKESPEARE

DOVER PUBLICATIONS, INC.
Mineola, New York

Copyright

Copyright © 2010 by Dover Publications, Inc.
Pages 89–147 copyright © 1996 by Research & Education Association, Inc.
All rights reserved.

Bibliographical Note

This Dover edition, first published in 2010, contains the unabridged text of *The Merchant of Venice,* as published in Volume II of *The Caxton Edition of the Complete Works of William Shakespeare,* Caxton Publishing Company, London, n.d., plus literary analysis and perspectives from *MAXnotes® for The Merchant of Venice,* published in 1996 by Research and Education Association, Inc., Piscataway, New Jersey. The explanatory footnotes to the play were prepared specially for the present edition.

Library of Congress Cataloging-in-Publication Data

Shakespeare, William, 1564–1616.
   The Merchant of Venice / William Shakespeare.
      p. cm. — (Dover thrift study edition)
   "This Dover edition, first published in 2010, contains the unabridged text of The Merchant of Venice, as published in Volume II of The Caxton Edition of the Complete Works of William Shakespeare, Caxton Publishing Company, London, n.d., plus literary analysis and perspectives from MAXnotes® for The Merchant of Venice, published in 1996 by Research and Education Association, Inc., Piscataway, New Jersey."
   Includes bibliographical references.
   ISBN-13: 978-0-486-47578-3
   ISBN-10: 0-486-47578-6
   1. Shylock (Fictitious character)—Drama. 2. Jews—Italy—Drama. 3. Moneylenders—Drama. 4. Venice (Italy)—Drama. 5. Shakespeare, William, 1564–1616. Merchant of Venice—Examinations—Study guides. I. Title.

PR2825.A1 2010
822.3'3—dc22

2009052493

Manufactured in the United States by Courier Corporation
47578601
www.doverpublications.com

Publisher's Note

Combining the complete text of a classic novel or drama with a comprehensive study guide, Dover Thrift Study Editions are the most effective way to gain a thorough understanding of the major works of world literature.

The study guide features up-to-date and expert analysis of every chapter or section from the source work. Questions and fully explained answers follow, allowing readers to analyze the material critically. Character lists, author bios, and discussions of the work's historical context are also provided.

Each Dover Thrift Study Edition includes everything a student needs to prepare for homework, discussions, reports, and exams.

Contents

The Merchant
of Venice

WILLIAM SHAKESPEARE

Contents

DRAMATIS PERSONÆ

THE DUKE OF VENICE.
THE PRINCE OF MOROCCO,} suitors to Portia.
THE PRINCE OF ARRAGON, }
ANTONIO, a merchant of Venice.
BASSANIO, his friend, suitor likewise to Portia.
SALANIO, }
SALARINO, } friends to Antonio and Bassanio.
GRATIANO, }
SALERIO, }
LORENZO, in love with Jessica.
SHYLOCK, a rich Jew.
TUBAL, a Jew, his friend.
LAUNCELOT GOBBO, the clown, servant to Shylock.
OLD GOBBO, father to Launcelot.
LEONARDO, servant to Bassanio.
BALTHASAR, } servants to Portia.
STEPHANO, }
PORTIA, a rich heiress.
NERISSA, her waiting-maid.
JESSICA, daughter to Shylock.

Magnificoes of Venice, Officers of the Court of Justice, Gaoler,
Servants to Portia, and other Attendants.

SCENE —*Partly at Venice, and partly at Belmont, the seat of Portia,
on the Continent*

ix

ACT I.

SCENE I. *Venice. A Street.*

Enter ANTONIO, SALARINO, *and* SALANIO

ANT.   In sooth, I know not why I am so sad:
    It wearies me; you say it wearies you;
    But how I caught it, found it, or came by it,
    What stuff 't is made of, whereof it is born,
    I am to learn;
    And such a want-wit sadness makes of me,
    That I have much ado to know myself.
SALAR.   Your mind is tossing on the ocean;
    There, where your argosies with portly sail,
    Like signiors and rich burghers on the flood,
    Or, as it were, the pageants[1] of the sea,
    Do overpeer the petty traffickers,
    That curt'sy to them, do them reverence,
    As they fly by them with their woven wings.
SALAN.   Believe me, sir, had I such venture forth,
    The better part of my affections would
    Be with my hopes abroad. I should be still
    Plucking the grass, to know where sits the wind;
    Peering in maps for ports, and piers, and roads;
    And every object, that might make me fear

---

1. *pageants*] An allusion to the huge, towering machines in the shape of castles, dragons, giants, and the like, which formed part of ancient shows, and were drawn on ceremonial occasions through the streets.

          Misfortune to my ventures, out of doubt
          Would make me sad.
SALAR.   My wind, cooling my broth,
          Would blow me to an ague, when I thought
          What harm a wind too great at sea might do.
          I should not see the sandy hour-glass run,
          But I should think of shallows and of flats,
          And see my wealthy Andrew[2] dock'd in sand
          Vailing her high top lower than her ribs
          To kiss her burial.[3] Should I go to church
          And see the holy edifice of stone,
          And not bethink me straight of dangerous rocks,
          Which touching but my gentle vessel's side
          Would scatter all her spices on the stream,
          Enrobe the roaring waters with my silks;
          And, in a word, but even now worth this,
          And now worth nothing? Shall I have the thought
          To think on this; and shall I lack the thought,
          That such a thing bechanced would make me sad?
          But tell not me; I know, Antonio
          Is sad to think upon his merchandise.
ANT.   Believe me, no: I thank my fortune for it,
          My ventures are not in one bottom trusted,
          Nor to one place; nor is my whole estate
          Upon the fortune of this present year:
          Therefore my merchandise makes me not sad.
SALAR.   Why, then you are in love.
ANT.   Fie, fie!
SALAR.   Not in love neither? Then let us say you are sad,
          Because you are not merry: and 't were as easy
          For you to laugh, and leap, and say you are merry,
          Because you are not sad. Now, by two-headed Janus,[4]
          Nature hath framed strange fellows in her time:
          Some that will evermore peep through their eyes,

------

2. *Andrew*] the name of a ship.
3. *kiss her burial*] touch her burial place, sink.
4. *two-headed Janus*] The Roman god Janus was often depicted with two faces.

And laugh like parrots at a bag-piper;
And other of such vinegar aspect,
That they 'll not show their teeth in way of smile,
Though Nestor[5] swear the jest be laughable.

Enter BASSANIO, LORENZO, *and* GRATIANO

SALAN.   Here comes Bassanio, your most noble kinsman,
Gratiano, and Lorenzo. Fare ye well:
We leave you now with better company.
SALAR.   I would have stay'd till I had made you merry,
If worthier friends had not prevented me.
ANT.   Your worth is very dear in my regard.
I take it, your own business calls on you,
And you embrace the occasion to depart.
SALAR.   Good morrow, my good lords.
BASS.   Good signiors both, when shall we laugh? say, when?
You grow exceeding strange: must it be so?
SALAR.   We 'll make our leisures to attend on yours.
                           [*Exeunt* SALARINO *and* SALANIO.]
LOR.   My Lord Bassanio, since you have found Antonio,
We two will leave you: but, at dinner-time,
I pray you, have in mind where we must meet.
BASS.   I will not fail you.
GRA.   You look not well, Signior Antonio;
You have too much respect upon the world:[6]
They lose it that do buy it with much care:
Believe me, you are marvellously changed.
ANT.   I hold the world but as the world, Gratiano;
A stage, where every man must play a part,
And mine a sad one.
GRA.   Let me play the fool:
With mirth and laughter let old wrinkles come;
And let my liver rather heat with wine
Than my heart cool with mortifying groans.

---

5. *Nestor*] a king of Pylos who served in his old age as a counselor to the Greeks at Troy.
6. *respect upon the world*] worldly care, anxiety.

Why should a man, whose blood is warm within,
Sit like his grandsire cut in alabaster?
Sleep when he wakes, and creep into the jaundice
By being peevish? I tell thee what, Antonio —
I love thee, and it is my love that speaks, —
There are a sort of men, whose visages
Do cream and mantle like a standing pond;[7]
And do a wilful stillness entertain,
With purpose to be dress'd in an opinion
Of wisdom, gravity, profound conceit;
As who should say, "I am Sir Oracle,
And, when I ope my lips, let no dog bark!"
O my Antonio, I do know of these,
That therefore only are reputed wise
For saying nothing; when, I am very sure,
If they should speak, would almost damn those ears,
Which, hearing them, would call their brothers fools.
I 'll tell thee more of this another time:
But fish not, with this melancholy bait,
For this fool gudgeon,[8] this opinion.
Come, good Lorenzo. Fare ye well awhile:
I 'll end my exhortation after dinner.

LOR.   Well, we will leave you, then, till dinner-time:
I must be one of these same dumb wise men,
For Gratiano never lets me speak.

GRA.   Well, keep me company but two years moe,
Thou shalt not know the sound of thine own tongue.

ANT.   Farewell: I 'll grow a talker for this gear.[9]

GRA.   Thanks, i' faith; for silence is only commendable
In a neat's tongue[10] dried, and a maid not vendible.
                    [*Exeunt* GRATIANO *and* LORENZO.]

ANT.   Is that any thing now?

---

7. *Do cream . . . pond*] Acquire the cream-like mantle or coating that gathers on a
   stagnant pool.
8. *gudgeon*] a small fish that is easily caught; here, a person easily duped.
9. *gear*] stuff, business.
10. *neat's tongue*] "neat" refers to horned cattle; beef tongue.

BASS.   Gratiano speaks an infinite deal of nothing, more than any man
in all Venice. His reasons are as two grains of wheat hid in two
bushels of chaff: you shall seek all day ere you find them: and when
you have them, they are not worth the search.

ANT.   Well, tell me now, what lady is the same
To whom you swore a secret pilgrimage,
That you to-day promised to tell me of?

BASS.   'T is not unknown to you, Antonio,
How much I have disabled mine estate,
By something showing a more swelling port
Than my faint means would grant continuance:
Nor do I now make moan to be abridged
From such a noble rate; but my chief care
Is, to come fairly off from the great debts,
Wherein my time, something too prodigal,
Hath left me gaged. To you, Antonio,
I owe the most, in money and in love;
And from your love I have a warranty
To unburthen all my plots and purposes
How to get clear of all the debts I owe.

ANT.   I pray you, good Bassanio, let me know it;
And if it stand, as you yourself still do,
Within the eye of honour, be assured,
My purse, my person, my extremest means,
Lie all unlock'd to your occasions.

BASS.   In my school-days, when I had lost one shaft,
I shot his fellow of the self-same flight
The self-same way with more advised watch,
To find the other forth; and by adventuring both,
I oft found both: I urge this childhood proof,
Because what follows is pure innocence.
I owe you much; and, like a wilful youth,
That which I owe is lost: but if you please
To shoot another arrow that self way
Which you did shoot the first, I do not doubt,
As I will watch the aim, or to find both,
Or bring your latter hazard back again,

And thankfully rest debtor for the first.

ANT.   You know me well; and herein spend but time
  To wind about my love with circumstance;
  And out of doubt you do me now more wrong
  In making question of my uttermost,
  Than if you had made waste of all I have:
  Then do but say to me what I should do,
  That in your knowledge may by me be done,
  And I am prest[11] unto it: therefore, speak.

BASS.   In Belmont is a lady richly left;
  And she is fair, and, fairer than that word,
  Of wondrous virtues: sometimes from her eyes
  I did receive fair speechless messages:
  Her name is Portia; nothing undervalued
  To Cato's daughter, Brutus' Portia:
  Nor is the wide world ignorant of her worth;
  For the four winds blow in from every coast
  Renowned suitors: and her sunny locks
  Hang on her temples like a golden fleece;
  Which makes her seat of Belmont Colchos' strond,[12]
  And many Jasons come in quest of her.
  O my Antonio, had I but the means
  To hold a rival place with one of them,
  I have a mind presages me such thrift,[13]
  That I should questionless be fortunate!

ANT.   Thou know'st that all my fortunes are at sea;
  Neither have I money, nor commodity
  To raise a present sum: therefore go forth;
  Try what my credit can in Venice do:
  That shall be rack'd, even to the uttermost,
  To furnish thee to Belmont, to fair Portia.
  Go, presently inquire, and so will I,

---

11. *prest*] ready, from the French, *prêt*.
12. *Colchos' strond*] Colchis was the country of the golden fleece; strond is "strand," or beach, shore.
13. *such thrift*] such thriving, good success.

Where money is; and I no question make,
To have it of my trust, or for my sake.   [*Exeunt.*]

SCENE II. *Belmont. A room in* PORTIA'S *house.*

Enter PORTIA *and* NERISSA

POR.   By my troth, Nerissa, my little body is aweary of this great world.

NER.   You would be, sweet madam, if your miseries were in the same
abundance as your good fortunes are: and yet, for aught I see, they
are as sick that surfeit with too much, as they that starve with
nothing. It is no mean happiness, therefore, to be seated in the
mean: superfluity comes sooner by white hairs; but competency
lives longer.

POR.   Good sentences,[1] and well pronounced.

NER.   They would be better, if well followed.

POR.   If to do were as easy as to know what were good to do, chapels
had been churches, and poor men's cottages princes' palaces. It is a
good divine that follows his own instructions: I can easier teach
twenty what were good to be done, than be one of the twenty to
follow mine own teaching. The brain may devise laws for the
blood; but a hot temper leaps o'er a cold decree: such a hare is
madness the youth, to skip o'er the meshes of good counsel the
cripple. But this reasoning is not in the fashion to choose me a
husband. O me, the word "choose"! I may neither choose whom I
would, nor refuse whom I dislike; so is the will of a living daughter
curbed by the will of a dead father. Is it not hard, Nerissa, that I
cannot choose one, nor refuse none?

NER.   Your father was ever virtuous; and holy men, at their death, have
good inspirations: therefore, the lottery, that he hath devised in

---

1. *sentences*] maxims.

these three chests of gold, silver, and lead, — whereof who chooses his meaning chooses you, — will, no doubt, never be chosen by any rightly, but one who shall rightly love. But what warmth is there in your affection towards any of these princely suitors that are already come?

POR.   I pray thee, over-name them; and as thou namest them, I will describe them; and, according to my description, level at[2] my affection.

NER.   First, there is the Neapolitan prince.

POR.   Ay, that's a colt indeed, for he doth nothing but talk of his horse; and he makes it a great appropriation to his own good parts, that he can shoe him himself. I am much afeard my lady his mother played false with a smith.

NER.   Then there is the County Palatine.

POR.   He doth nothing but frown; as who should say, "if you will not have me, choose:" he hears merry tales, and smiles not: I fear he will prove the weeping philosopher[3] when he grows old, being so full of unmannerly sadness in his youth. I had rather be married to a death's-head with a bone in his mouth than to either of these. God defend me from these two!

NER.   How say you by the French lord, Monsieur Le Bon?

POR.   God made him, and therefore let him pass for a man. In truth, I know it is a sin to be a mocker: but, he! — why, he hath a horse better than the Neapolitan's; a better bad habit of frowning than the Count Palatine: he is every man in no man; if a throstle sing, he falls straight a capering: he will fence with his own shadow: if I should marry him, I should marry twenty husbands. If he would despise me, I would forgive him; for if he love me to madness, I shall never requite him.

NER.   What say you, then, to Falconbridge, the young baron of England?

POR.   You know I say nothing to him; for he understands not me, nor I him: he hath neither Latin, French, nor Italian; and you will come

---

2. *level at*] aim at, guess at.

3. *weeping philosopher*] An allusion to the Greek philosopher, Heraclitus, who is usually contrasted with Democritus, "the laughing philosopher."

into the court and swear that I have a poor pennyworth in the
English. He is a proper man's picture; but, alas, who can converse
with a dumb-show? How oddly he is suited! I think he bought his
doublet in Italy, his round hose in France, his bonnet in Germany,
and his behaviour every where.

NER.   What think you of the Scottish lord, his neighbour?

POR.   That he hath a neighbourly charity in him; for he borrowed a
box of the ear of the Englishman, and swore he would pay him
again when he was able: I think the Frenchman became his surety,
and sealed under[4] for another.

NER.   How like you the young German, the Duke of Saxony's
nephew?

POR.   Very vilely in the morning, when he is sober; and most vilely in
the afternoon, when he is drunk· when he is best, he is a little worse
than a man; and when he is worst, he is little better than a beast: an
the worst fall that ever fell, I hope I shall make shift to go without
him.

NER.   If he should offer to choose, and choose the right casket, you
should refuse to perform your father's will, if you should refuse to
accept him.

POR.   Therefore, for fear of the worst, I pray thee, set a deep glass of
Rhenish wine on the contrary casket; for, if the devil be within and
that temptation without, I know he will choose it. I will do any
thing, Nerissa, ere I'll be married to a sponge.

NER.   You need not fear, lady, the having any of these lords: they have
acquainted me with their determinations; which is, indeed, to
return to their home, and to trouble you with no more suit, unless
you may be won by some other sort than your father's imposition,
depending on the caskets.

POR.   If I live to be as old as Sibylla,[5] I will die as chaste as Diana,
unless I be obtained by the manner of my father's will. I am glad
this parcel of wooers are so reasonable; for there is not one among

---

4. *sealed under*] A legal expression implying that the bond or surety was entered into
vicariously, in behalf of some other person who was responsible.

5. *Sibylla*] An obvious reference to the story of Sibylla, the Cumæan Sibyl, in Ovid's
Metamorphoses, XIV, where Apollo promises her as many years of life as the grains of
sand she holds in her hand.

them but I dote on his very absence; and I pray God grant them a
fair departure.

NER.   Do you not remember, lady, in your father's time, a Venetian, a
scholar, and a soldier, that came hither in company of the Marquis
of Montferrat?

POR.   Yes, yes, it was Bassanio; as I think he was so called.

NER.   True, madam: he, of all the men that ever my foolish eyes looked
upon, was the best deserving a fair lady.

POR.   I remember him well; and I remember him worthy of thy praise.

Enter a Serving-man

How now! what news?

SERV.   The four strangers[6] seek for you, madam, to take their leave:
and there is a forerunner come from a fifth, the Prince of Morocco;
who brings word, the prince his master will be here to-night.

POR.   If I could bid the fifth welcome with so good a heart as I can bid
the other four farewell, I should be glad of his approach: if he have
the condition of a saint and the complexion of a devil, I had rather
he should shrive me than wive me.
Come, Nerissa. Sirrah, go before.
Whiles we shut the gates upon one wooer, another knocks at the
door.   [*Exeunt.*]

SCENE III. *Venice. A public place.*

Enter BASSANIO *and* SHYLOCK

SHY.   Three thousand ducats;[1] well.

---

6. *The four strangers*] Portia has already described the suitors who are about to take leave of
her as six in number. "*Four*," which is repeated a few lines later, is either a misprint for
six, or this passage may present an unrevised relic of a first draft of the play.

1. *Three thousand ducats*] "Ducat" was the name of a Venetian coin cast both in gold and
silver. The gold ducat was worth about ten shillings, and the silver ducat under five

BASS. Ay, sir, for three months.

SHY. For three months; well.

BASS. For the which, as I told you, Antonio shall be bound.

SHY. Antonio shall become bound; well.

BASS. May you stead me? will you pleasure me? shall I know your answer?

SHY. Three thousand ducats for three months, and Antonio bound.

BASS. Your answer to that.

SHY. Antonio is a good man.

BASS. Have you heard any imputation to the contrary?

SHY. Ho, no, no, no, no: my meaning, in saying he is a good man, is to have you understand me, that he is sufficient. Yet his means are in supposition: he hath an argosy bound to Tripolis, another to the Indies; I understand, moreover, upon the Rialto,[2] he hath a third at Mexico, a fourth for England, and other ventures he hath, squandered abroad. But ships are but boards, sailors but men: there be land-rats and water-rats, water-thieves and land-thieves, I mean pirates; and then there is the peril of waters, winds, and rocks. The man is, notwithstanding, sufficient. Three thousand ducats; I think I may take his bond.

BASS. Be assured you may.

SHY. I will be assured I may; and, that I may be assured, I will bethink me. May I speak with Antonio?

BASS. If it please you to dine with us.

SHY. Yes, to smell pork; to eat of the habitation which your prophet the Nazarite conjured the devil into. I will buy with you, sell with you, talk with you, walk with you, and so following; but I will not eat with you, drink with you, nor pray with you. What news on the Rialto? Who is he comes here?

Enter ANTONIO

BASS. This is Signior Antonio.

---

shillings. Like other Elizabethan writers, Shakespeare seems to use the term here to mean a coin of great worth without attaching to it a very precise value.

2. *Rialto*] The Venetian financial district, similar to the London Exchange. The famous bridge at Venice, called after the Exchange, Ponte di Rialto, was not built until 1591.

SHY.   [*Aside*] How like a fawning publican he looks!
        I hate him for he is a Christian;
        But more for that in low simplicity
        He lends out money gratis and brings down
        The rate of usance[3] here with us in Venice.
        If I can catch him once upon the hip,
        I will feed fat the ancient grudge I bear him.
        He hates our sacred nation; and he rails,
        Even there where merchants most do congregate,
        On me, my bargains, and my well-won thrift,
        Which he calls interest. Cursed be my tribe,
        If I forgive him!

BASS.   Shylock, do you hear?

SHY.   I am debating of my present store;
        And, by the near guess of my memory,
        I cannot instantly raise up the gross
        Of full three thousand ducats. What of that?
        Tubal, a wealthy Hebrew of my tribe,
        Will furnish me. But soft! how many months
        Do you desire? [*To Ant.*] Rest you fair, good signior;
        Your worship was the last man in our mouths.

ANT.   Shylock, although I neither lend nor borrow,
        By taking nor by giving of excess,[4]
        Yet, to supply the ripe wants of my friend,
        I 'll break a custom. Is he yet possess'd
        How much ye would?

SHY.   Ay, ay, three thousand ducats.

ANT.   And for three months.

SHY.   I had forgot; three months, you told me so.
        Well then, your bond; and let me see; but hear you;
        Methought you said you neither lend nor borrow
        Upon advantage.

ANT.   I do never use it.

---

3. *usance*] interest paid on money lent.
4. *excess*] interest.

SHY.   When Jacob grazed his uncle Laban's sheep, — [5]
　　This Jacob from our holy Abram was,
　　As his wise mother wrought in his behalf,
　　The third possessor; ay, he was the third, —
ANT.   And what of him? did he take interest?
SHY.   No, not take interest; not, as you would say,
　　Directly interest: mark what Jacob did.
　　When Laban and himself were compromised
　　That all the eanlings[6] which were streak'd and pied
　　Should fall as Jacob's hire, the ewes, being rank,
　　In the end of Autumn turned to the rams;
　　And when the work of generation was
　　Between these woolly breeders in the act,
　　The skilful shepherd peel'd me certain wands,
　　And, in the doing of the deed of kind,
　　He stuck them up before the fulsome ewes,
　　Who, then conceiving, did in eanling time
　　Fall parti-colour'd lambs, and those were Jacob's.
　　This was a way to thrive, and he was blest:
　　And thrift is blessing, if men steal it not.
ANT.   This was a venture, sir, that Jacob served for;
　　A thing not in his power to bring to pass,
　　But sway'd and fashion'd by the hand of heaven.
　　Was this inserted to make interest good?
　　Or is your gold and silver ewes and rams?
SHY.   I cannot tell; I make it breed as fast:
　　But note me, signior.
ANT.　　　　　　　　　Mark you this, Bassanio,
　　The devil can cite Scripture for his purpose.
　　An evil soul, producing holy witness,
　　Is like a villain with a smiling cheek;
　　A goodly apple rotten at the heart:
　　O, what a goodly outside falsehood hath!

―――――――――

5. *When Jacob grazed . . . steal it not.*] Shakespeare here paraphrases and interprets the passage from *Genesis* 30:37 and following.
6. *eanlings*] newborn lambs.

SHY.   Three thousand ducats; 't is a good round sum.
     Three months from twelve; then, let me see; the rate —
ANT.   Well, Shylock, shall we be beholding to you?
SHY.   Signior Antonio, many a time and oft
     In the Rialto you have rated me
     About my moneys and my usances:
     Still have I borne it with a patient shrug;
     For sufferance is the badge of all our tribe.
     You call me misbeliever, cut-throat dog,
     And spit upon my Jewish gaberdine,
     And all for use of that which is mine own.
     Well then, it now appears you need my help:
     Go to, then; you come to me, and you say
     "Shylock, we would have moneys:" you say so;
     You, that did void your rheum upon my beard,
     And foot me as you spurn a stranger cur
     Over your threshold: moneys is your suit.
     What should I say to you? Should I not say
     "Hath a dog money? is it possible
     A cur can lend three thousand ducats?" or
     Shall I bend low and in a bondman's key,
     With bated breath and whispering humbleness,
     Say this, —
     "Fair sir, you spit on me on Wednesday last;
     You spurn'd me such a day; another time
     You call'd me dog; and for these courtesies
     I 'll lend you thus much moneys"?
ANT.   I am as like to call thee so again,
     To spit on thee again, to spurn thee too.
     If thou wilt lend this money, lend it not
     As to thy friends; for when did friendship take
     A breed[7] for barren metal of his friend?
     But lend it rather to thine enemy;
     Who if he break, thou mayst with better face
     Exact the penalty.

---

7. *breed*] offspring; used figuratively here for interest.

SHY.　　　　　　　　Why, look you, how you storm!
　　I would be friends with you, and have your love,
　　Forget the shames that you have stain'd me with,
　　Supply your present wants, and take no doit[8]
　　Of usance for my moneys, and you 'll not hear me:
　　This is kind I offer.
BASS.　　This were kindness.
SHY.　　　　　　　　This kindness will I show.
　　Go with me to a notary, seal me there
　　Your single bond;[9] and, in a merry sport,
　　If you repay me not on such a day,
　　In such a place, such sum or sums as are
　　Express'd in the condition, let the forfeit
　　Be nominated for an equal pound
　　Of your fair flesh, to be cut off and taken
　　In what part of your body pleaseth me.
ANT.　　Content, i' faith: I 'll seal to such a bond,
　　And say there is much kindness in the Jew.
BASS.　　You shall not seal to such a bond for me:
　　I 'll rather dwell in my necessity.
ANT.　　Why, fear not, man; I will not forfeit it:
　　Within these two months, that 's a month before
　　This bond expires, I do expect return
　　Of thrice three times the value of this bond.
SHY.　　O father Abram, what these Christians are,
　　Whose own hard dealings teaches them suspect
　　The thoughts of others! Pray you, tell me this;
　　If he should break his day, what should I gain
　　By the exaction of the forfeiture?
　　A pound of man's flesh taken from a man
　　Is not so estimable, profitable neither,
　　As flesh of muttons, beefs, or goats. I say,
　　To buy his favour, I extend this friendship:

---

8. *doit*] the smallest piece of money, a trifle.
9. *single bond*] a bond involving one person exclusively; an engagement, responsibility for which cannot be devolved on another.

  If he will take it, so; if not, adieu;
  And, for my love, I pray you wrong me not.
ANT. Yes, Shylock, I will seal unto this bond.
SHY. Then meet me forthwith at the notary's;
  Give him direction for this merry bond;
  And I will go and purse the ducats straight;
  See to my house, left in the fearful guard
  Of an unthrifty knave; and presently
  I will be with you.
ANT.   Hie thee, gentle Jew.   [*Exit* SHYLOCK.]
  The Hebrew will turn Christian: he grows kind.
BASS. I like not fair terms and a villain's mind.
ANT. Come on: in this there can be no dismay;
  My ships come home a month before the day.   [*Exeunt.*]

ACT II.

SCENE I. *Belmont. A room in* PORTIA'S *house.*

Flourish of Cornets. Enter the PRINCE OF MOROCCO *and his train;*
PORTIA, NERISSA, *and others attending*

MOR.   Mislike me not for my complexion,
    The shadow'd livery of the burnish'd sun,
    To whom I am a neighbour and near bred.
    Bring me the fairest creature northward born,
    Where Phœbus' fire scarce thaws the icicles,
    And let us make incision for your love,
    To prove whose blood is reddest, his or mine.
    I tell thee, lady, this aspect of mine
    Hath fear'd the valiant: by my love, I swear
    The best-regarded virgins of our clime
    Have loved it too: I would not change this hue,
    Except to steal your thoughts, my gentle queen.
POR.   In terms of choice I am not solely led
    By nice direction of a maiden's eyes;
    Besides, the lottery of my destiny
    Bars me the right of voluntary choosing:
    But if my father had not scanted me
    And hedged me by his wit, to yield myself
    His wife who wins me by that means I told you,
    Yourself, renowned prince, then stood as fair
    As any comer I have look'd on yet
    For my affection.

17

MOR.   Even for that I thank you:
    Therefore, I pray you, lead me to the caskets,
    To try my fortune. By this scimitar
    That slew the Sophy and a Persian prince
    That won three fields of Sultan Solyman,[1]
    I would outstare the sternest eyes that look,
    Outbrave the heart most daring on the earth,
    Pluck the young sucking cubs from the she-bear,
    Yea, mock the lion when he roars for prey,
    To win thee, lady. But, alas the while!
    If Hercules and Lichas[2] play at dice
    Which is the better man, the greater throw
    May turn by fortune from the weaker hand
    So is Alcides[3] beaten by his page;
    And so may I, blind fortune leading me,
    Miss that which one unworthier may attain,
    And die with grieving.
POR.   You must take your chance;
    And either not attempt to choose at all,
    Or swear before you choose, if you choose wrong,
    Never speak to lady afterward
    In way of marriage: therefore be advised.
MOR.   Nor will not. Come, bring me unto my chance.
POR.   First, forward to the temple: after dinner
    Your hazard shall be made.
MOR.   Good fortune then!
    To make me blest or cursed'st among men.

                                    [*Cornets, and exeunt.*]

---

1. *Sophy . . . Solyman*] The "Sophy" was a title commonly bestowed on the Shah or
   Emperor of Persia. Suleiman the Magnificent, the greatest of the sultans of the Ottoman
   Empire, was defeated in an attack on Persia in 1535.
2. *Lichas*] The servant of Hercules who unwittingly brought him the poisoned shirt of
   Nessus, which caused the hero's death.
3. *Alcides*] Hercules.

SCENE II. *Venice. A street.*

Enter LAUNCELOT

LAUN. Certainly my conscience will serve me to run from this Jew my
    master. The fiend is at mine elbow, and tempts me, saying to me,
    "Gobbo, Launcelot Gobbo, good Launcelot," or "good Gobbo," or
    "good Launcelot Gobbo, use your legs, take the start, run away."
    My conscience says, "No; take heed, honest Launcelot; take heed,
    honest Gobbo," or, as aforesaid, "honest Launcelot Gobbo, do not
    run; scorn running with thy heels." Well, the most courageous
    fiend bids me pack: "Via!" says the fiend; "away!" says the fiend,
    "for the heavens, rouse up a brave mind," says the fiend, "and run."
    Well, my conscience, hanging about the neck of my heart, says very
    wisely to me, "My honest friend Launcelot, being an honest man's
    son," — or rather an honest woman's son; — for, indeed, my father
    did something smack, something grow to, he had a kind of taste; —
    well, my conscience says, "Launcelot, budge not." "Budge," says
    the fiend. "Budge not," says my conscience. "Conscience," say I,
    "you counsel well;" "Fiend," say I, "you counsel well:" to be ruled
    by my conscience, I should stay with the Jew my master, who, God
    bless the mark, is a kind of devil; and, to run away from the Jew, I
    should be ruled by the fiend, who, saving your reverence, is the
    devil himself. Certainly the Jew is the very devil incarnal; and, in
    my conscience, my conscience is but a kind of hard conscience, to
    offer to counsel me to stay with the Jew. The fiend gives the more
    friendly counsel: I will run, fiend; my heels are at your command; I
    will run.

Enter Old GOBBO, *with a basket*

GOB. Master young man, you, I pray you, which is the way to master
    Jew's?
LAUN. [*Aside*] O heavens, this is my true-begotten father! who, being

more than sand-blind, high-gravel blind,[1] knows me not: I will try confusions with him.

GOB.　Master young gentleman, I pray you, which is the way to master Jew's?

LAUN.　Turn up on your right hand at the next turning, but, at the next turning of all, on your left; marry, at the very next turning, turn of no hand, but turn down indirectly to the Jew's house.

GOB.　By God's sonties,[2] 't will be a hard way to hit. Can you tell me whether one Launcelot, that dwells with him, dwell with him or no?

LAUN.　Talk you of young Master Launcelot? [*Aside*] Mark me now; now will I raise the waters. Talk you of young Master Launcelot?

GOB.　No master, sir, but a poor man's son: his father, though I say it, is an honest exceeding poor man, and, God be thanked, well to live.

LAUN.　Well, let his father be what a' will, we talk of young Master Launcelot.

GOB.　Your worship's friend, and Launcelot, sir.

LAUN.　But I pray you, ergo, old man, ergo, I beseech you, talk you of young Master Launcelot?

GOB.　Of Launcelot, an 't please your mastership.

LAUN.　Ergo, Master Launcelot. Talk not of Master Launcelot, father; for the young gentleman, according to Fates and Destinies and such odd sayings, the Sisters Three and such branches of learning, is indeed deceased; or, as you would say in plain terms, gone to heaven.

GOB.　Marry, God forbid! the boy was the very staff of my age, my very prop.

LAUN.　Do I look like a cudgel or a hovel-post, a staff or a prop? Do you know me, father?

GOB.　Alack the day, I know you not, young gentleman: but, I pray you, tell me, is my boy, God rest his soul, alive or dead?

LAUN.　Do you not know me, father?

---

1. *sand-blind, high-gravel blind*] Launcelot here duplicates synonyms for "purblind." With "sand-blind" and "gravel-blind" compare "stone-blind," which was in common use for "completely blind."

2. *sonties*] Possibly old Gobbo's corruption of *santé* (health) or sanctity.

GOB.   Alack, sir, I am sand-blind; I know you not.

LAUN.   Nay, indeed, if you had your eyes, you might fail of the knowing me: it is a wise father that knows his own child. Well, old man, I will tell you news of your son: give me your blessing: truth will come to light; murder cannot be hid long; a man's son may; but, at the length, truth will out.

GOB.   Pray you, sir, stand up: I am sure you are not Launcelot, my boy.

LAUN.   Pray you, let 's have no more fooling about it, but give me your blessing: I am Launcelot, your boy that was, your son that is, your child that shall be.

GOB.   I cannot think you are my son.

LAUN.   I know not what I shall think of that: but I am Launcelot, the Jew's man; and I am sure Margery your wife is my mother.

GOB.   Her name is Margery, indeed: I 'll be sworn, if thou be Launcelot, thou art mine own flesh and blood. Lord worshipped might he be! what a beard[3] hast thou got! thou hast got more hair on thy chin than Dobbin my fill-horse has on his tail.

LAUN.   It should seem, then, that Dobbin's tail grows backward: I am sure he had more hair of his tail than I have of my face when I last saw him.

GOB.   Lord, how art thou changed! How dost thou and thy master agree? I have brought him a present. How 'gree you now?

LAUN.   Well, well: but, for my own part, as I have set up my rest to run away, so I will not rest till I have run some ground. My master 's a very Jew: give him a present! give him a halter: I am famished in his service; you may tell every finger I have with my ribs. Father, I am glad you are come: give me your present to one Master Bassanio, who, indeed, gives rare new liveries: if I serve not him, I will run as far as God has any ground. O rare fortune! here comes the man: to him, father; for I am a Jew, if I serve the Jew any longer.

Enter BASSANIO, *with* LEONARDO *and other followers*

BASS.   You may do so; but let it be so hasted, that supper be ready at the farthest by five of the clock. See these letters delivered; put the

---

3. *what a beard, etc.*] According to stage tradition, Launcelot kneels down with his back towards old Gobbo, who, touching the hair of his son's head, mistakes it for a beard.

liveries to making; and desire Gratiano to come anon to my lodging.   [*Exit a* Servant.]

LAUN.   To him, father.

GOB.   God bless your worship!

BASS.   Gramercy!⁴ wouldst thou aught with me?

GOB.   Here's my son, sir, a poor boy, —

LAUN.   Not a poor boy, sir, but the rich Jew's man; that would, sir, — as my father shall specify, —

GOB.   He hath a great infection, sir, as one would say, to serve —

LAUN.   Indeed, the short and the long is, I serve the Jew, and have a desire, — as my father shall specify, —

GOB.   His master and he, saving your worship's reverence, are scarce cater-cousins, — ⁵

LAUN.   To be brief, the very truth is that the Jew, having done me wrong, doth cause me, — as my father, being, I hope, an old man, shall frutify⁶ unto you, —

GOB.   I have here a dish of doves that I would bestow upon your worship, and my suit is, —

LAUN.   In very brief, the suit is impertinent to myself, as your worship shall know by this honest old man; and, though I say it, though old man, yet poor man, my father.

BASS.   One speak for both. What would you?

LAUN.   Serve you, sir.

GOB.   That is the very defect of the matter, sir.

BASS.   I know thee well; thou hast obtain'd thy suit:
Shylock thy master spoke with me this day,
And hath preferr'd thee, if it be preferment
To leave a rich Jew's service, to become
The follower of so poor a gentleman.

LAUN.   The old proverb is very well parted between my master Shylock

---

4. *Gramercy!*] Great thanks!

5. *cater-cousins*] quatre-cousins, remote relations. Old Gobbo misapplies the term here to mean persons who peaceably eat together.

6. *frutify*] used by Launcelot for "notify."

and you, sir: you have the grace of God, sir, and he hath enough.
BASS.   Thou speak'st it well. Go, father, with thy son.
　　Take leave of thy old master and inquire
　　My lodging out. Give him a livery
　　More guarded[7] than his fellows': see it done.
LAUN.   Father, in. I cannot get a service, no; I have ne'er a tongue in
　　my head. Well, if any man in Italy have a fairer table[8] which doth
　　offer to swear upon a book,[9] I shall have good fortune. Go to, here's
　　a simple line of life: here's a small trifle of wives: alas, fifteen wives
　　is nothing! a 'leven widows and nine maids is a simple coming-in
　　for one man: and then to 'scape drowning thrice, and to be in peril
　　of my life with the edge of a feather-bed; here are simple scapes.
　　Well, if Fortune be a woman, she's a good wench for this gear.
　　Father, come; I'll take my leave of the Jew in the twinkling of
　　an eye.　　　　　　　　[Exeunt LAUNCELOT and Old GOBBO.]
BASS.   I pray thee, good Leonardo, think on this:
　　These things being bought and orderly bestow'd,
　　Return in haste, for I do feast to-night
　　My best-esteem'd acquaintance: hie thee, go.
LEON.   My best endeavours shall be done herein.

Enter GRATIANO

GRA.   Where is your master?
LEON.　　　　　　　　　　Yonder, sir, he walks.　　　　　　[Exit.]
GRA.   Signior Bassanio, —
BASS.   Gratiano!
GRA.   I have a suit to you.
BASS.　　　　　　　　　You have obtain'd it.
GRA.   You must not deny me: I must go with you to Belmont.

---

7. *More guarded*] Better trimmed, ornamented with more lace or gold braid, which
　usually edged a garment and "guarded" it from fraying.
8. *table*] The speaker is here looking at the palm of his hand, which in palmistry was
　technically known as the "table."
9. *which doth offer . . . book*] which gives positive assurance. To "swear upon a book" is to
　take an oath of the most binding force.

BASS.   Why, then you must. But hear thee, Gratiano:
        Thou art too wild, too rude, and bold of voice;
        Parts that become thee happily enough,
        And in such eyes as ours appear not faults;
        But where thou art not known, why there they show
        Something too liberal. Pray thee, take pain
        To allay with some cold drops of modesty
        Thy skipping spirit; lest, through thy wild behaviour,
        I be misconstrued in the place I go to,
        And lose my hopes.

GRA.   Signior Bassanio, hear me:
        If I do not put on a sober habit,
        Talk with respect, and swear but now and then,
        Wear prayer-books in my pocket, look demurely;
        Nay more, while grace is saying, hood mine eyes
        Thus with my hat, and sigh, and say "amen;"
        Use all the observance of civility,
        Like one well studied in a sad ostent[10]
        To please his grandam, never trust me more.

BASS.   Well, we shall see your bearing.

GRA.   Nay, but I bar to-night: you shall not gauge me
        By what we do to-night.

BASS.   No, that were pity:
        I would entreat you rather to put on
        Your boldest suit of mirth, for we have friends
        That purpose merriment. But fare you well:
        I have some business.

GRA.   And I must to Lorenzo and the rest:
        But we will visit you at supper-time.   [*Exeunt.*]

---

10. *sad ostent*] serious aspect or demeanor.

SCENE III. *The same. A room in* SHYLOCK'S *house.*

Enter JESSICA *and* LAUNCELOT

JES.   I am sorry thou wilt leave my father so:
        Our house is hell; and thou, a merry devil,
        Didst rob it of some taste of tediousness.
        But fare thee well; there is a ducat for thee:
        And, Launcelot, soon at supper shalt thou see
        Lorenzo, who is thy new master's guest:
        Give him this letter; do it secretly;
        And so farewell: I would not have my father
        See me in talk with thee.

LAUN.   Adieu! tears exhibit my tongue.[1] Most beautiful pagan, most
        sweet Jew! if a Christian did not play the knave, and get[2] thee, I am
        much deceived. But, adieu: these foolish drops do something
        drown my manly spirit: adieu.

JES.   Farewell, good Launcelot.   [*Exit* LAUNCELOT.]
        Alack, what heinous sin is it in me
        To be ashamed to be my father's child!
        But though I am a daughter to his blood,
        I am not to his manners. O Lorenzo,
        If thou keep promise, I shall end this strife,
        Become a Christian, and thy loving wife.   [*Exit.*]

---

1. *exhibit my tongue*] show what my tongue ought to express.
2. *get*] beget.

SCENE IV. *The same. A street.*

Enter GRATIANO, LORENZO, SALARINO, *and* SALANIO

LOR.　Nay, we will slink away in supper-time,
　　Disguise us at my lodging, and return
　　All in an hour.
GRA.　We have not made good preparation.
SALAR.　We have not spoke us yet of torch-bearers.
SALAN.　'T is vile, unless it may be quaintly order'd,[1]
　　And better in my mind not undertook.
LOR.　'T is now but four o'clock: we have two hours
　　To furnish us.

Enter LAUNCELOT *with a letter*

　　　　　　　　Friend Launcelot, what 's the news?
LAUN.　An it shall please you to break up this, it shall seem to signify.
LOR.　I know the hand: in faith, 't is a fair hand;
　　And whiter than the paper it writ on
　　Is the fair hand that writ.
GRA.　　　　　　　　　　Love-news, in faith.
LAUN.　By your leave, sir.
LOR.　Whither goest thou?
LAUN.　Marry, sir, to bid my old master the Jew to sup to-night with my
　　new master the Christian.
LOR.　Hold here, take this: tell gentle Jessica
　　I will not fail her; speak it privately.
　　Go, gentlemen,　　　　　　　　　　[*Exit* LAUNCELOT.]
　　Will you prepare you for this masque to-night?
　　I am provided of a torch-bearer.
SALAR.　Ay, marry, I 'll be gone about it straight.
SALAN.　And so will I.

---

1. *quaintly order'd*] ingeniously, cleverly arranged.

LOR.   Meet me and Gratiano
   At Gratiano's lodging some hour hence.
SALAR.   'T is good we do so.   [*Exeunt* SALARINO *and* SALANIO.]
GRA.   Was not that letter from fair Jessica?
LOR.   I must needs tell thee all. She hath directed
   How I shall take her from her father's house;
   What gold and jewels she is furnish'd with;
   What page's suit she hath in readiness.
   If e'er the Jew her father come to heaven,
   It will be for his gentle daughter's sake:
   And never dare misfortune cross her foot,
   Unless she do it under this excuse,
   That she is issue to a faithless Jew.
   Come, go with me; peruse this as thou goest·
   Fair Jessica shall be my torch-bearer.   [*Exeunt.*]

SCENE V. *The same. Before* SHYLOCK'S *house.*

Enter SHYLOCK *and* LAUNCELOT

SHY.   Well, thou shalt see, thy eyes shall be thy judge,
   The difference of old Shylock and Bassanio: —
   What, Jessica! — thou shalt not gormandise,
   As thou hast done with me: — What, Jessica! —
   And sleep and snore, and rend apparel out; —
   Why, Jessica, I say!
LAUN.   Why, Jessica!
SHY.   Who bids thee call? I do not bid thee call.
LAUN.   Your worship was wont to tell me that I could do nothing
   without bidding.

Enter JESSICA

JES.   Call you? what is your will?

SHY.   I am bid forth to supper, Jessica:
          There are my keys. But wherefore should I go?
          I am not bid for love; they flatter me:
          But yet I 'll go in hate, to feed upon
          The prodigal Christian. Jessica, my girl,
          Look to my house. I am right loath to go:
          There is some ill a-brewing towards my rest,
          For I did dream of money-bags to-night.
LAUN.   I beseech you, sir, go: my young master doth expect your
          reproach.
SHY.   So do I his.
LAUN.   And they have conspired together, I will not say you shall see a
          masque; but if you do, then it was not for nothing that my nose fell
          a-bleeding on Black-Monday last at six o'clock i' the morning,
          falling out that year on Ash-Wednesday was four year, in the
          afternoon.
SHY.   What, are there masques? Hear you me, Jessica:
          Lock up my doors; and when you hear the drum,
          And the vile squealing of the wry-neck'd fife,
          Clamber not you up to the casements then,
          Nor thrust your head into the public street
          To gaze on Christian fools with varnish'd faces;
          But stop my house's ears, I mean my casements:
          Let not the sound of shallow foppery enter
          My sober house. By Jacob's staff, I swear
          I have no mind of feasting forth to-night:
          But I will go. Go you before me, sirrah;
          Say I will come.
LAUN.   I will go before, sir. Mistress, look out at window, for all this;

                    There will come a Christian by,
                    Will be worth a Jewess' eye.   [*Exit.*]

SHY.   What says that fool of Hagar's offspring, ha?
JES.   His words were, "Farewell, mistress;" nothing else.
SHY.   The patch[1] is kind enough, but a huge feeder;

---

1. *patch*] a paltry fellow, interpreted in this passage as a domestic fool, called "patch"
   because of his parti-colored dress.

Snail-slow in profit, and he sleeps by day
More than the wild-cat: drones hive not with me;
Therefore I part with him; and part with him
To one that I would have him help to waste
His borrow'd purse. Well, Jessica, go in:
Perhaps I will return immediately:
Do as I bid you; shut doors after you:
Fast bind, fast find,
A proverb never stale in thrifty mind.   [*Exit.*]
JES.   Farewell; and if my fortune be not crost,
I have a father, you a daughter, lost.   [*Exit.*]

SCENE **VI**. *The same.*

Enter GRATIANO *and* SALARINO, *masqued*

GRA.   This is the pent-house under which Lorenzo
Desired us to make stand.
SALAR.   His hour is almost past.
GRA.   And it is marvel he out-dwells his hour,
For lovers ever run before the clock.
SALAR.   O, ten times faster Venus' pigeons fly
To seal love's bonds new-made, than they are wont
To keep obliged faith unforfeited!
GRA.   That ever holds: who riseth from a feast
With that keen appetite that he sits down?
Where is the horse that doth untread again
His tedious measures with the unbated fire
That he did pace them first? All things that are,
Are with more spirit chased than enjoy'd.
How like a younker[1] or a prodigal

---

1. *younker*] a stripling.

The scarfed bark puts from her native bay,
Hugg'd and embraced by the strumpet wind!
How like the prodigal doth she return,
With over-weather'd ribs and ragged sails,
Lean, rent, and beggar'd by the strumpet wind!

SALAR.   Here comes Lorenzo: more of this hereafter.

Enter LORENZO

LOR.   Sweet friends, your patience for my long abode;
Not I, but my affairs, have made you wait:
When you shall please to play the thieves for wives,
I 'll watch as long for you then. Approach;
Here dwells my father Jew. Ho! who 's within?

Enter JESSICA, *above, in boy's clothes*

JES.   Who are you? Tell me, for more certainty,
Albeit I 'll swear that I do know your tongue.

LOR.   Lorenzo, and thy love.

JES.   Lorenzo, certain; and my love, indeed,
For who love I so much? And now who knows
But you, Lorenzo, whether I am yours?

LOR.   Heaven and thy thoughts are witness that thou art.

JES.   Here, catch this casket; it is worth the pains.
I am glad 't is night, you do not look on me,
For I am much ashamed of my exchange:
But love is blind, and lovers cannot see
The pretty follies that themselves commit;
For if they could, Cupid himself would blush
To see me thus transformed to a boy.

LOR.   Descend, for you must be my torch-bearer.

JES.   What, must I hold a candle to my shames?
They in themselves, good sooth, are too too light.
Why, 't is an office of discovery, love;
And I should be obscured.

LOR.   So are you, sweet,
Even in the lovely garnish² of a boy.

---

2. *garnish*] outfit or dress.

But come at once;
For the close night doth play the runaway,
And we are stay'd for at Bassanio's feast.
JES.   I will make fast the doors, and gild myself
With some mo ducats, and be with you straight.   [*Exit above.*]
GRA.   Now, by my hood,³ a Gentile, and no Jew.
LOR.   Beshrew me⁴ but I love her heartily;
For she is wise, if I can judge of her;
And fair she is, if that mine eyes be true;
And true she is, as she hath proved herself;
And therefore, like herself, wise, fair, and true,
Shall she be placed in my constant soul.

Enter JESSICA, *below*

What, art thou come? On, gentlemen; away!
Our masquing mates by this time for us stay.
                    [*Exit with* JESSICA *and* SALARINO.]

Enter ANTONIO

ANT.   Who's there?
GRA.   Signior Antonio!
ANT.   Fie, fie, Gratiano; where are all the rest?
'T is nine o'clock: our friends all stay for you.
No masque to-night: the wind is come about,
Bassanio presently will go aboard:
I have sent twenty out to seek for you.
GRA.   I am glad on 't: I desire no more delight
Than to be under sail and gone to-night.   [*Exeunt.*]

---

3. *by my hood*] An expletive objurgation, which may have originally been employed by hooded monks or friars.
4. *Beshrew me*] A simple assertion, such as "Indeed."

SCENE VII. *Belmont. A room in* PORTIA'S *house.*

Flourish of cornets. Enter PORTIA, *with the* PRINCE OF MOROCCO, *and their trains*

POR.　Go draw aside the curtains, and discover[1]
　　　The several caskets to this noble prince.
　　　Now make your choice.
MOR.　The first, of gold, who this inscription bears,
　　　"Who chooseth me shall gain what many men desire;"
　　　The second, silver, which this promise carries,
　　　"Who chooseth me shall get as much as he deserves;"
　　　This third, dull lead, with warning all as blunt,
　　　"Who chooseth me must give and hazard all he hath."
　　　How shall I know if I do choose the right?
POR.　The one of them contains my picture, prince:
　　　If you choose that, then I am yours withal.
MOR.　Some god direct my judgement! Let me see;
　　　I will survey the inscriptions back again.
　　　What says this leaden casket?
　　　"Who chooseth me must give and hazard all he hath."
　　　Must give, — for what? for lead? hazard for lead?
　　　This casket threatens. Men that hazard all
　　　Do it in hope of fair advantages:
　　　A golden mind stoops not to shows of dross;
　　　I 'll then nor give nor hazard aught for lead.
　　　What says the silver with her virgin hue?
　　　"Who chooseth me shall get as much as he deserves."
　　　As much as he deserves! Pause there, Morocco,
　　　And weigh thy value with an even hand:
　　　If thou be'st rated by thy estimation,
　　　Thou dost deserve enough; and yet enough

---

1. *discover*] reveal.

May not extend so far as to the lady:
And yet to be afeard of my deserving
Were but a weak disabling of myself.
As much as I deserve! Why, that 's the lady:
I do in birth deserve her, and in fortunes,
In graces and in qualities of breeding;
But more than these, in love I do deserve.
What if I stray'd no further, but chose here?
Let 's see once more this saying graved in gold;
"Who chooseth me shall gain what many men desire."
Why, that 's the lady; all the world desires her;
From the four corners of the earth they come,
To kiss this shrine, this mortal-breathing saint:
The Hyrcanian deserts[2] and the vasty wilds
Of wide Arabia are as throughfares now
For princes to come view fair Portia.
The watery kingdom, whose ambitious head
Spits in the face of heaven, is no bar
To stop the foreign spirits; but they come,
As o'er a brook, to see fair Portia.
One of these three contains her heavenly picture.
Is 't like that lead contains her? 'T were damnation
To think so base a thought: it were too gross
To rib her cerecloth[3] in the obscure grave.
Or shall I think in silver she 's immured,
Being ten times undervalued to tried gold?
O sinful thought! Never so rich a gem
Was set in worse than gold. They have in England
A coin that bears the figure of an angel[4]
Stamped in gold, but that 's insculp'd upon;
But here an angel in a golden bed

---

2. *Hyrcanian deserts*] wild tracts to the southeast of the Caspian Sea where tigers were
   reputed to abound.
3. *rib her cerecloth*] enclose, encircle (like ribs) her winding sheet.
4. *angel*] A gold coin worth about ten shillings, on one side of which was stamped in high
   relief a figure of the archangel Michael.

Lies all within. Deliver me the key:
Here do I choose, and thrive I as I may!
POR.   There, take it, prince; and if my form lie there,
Then I am yours.   [*He unlocks the golden casket.*]
MOR.   O hell! what have we here?
A carrion Death, within whose empty eye
There is a written scroll! I 'll read the writing.   [*Reads.*]

> All that glisters is not gold;
> Often have you heard that told:
> Many a man his life hath sold
> But my outside to behold:
> Gilded tombs do worms infold.
> Had you been as wise as bold,
> Young in limbs, in judgement old,
> Your answer had not been inscroll'd:
> Fare you well; your suit is cold.

Cold, indeed and labour lost:
Then, farewell, heat, and welcome, frost!
Portia, adieu. I have too grieved a heart
To take a tedious leave: thus losers part.
                [*Exit with his train. Flourish of cornets.*]
POR.   A gentle riddance. Draw the curtains, go.
Let all of his complexion choose me so.   [*Exeunt.*]

SCENE VIII. *Venice. A street.*

Enter SALARINO *and* SALANIO

SALAR.   Why, man, I saw Bassanio under sail:
With him is Gratiano gone along;
And in their ship I am sure Lorenzo is not.
SALAN.   The villain Jew with outcries raised the Duke,
Who went with him to search Bassanio's ship.
SALAR.   He came too late, the ship was under sail:

But there the Duke was given to understand
That in a gondola were seen together
Lorenzo and his amorous Jessica:
Besides, Antonio certified the Duke
They were not with Bassanio in his ship.

SALAN.   I never heard a passion so confused,
So strange, outrageous, and so variable,
As the dog Jew did utter in the streets:
"My daughter! O my ducats! O my daughter!
Fled with a Christian! O my Christian ducats!
Justice! the law! my ducats, and my daughter!
A sealed bag, two sealed bags of ducats,
Of double ducats, stolen from me by my daughter!
And jewels, two stones, two rich and precious stones,
Stolen by my daughter! Justice! find the girl!
She hath the stones upon her, and the ducats!"

SALAR.   Why, all the boys in Venice follow him,
Crying, his stones, his daughter, and his ducats.

SALAR.   Let good Antonio look he keep his day,
Or he shall pay for this.

SALAR.   Marry, well remember'd.
I reason'd with a Frenchman yesterday,
Who told me, in the narrow seas that part
The French and English, there miscarried
A vessel of our country richly fraught:
I thought upon Antonio when he told me;
And wish'd in silence that it were not his.

SALAN.   You were best to tell Antonio what you hear;
Yet do not suddenly, for it may grieve him.

SALAR.   A kinder gentleman treads not the earth.
I saw Bassanio and Antonio part:
Bassanio told him he would make some speed
Of his return: he answer'd, "Do not so;
Slubber[1] not business for my sake, Bassanio,
But stay the very riping of the time;

---

1. *Slubber*] To do carelessly or negligently.

And for the Jew's bond which he hath of me,
Let it not enter in your mind of love:
Be merry; and employ your chiefest thoughts
To courtship, and such fair ostents[2] of love
As shall conveniently become you there:"
And even there, his eye being big with tears,
Turning his face, he put his hand behind him,
And with affection wondrous sensible
He wrung Bassanio's hand; and so they parted.

SALAN. I think he only loves the world for him.
I pray thee, let us go and find him out,
And quicken his embraced heaviness
With some delight or other.

SALAR.   Do we so.   [*Exeunt.*]

SCENE IX. *Belmont. A room in* PORTIA'S *house.*

Enter NERISSA *and a* Servitor

NER. Quick, quick, I pray thee: draw the curtain straight:
The Prince of Arragon hath ta'en his oath,
And comes to his election presently.

Flourish of cornets. Enter the PRINCE OF ARRAGON, PORTIA, *and
their trains*

POR. Behold, there stand the caskets, noble prince:
If you choose that wherein I am contain'd,
Straight shall our nuptial rites be solemnized:
But if you fail, without more speech, my lord,
You must be gone from hence immediately.

AR. I am enjoin'd by oath to observe three things:
First, never to unfold to any one

---

2. *ostents*] external shows.

Which casket 't was I chose; next, if I fail
Of the right casket, never in my life
To woo a maid in way of marriage:
Lastly,
If I do fail in fortune of my choice,
Immediately to leave you and be gone.

POR.   To these injunctions every one doth swear
That comes to hazard for my worthless self.

AR.   And so have I address'd me. Fortune now
To my heart's hope! Gold; silver; and base lead.
"Who chooseth me must give and hazard all he hath."
You shall look fairer, ere I give or hazard.
What says the golden chest? ha! let me see:
"Who chooseth me shall gain what many men desire."
What many men desire! that "many" may be meant
By the fool multitude, that choose by show,
Not learning more than the fond eye doth teach;
Which pries not to the interior, but, like the martlet,[1]
Builds in the weather on the outward wall,
Even in the force and road of casualty.
I will not choose what many men desire,
Because I will not jump with common spirits,
And rank me with the barbarous multitudes.
Why, then to thee, thou silver treasure-house;
Tell me once more what title thou dost bear:
"Who chooseth me shall get as much as he deserves:"
And well said too; for who shall go about
To cozen[2] fortune, and be honourable
Without the stamp of merit? Let none presume
To wear an undeserved dignity.
O, that estates, degrees and offices
Were not derived corruptly, and that clear honour
Were purchased by the merit of the wearer!
How many then should cover that stand bare!

---

1. *martlet*] Used here for the "house martin," but more properly the swift.
2. *cozen*] cheat.

How many be commanded that command!
How much low peasantry would then be glean'd
From the true seed of honour!³ and how much honour
Pick'd from the chaff and ruin of the times,
To be new-varnish'd! Well, but to my choice:
"Who chooseth me shall get as much as he deserves."
I will assume desert. Give me a key for this,
And instantly unlock my fortunes here.

> [*He opens the silver casket.*]

POR.   [*Aside*] Too long a pause for that which you find there.
AR.   What 's here? the portrait of a blinking idiot,
Presenting me a schedule! I will read it.
How much unlike art thou to Portia!
How much unlike my hopes and my deservings!
"Who chooseth me shall have as much as he deserves."
Did I deserve no more than a fool's head?
Is that my prize? are my deserts no better?
POR.   To offend, and judge, are distinct offices,
    And of opposed natures.
AR.   What is here?

[*Reads*]   The fire seven times tried this:
            Seven times tried that judgement is,
            That did never choose amiss.
            Some there be that shadows kiss;
            Such have but a shadow's bliss:
            There be fools alive, I wis,
            Silver'd o'er; and so was this.
            Take what wife you will to bed,
            I will ever be your head:
            So be gone: you are sped.

        Still more fool I shall appear
        By the time I linger here:

---

3. *How much low peasantry . . . honour!*] How much vulgarity or boorishness would then
be detected in those succeeding to high office by hereditary right.

> With one fool's head I came to woo,
> But I go away with two.
> Sweet, adieu. I 'll keep my oath,
> Patiently to bear my wroth.
>
> > [*Exeunt* ARRAGON *and train.*]

POR.   Thus hath the candle singed the moth.
O, these deliberate fools! when they do choose,
They have the wisdom by their wit to lose.

NER.   The ancient saying is no heresy,
Hanging and wiving goes by destiny.

POR   Come, draw the curtain, Nerissa.

Enter a Servant

SERV.   Where is my lady?

POR.   Here: what would my lord?

SERV.   Madam, there is alighted at your gate
A young Venetian, one that comes before
To signify the approaching of his lord;
From whom he bringeth sensible regreets,[4]
To wit, besides commends and courteous breath,
Gifts of rich value. Yet I have not seen
So likely an ambassador of love:
A day in April never came so sweet,
To show how costly summer was at hand,
As this fore-spurrer comes before his lord.

POR.   No more, I pray thee: I am half afeard
Thou wilt say anon he is some kin to thee,
Thou spend'st such high-day wit[5] in praising him.
Come, come, Nerissa; for I long to see
Quick Cupid's post that comes so mannerly.

NER.   Bassanio, lord Love, if thy will it be!   [*Exeunt.*]

---

4. *regreets*] greetings.
5. *high-day wit*] holiday, cheerful wit.

ACT III

SCENE I. *Venice. A street.*

Enter SALANIO *and* SALARINO

SALAN. Now, what news on the Rialto?

SALAR. Why, yet it lives there unchecked, that Antonio hath a ship of
rich lading wrecked on the narrow seas; the Goodwins, I think they
call the place; a very dangerous flat and fatal, where the carcases of
many a tall ship lie buried, as they say, if my gossip Report be an
honest woman of her word.

SALAN. I would she were as lying a gossip in that as ever knapped
ginger,[1] or made her neighbours believe she wept for the death of a
third husband. But it is true, without any slips of prolixity, or
crossing the plain highway of talk, that the good Antonio, the
honest Antonio, — O that I had a title good enough to keep his
name company! —

SALAR. Come, the full stop.

SALAN. Ha! what sayest thou? Why, the end is, he hath lost a ship.

SALAR. I would it might prove the end of his losses.

SALAN. Let me say "amen" betimes, lest the devil cross my prayer, for
here he comes in the likeness of a Jew.

Enter SHYLOCK

How now, Shylock! what news among the merchants?

---

1. *knapped ginger*] gnawed or nibbled off ginger. A taste for ginger was commonly held at
the time to be characteristic of old women.

SHY.   You knew, none so well, none so well as you, of my daughter's flight.

SALAR.   That's certain: I, for my part, knew the tailor that made the wings she flew withal.

SALAN.   And Shylock, for his own part, knew the bird was fledged; and then it is the complexion of them all to leave the dam.

SHY.   She is damned for it.

SALAR.   That's certain, if the devil may be her judge.

SHY.   My own flesh and blood to rebel!

SALAN.   Out upon it, old carrion! rebels it at these years?

SHY.   I say, my daughter is my flesh and blood.

SALAR.   There is more difference between thy flesh and hers than between jet and ivory; more between your bloods than there is between red wine and rhenish. But tell us, do you hear whether Antonio have had any loss at sea or no?

SHY.   There I have another bad match: a bankrupt, a prodigal, who dare scarce show his head on the Rialto; a beggar, that was used to come so smug upon the mart; let him look to his bond: he was wont to call me usurer; let him look to his bond: he was wont to lend money for a Christian courtesy; let him look to his bond.

SALAR.   Why, I am sure, if he forfeit, thou wilt not take his flesh: what's that good for?

SHY.   To bait fish withal: if it will feed nothing else, it will feed my revenge. He hath disgraced me, and hindered me half a million; laughed at my losses, mocked at my gains, scorned my nation, thwarted my bargains, cooled my friends, heated mine enemies; and what's his reason? I am a Jew. Hath not a Jew eyes? hath not a Jew hands, organs, dimensions, senses, affections, passions? fed with the same food, hurt with the same weapons, subject to the same diseases, healed by the same means, warmed and cooled by the same winter and summer, as a Christian is? If you prick us, do we not bleed? if you tickle us, do we not laugh? if you poison us, do we not die? and if you wrong us, shall we not revenge? if we are like you in the rest, we will resemble you in that. If a Jew wrong a Christian, what is his humility?[2] Revenge. If a Christian wrong a

---

2. *humility*] humanity, benevolence, kindness, not "humbleness."

Jew, what should his sufferance be by Christian example? Why, revenge. The villany you teach me, I will execute; and it shall go hard but I will better the instruction.

Enter a Servant

SERV.   Gentlemen, my master Antonio is at his house, and desires to speak with you both.

SALAR.   We have been up and down to seek him.

Enter TUBAL

SALAN.   Here comes another of the tribe: a third cannot be matched, unless the devil himself turn Jew.

[*Exeunt* SALANIO, SALARINO, *and* Servant.]

SHY.   How now, Tubal! what news from Genoa? hast thou found my daughter?

TUB.   I often came where I did hear of her, but cannot find her.

SHY.   Why, there, there, there, there! a diamond gone, cost me two thousand ducats in Frankfort! The curse never fell upon our nation till now; I never felt it till now: two thousand ducats in that; and other precious, precious jewels. I would my daughter were dead at my foot, and the jewels in her ear! would she were hearsed at my foot, and the ducats in her coffin! No news of them? Why, so: — and I know not what 's spent in the search: why, thou loss upon loss! the thief gone with so much, and so much to find the thief; and no satisfaction, no revenge: nor no ill luck stirring but what lights on my shoulders; no sighs but of my breathing; no tears but of my shedding.

TUB.   Yes, other men have ill luck too: Antonio, as I heard in Genoa, —

SHY.   What, what, what? ill luck, ill luck?

TUB.   Hath an argosy[3] cast away, coming from Tripolis.

SHY.   I thank God, I thank God! Is 't true, is 't true?

TUB.   I spoke with some of the sailors that escaped the wreck.

SHY.   I thank thee, good Tubal: good news, good news! ha, ha! where? in Genoa?

---

3. *argosy*] large merchantman.

TUB.   Your daughter spent in Genoa, as I heard, in one night fourscore ducats.

SHY.   Thou stick'st a dagger in me: I shall never see my gold again: fourscore ducats at a sitting! fourscore ducats!

TUB.   There came divers[4] of Antonio's creditors in my company to Venice, that swear he cannot choose but break.

SHY.   I am very glad of it: I 'll plague him; I 'll torture him: I am glad of it.

TUB.   One of them showed me a ring that he had of your daughter for a monkey.

SHY.   Out upon her! Thou torturest me, Tubal: it was my turquoise; I had it of Leah[5] when I was a bachelor: I would not have given it for a wilderness of monkeys.

TUB.   But Antonio is certainly undone.

SHY.   Nay, that 's true, that 's very true. Go, Tubal, fee me an officer; bespeak him a fortnight before. I will have the heart of him, if he forfeit; for, were he out of Venice, I can make what merchandise I will. Go, go, Tubal, and meet me at our synagogue; go, good Tubal; at our synagogue, Tubal.   [*Exeunt.*]

SCENE II. *Belmont. A room in* PORTIA'S *house.*

Enter BASSANIO, PORTIA, GRATIANO, NERISSA, *and* Attendants

POR.   I pray you, tarry: pause a day or two
Before you hazard; for, in choosing wrong,
I lose your company: therefore forbear awhile.
There 's something tells me, but it is not love,
I would not lose you; and you know yourself,

---

4. *divers*] several, sundry.
5. *I had it of Leah*] Shylock received the ring from his dead wife Leah.

Hate counsels not in such a quality.
But lest you should not understand me well, —
And yet a maiden hath no tongue but thought,[1] —
I would detain you here some month or two
Before you venture for me. I could teach you
How to choose right, but I am then forsworn;
So will I never be: so may you miss me;
But if you do, you 'll make me wish a sin,
That I had been forsworn. Beshrew your eyes,
They have o'er-look'd me, and divided me;
One half of me is yours, the other half yours,
Mine own, I would say; but if mine, then yours,
And so all yours! O, these naughty times
Put bars between the owners and their rights!
And so, though yours, not yours. Prove it so,
Let fortune go to hell for it, not I.
I speak too long; but 't is to peize[2] the time,
To eke it and to draw it out in length,
To stay you from election.

BASS.   Let me choose;
For as I am, I live upon the rack.

POR.   Upon the rack, Bassanio! then confess
What treason there is mingled with your love.

BASS.   None but that ugly treason of mistrust,
Which makes me fear the enjoying of my love:
There may as well be amity and life
'Tween snow and fire, as treason and my love.

POR.   Ay, but I fear you speak upon the rack,
Where men enforced do speak any thing.

BASS.   Promise me life, and I 'll confess the truth.

POR.   Well then, confess and live.

BASS.   "Confess," and "love,"

---

1. *a maiden . . . thought*] a maiden is restrained by modesty from giving expression to her
   love, and must only cherish it in thought.
2. *to peize*] to poise; here, to retard time by hanging weights on it.

Had been the very sum of my confession:
O happy torment, when my torturer
Doth teach me answers for deliverance!
But let me to my fortune and the caskets.

POR. Away, then! I am lock'd in one of them:
If you do love me, you will find me out.
Nerissa and the rest, stand all aloof.
Let music sound while he doth make his choice;
Then, if he lose, he makes a swan-like end,
Fading in music: that the comparison
May stand more proper, my eye shall be the stream,
And watery death-bed for him. He may win;
And what is music then? Then music is
Even as the flourish when true subjects bow
To a new-crowned monarch: such it is
As are those dulcet sounds in break of day
That creep into the dreaming bridegroom's ear,
And summon him to marriage. Now he goes,
With no less presence, but with much more love,
Than young Alcides,[3] when he did redeem
The virgin tribute paid by howling Troy
To the sea-monster: I stand for sacrifice;
The rest aloof are the Dardanian[4] wives,
With bleared visages, come forth to view
The issue of the exploit. Go, Hercules!
Live thou, I live: with much much more dismay
I view the fight than thou that makest the fray.

---

3. *young Alcides*] Ovid tells the story, in *Metamorphoses*, XI, how Hercules rescued from
   the sea monster the Trojan maiden Hesione, who had been sacrificed to free the town
   of Troy from pestilence, not for love of her, but on condition of receiving a gift of horses,
   from the girl's father, Laomedon.
4. *Dardanian*] Trojan.

Music, whilst BASSANIO *comments on the caskets to himself*

SONG

> Tell me where is fancy bred,
> Or in the heart or in the head?
> How begot, how nourished?
>   Reply, reply.
> It is engender'd in the eyes,
> With gazing fed; and fancy dies
> In the cradle where it lies.
>   Let us all ring fancy's knell;
>   I 'll begin it, — Ding, dong, bell.

ALL.   Ding, dong, bell.

BASS.   So may the outward shows be least themselves:
The world is still deceived with ornament.
In law, what plea so tainted and corrupt,
But, being season'd with a gracious voice,
Obscures the show of evil? In religion,
What damned error, but some sober brow
Will bless it, and approve it with a text,
Hiding the grossness with fair ornament?
There is no vice so simple, but assumes
Some mark of virtue on his outward parts:
How many cowards, whose hearts are all as false
As stairs of sand, wear yet upon their chins
The beards of Hercules and frowning Mars;
Who, inward search'd, have livers white as milk;
And these assume but valour's excrement
To render them redoubted! Look on beauty,
And you shall see 't is purchased by the weight;
Which therein works a miracle in nature,
Making them lightest that wear most of it:
So are those crisped snaky golden locks
Which make such wanton gambols with the wind,
Upon supposed fairness, often known

To be the dowry of a second head,[5]
The skull that bred them in the sepulchre.
Thus ornament is but the guiled shore
To a most dangerous sea; the beauteous scarf
Veiling an Indian beauty; in a word,
The seeming truth which cunning times put on
To entrap the wisest. Therefore, thou gaudy gold,
Hard food for Midas, I will none of thee;
Nor none of thee, thou pale and common drudge
'Tween man and man: but thou, thou meagre lead,
Which rather threatenest than dost promise aught,
Thy paleness moves me more than eloquence;
And here choose I: joy be the consequence!

POR. [*Aside*] How all the other passions fleet to air,
As doubtful thoughts, and rash-embraced despair,
And shuddering fear, and green-eyed jealousy!
O love, be moderate; allay thy ecstasy;
In measure rain thy joy; scant this excess!
I feel too much thy blessing: make it less,
For fear I surfeit!

BASS.   What find I here? [*Opening the leaden casket.*]
Fair Portia's counterfeit! What demi-god
Hath come so near creation? Move these eyes?
Or whether, riding on the balls of mine,
Seem they in motion? Here are sever'd lips,
Parted with sugar breath: so sweet a bar
Should sunder such sweet friends. Here in her hairs
The painter plays the spider, and hath woven
A golden mesh to entrap the hearts of men,
Faster than gnats in cobwebs: but her eyes, —
How could he see to do them? having made one,
Methinks it should have power to steal both his
And leave itself unfurnish'd. Yet look, how far
The substance of my praise doth wrong this shadow

---

5. *a second head*] It was a common practice to wear false hair or hair cut from the heads of corpses.

In underprizing it, so far this shadow
Doth limp behind the substance. Here 's the scroll,
The continent and summary of my fortune.

> [*Reads*] You that choose not by the view,
> Chance as fair, and choose as true!
> Since this fortune falls to you,
> Be content and seek no new.
> If you be well pleased with this,
> And hold your fortune for your bliss,
> Turn you where your lady is,
> And claim her with a loving kiss.

A gentle scroll. Fair lady, by your leave;
I come by note, to give and to receive.
Like one of two contending in a prize,
That thinks he hath done well in people's eyes,
Hearing applause and universal shout,
Giddy in spirit, still gazing in a doubt
Whether those peals of praise be his or no;
So, thrice-fair lady, stand I, even so;
As doubtful whether what I see be true,
Until confirm'd, sign'd, ratified by you.
POR. You see me, Lord Bassanio, where I stand,
Such as I am: though for myself alone
I would not be ambitious in my wish,
To wish myself much better; yet, for you
I would be treble twenty times myself;
A thousand times more fair, ten thousand times
More rich;
That only to stand high in your account,
I might in virtues, beauties, livings, friends,
Exceed account; but the full sum of me
Is sum of something, which, to term in gross,
Is an unlesson'd girl, unschool'd, unpractised;
Happy in this, she is not yet so old
But she may learn; happier than this,
She is not bred so dull but she can learn;
Happiest of all is that her gentle spirit

Commits itself to yours to be directed,
As from her lord, her governor, her king.
Myself and what is mine to you and yours
Is now converted: but now I was the lord
Of this fair mansion, master of my servants,
Queen o'er myself; and even now, but now,
This house, these servants, and this same myself,
Are yours, my lord: I give them with this ring;
Which when you part from, lose, or give away,
Let it presage the ruin of your love,
And be my vantage to exclaim on you.

BASS.   Madam, you have bereft me of all words,
Only my blood speaks to you in my veins;
And there is such confusion in my powers,
As, after some oration fairly spoke
By a beloved prince, there doth appear
Among the buzzing pleased multitude;
Where every something, being blent together,
Turns to a wild of nothing, save of joy,
Express'd and not express'd. But when this ring
Parts from this finger, then parts life from hence:
O, then be bold to say Bassanio 's dead!

NER.   My lord and lady, it is now our time,
That have stood by and seen our wishes prosper,
To cry, good joy: good joy, my lord and lady!

GRA.   My Lord Bassanio and my gentle lady,
I wish you all the joy that you can wish;
For I am sure you can wish none from me:
And when your honours mean to solemnize
The bargain of your faith, I do beseech you,
Even at that time I may be married too.

BASS.   With all my heart, so thou canst get a wife.

GRA.   I thank your lordship, you have got me one.
My eyes, my lord, can look as swift as yours:
You saw the mistress, I beheld the maid;
You loved, I loved for intermission.[6]

---

6. *for intermission*] here, for want of something to do.

No more pertains to me, my lord, than you.
Your fortune stood upon the casket there,
And so did mine too, as the matter falls;
For wooing here until I sweat again,
And swearing till my very roof was dry
With oaths of love, at last, if promise last,
I got a promise of this fair one here
To have her love, provided that your fortune
Achieved her mistress.

POR.　　　　　　　　Is this true, Nerissa?
NER.　Madam, it is, so you stand pleased withal.
BASS.　And do you, Gratiano, mean good faith?
GRA.　Yes, faith, my lord.
BASS.　Our feast shall be much honoured in your marriage.
GRA.　We 'll play with them the first boy for a thousand ducats.
NER.　What, and stake down?
GRA.　No; we shall ne'er win at that sport, and stake down.
　　　But who comes here? Lorenzo and his infidel?
　　　What, and my old Venetian friend Salerio?

Enter LORENZO, JESSICA, *and* SALERIO, *a Messenger from Venice*

BASS.　Lorenzo and Salerio, welcome hither;
　　　If that the youth of my new interest here
　　　Have power to bid you welcome. By your leave,
　　　I bid my very friends and countrymen,
　　　Sweet Portia, welcome.
POR.　　　　　　　　So do I, my lord:
　　　They are entirely welcome.
LOR.　I thank your honour. For my part, my lord,
　　　My purpose was not to have seen you here;
　　　But meeting with Salerio by the way,
　　　He did entreat me, past all saying nay,
　　　To come with him along.
SALER.　　　　　　　I did, my lord;
　　　And I have reason for it. Signior Antonio
　　　Commends him to you.　　　　　[*Gives* BASSANIO *a letter.*]
BASS.　　　　　　　Ere I ope his letter,
　　　I pray you, tell me how my good friend doth.

SALER. Not sick, my lord, unless it be in mind;
   Nor well, unless in mind: his letter there
   Will show you his estate.

GRA. Nerissa, cheer yon stranger; bid her welcome.
   Your hand, Salerio: what 's the news from Venice?
   How doth that royal merchant,[7] good Antonio?
   I know he will be glad of our success;
   We are the Jasons, we have won the fleece.

SALER. I would you had won the fleece that he hath lost.

POR. There are some shrewd contents in yon same paper,
   That steals the colour from Bassanio's cheek:
   Some dear friend dead; else nothing in the world
   Could turn so much the constitution
   Of any constant man. What, worse and worse!
   With leave, Bassanio; I am half yourself,
   And I must freely have the half of anything
   That this same paper brings you.

BASS.   O sweet Portia,
   Here are a few of the unpleasant'st words
   That ever blotted paper! Gentle lady,
   When I did first impart my love to you,
   I freely told you, all the wealth I had
   Ran in my veins, I was a gentleman;
   And then I told you true: and yet, dear lady,
   Rating myself at nothing, you shall see
   How much I was a braggart. When I told you
   My state was nothing, I should then have told you
   That I was worse than nothing; for, indeed,
   I have engaged myself to a dear friend,
   Engaged my friend to his mere enemy,
   To feed my means. Here is a letter, lady;
   The paper as the body of my friend,

---

7. *royal merchant*] This term was specifically allotted to the Venetian merchants who
   enjoyed a license from the Republic to occupy and govern islands in the Greek
   Archipelago on the sole condition of acknowledging the suzerainty of the Republic. But
   it may well be that the epithet "royal" has no more recondite significance than that of
   "great" or "magnificent."

And every word in it a gaping wound,
Issuing life-blood. But is it true, Salerio?
Have all his ventures fail'd? What, not one hit?
From Tripolis, from Mexico, and England,
From Lisbon, Barbary, and India?
And not one vessel scape the dreadful touch
Of merchant-marring rocks?

SALER.   Not one, my lord.
Besides, it should appear, that if he had
The present money to discharge the Jew,
He would not take it. Never did I know
A creature, that did bear the shape of man,
So keen and greedy to confound a man:
He plies the Duke at morning and at night;
And doth impeach the freedom of the state,
If they deny him justice: twenty merchants,
The Duke himself, and the magnificoes
Of greatest port, have all persuaded with him;
But none can drive him from the envious plea
Of forfeiture, of justice, and his bond.

JES.   When I was with him I have heard him swear
To Tubal and to Chus, his countrymen,
That he would rather have Antonio's flesh
Than twenty times the value of the sum
That he did owe him: and I know, my lord,
If law, authority and power deny not,
It will go hard with poor Antonio.

POR.   Is it your dear friend that is thus in trouble?

BASS.   The dearest friend to me, the kindest man,
The best-condition'd and unwearied spirit
In doing courtesies; and one in whom
The ancient Roman honour more appears
Than any that draws breath in Italy.

POR.   What sum owes he the Jew?

BASS.   For me three thousand ducats.

POR.   What, no more?
Pay him six thousand, and deface the bond;

Double six thousand, and then treble that,
Before a friend of this description
Shall lose a hair through Bassanio's fault.
First go with me to church and call me wife,
And then away to Venice to your friend;
For never shall you lie by Portia's side
With an unquiet soul. You shall have gold
To pay the petty debt twenty times over:
When it is paid, bring your true friend along.
My maid Nerissa and myself meantime
Will live as maids and widows. Come, away!
For you shall hence upon your wedding-day:
Bid your friends welcome, show a merry cheer:
Since you are dear bought, I will love you dear.
But let me hear the letter of your friend.

BASS. [*Reads*] Sweet Bassanio, my ships have all miscarried, my creditors grow cruel, my estate is very low, my bond to the Jew is forfeit; and since in paying it, it is impossible I should live, all debts are cleared between you and I, if I might but see you at my death. Notwithstanding, use your pleasure: if your love do not persuade you to come, let not my letter.

POR. O love, dispatch all business, and be gone!
BASS. Since I have your good leave to go away,
　　　I will make haste: but, till I come again,
　　　No bed shall e'er be guilty of my stay,
　　　No rest be interposer 'twixt us twain.　　　　　[*Exeunt.*]

SCENE III. *Venice. A street.*

Enter SHYLOCK, SALARINO, ANTONIO, *and* GAOLER

SHY.   Gaoler, look to him: tell not me of mercy;
This is the fool that lent out money gratis:
Gaoler, look to him.
ANT.   Hear me yet, good Shylock.
SHY.   I 'll have my bond; speak not against my bond:
I have sworn an oath that I will have my bond.
Thou call'dst me dog before thou hadst a cause;
But, since I am a dog, beware my fangs:
The Duke shall grant me justice. I do wonder,
Thou naughty gaoler, that thou art so fond
To come abroad with him at his request.
ANT.   I pray thee, hear me speak.
SHY.   I 'll have my bond; I will not hear thee speak:
I 'll have my bond; and therefore speak no more.
I 'll not be made a soft and dull-eyed fool,
To shake the head, relent, and sigh, and yield
To Christian intercessors. Follow not;
I 'll have no speaking: I will have my bond.   [*Exit.*]
SALAR.   It is the most impenetrable cur
That ever kept with men.
ANT.   Let him alone:
I 'll follow him no more with bootless prayers.
He seeks my life; his reason well I know:
I oft deliver'd from his forfeitures
Many that have at times made moan to me;
Therefore he hates me.
SALAR.   I am sure the Duke
Will never grant this forfeiture to hold.
ANT.   The Duke cannot deny the course of law:
For the commodity that strangers have

With us in Venice, if it be denied,
Will much impeach the justice of his state;
Since that the trade and profit of the city
Consisteth of all nations. Therefore, go:
These griefs and losses have so bated me,
That I shall hardly spare a pound of flesh
To-morrow to my bloody creditor.
Well, gaoler, on. Pray God, Bassanio come
To see me pay his debt, and then I care not!   [*Exeunt.*]

SCENE IV. *Belmont. A room in* PORTIA'S *house.*

Enter PORTIA, NERISSA, LORENZO, JESSICA, *and* BALTHASAR

LOR.   Madam, although I speak it in your presence,
You have a noble and a true conceit
Of god-like amity; which appears most strongly
In bearing thus the absence of your lord.
But if you knew to whom you show this honour,
How true a gentleman you send relief,
How dear a lover of my lord your husband,
I know you would be prouder of the work
Than customary bounty can enforce you.

POR.   I never did repent for doing good,
Nor shall not now: for in companions
That do converse and waste the time together,
Whose souls do bear an equal yoke of love,
There must be needs a like proportion
Of lineaments, of manners and of spirit;
Which makes me think that this Antonio,
Being the bosom lover of my lord,
Must needs be like my lord. If it be so,
How little is the cost I have bestow'd
In purchasing the semblance of my soul

From out the state of hellish misery!
This comes too near the praising of myself;
Therefore no more of it: hear other things.
Lorenzo, I commit into your hands
The husbandry and manage of my house
Until my lord's return: for mine own part,
I have toward heaven breathed a secret VOW
To live in prayer and contemplation,
Only attended by Nerissa here,
Until her husband and my lord's return:
There is a monastery two miles off;
And there will we abide. I do desire you
Not to deny this imposition;
The which my love and some necessity
Now lays upon you.

LOR.   Madam, with all my heart;
I shall obey you in all fair commands.

POR.   My people do already know my mind,
And will acknowledge you and Jessica
In place of Lord Bassanio and myself.
And so farewell, till we shall meet again.

LOR.   Fair thoughts and happy hours attend on you!

JES.   I wish your ladyship all heart's content.

POR.   I thank you for your wish, and am well pleased
To wish it back on you: fare you well, Jessica.

                    [*Exeunt* JESSICA *and* LORENZO.]
Now, Balthasar,
As I have ever found thee honest-true,
So let me find thee still. Take this same letter,
And use thou all the endeavour of a man
In speed to Padua: see thou render this
Into my cousin's hand, Doctor Bellario;
And, look, what notes and garments he doth give thee,
Bring them, I pray thee, with imagined speed
Unto the tranect,[1] to the common ferry

---

1. *tranect*] a word possibly corrupted from the Italian *traghetto* (ferry).

Which trades to Venice. Waste no time in words,
But get thee gone: I shall be there before thee.

BALTH.　Madam, I go with all convenient speed.　　　　[*Exit.*]

POR.　Come on, Nerissa; I have work in hand
That you yet know not of; we'll see our husbands
Before they think of us.

NER.　　　　　　　　Shall they see us?

POR.　They shall, Nerissa; but in such a habit,
That they shall think we are accomplished
With that we lack. I 'll hold thee any wager,
When we are both accoutred like young men,
I 'll prove the prettier fellow of the two,
And wear my dagger with the braver grace,
And speak between the change of man and boy
With a reed voice, and turn two mincing steps
Into a manly stride, and speak of frays
Like a fine bragging youth; and tell quaint lies
How honourable ladies sought my love,
Which I denying, they fell sick and died;
I could not do withal:[2] then I 'll repent,
And wish, for all that, that I had not kill'd them;
And twenty of these puny lies I 'll tell,
That men shall swear I have discontinued school
Above a twelvemonth. I have within my mind
A thousand raw tricks of these bragging Jacks,
Which I will practise.

NER.　　　　　　Why, shall we turn to men?

POR.　Fie, what a question 's that,
If thou wert near a lewd interpreter!
But come, I 'll tell thee all my whole device
When I am in my coach, which stays for us
At the park-gate; and therefore haste away,
For we must measure twenty miles to-day.　　　　[*Exeunt.*]

---

2. *I could not do withal*] I could not help it; a common phrase in contemporary authors.

SCENE V. *The same. A garden.*

Enter LAUNCELOT *and* JESSICA

LAUN.   Yes, truly; for, look you, the sins of the father are to be laid upon the children: therefore, I promise ye, I fear you.[1] I was always plain with you, and so now I speak my agitation[2] of the matter; therefore be of good cheer; for, truly, I think you are damned. There is but one hope in it that can do you any good; and that is but a kind of bastard hope neither.

JES.   And what hope is that, I pray thee?

LAUN.   Marry, you may partly hope that your father got you not, that you are not the Jew's daughter.

JES.   That were a kind of bastard hope, indeed: so the sins of my mother should be visited upon me.

LAUN.   Truly then I fear you are damned both by father and mother: thus when I shun Scylla, your father, I fall into Charybdis, your mother:[3] well, you are gone both ways.

JES.   I shall be saved by my husband; he hath made me a Christian.

LAUN.   Truly, the more to blame he: we were Christians enow before; e'en as many as could well live, one by another. This making of Christians will raise the price of hogs: if we grow all to be pork-eaters, we shall not shortly have a rasher on the coals for money.

Enter LORENZO

JES.   I 'll tell my husband, Launcelot, what you say: here he comes.

---

1. *I fear you*] I fear for you.
2. *agitation*] A clownish blunder for "cogitation."
3. *Scylla . . . Charybdis*] This proverb, which is very common in Elizabethan authors, seems to have been the invention of a twelfth-century Latin poet, Philippe Gualtier de Chatillon, whose Latin epic *Alexandreis* includes the line: "Incidis in Scyllam, cupiens vitare Charybdim" ("You encounter Scylla when attempting to avoid Charybdis").

LOR.   I shall grow jealous of you shortly, Launcelot, if you thus get my
wife into corners.

JES.   Nay, you need not fear us, Lorenzo: Launcelot and I are out. He
tells me flatly, there is no mercy for me in heaven, because I am a
Jew's daughter: and he says, you are no good member of the
commonwealth; for, in converting Jews to Christians, you raise the
price of pork.

LOR.   I shall answer that better to the commonwealth than you can the
getting up of the negro's belly: the Moor is with child by you,
Launcelot.

LAUN.   It is much that the Moor should be more than reason: but if she
be less than an honest woman, she is indeed more than I took her
for.

LOR.   How every fool can play upon the word! I think the best grace of
wit will shortly turn into silence; and discourse grow commendable
in none only but parrots. Go in, sirrah; bid them prepare for dinner.

LAUN.   That is done, sir; they have all stomachs.

LOR.   Goodly Lord, what a wit-snapper are you! then bid them prepare
dinner.

LAUN.   That is done too, sir; only "cover" is the word.

LOR.   Will you cover,[4] then, sir?

LAUN.   Not so, sir, neither; I know my duty.

LOR.   Yet more quarrelling with occasion! Wilt thou show the whole
wealth of thy wit in an instant? I pray thee, understand a plain man
in his plain meaning: go to thy fellows; bid them cover the table,
serve in the meat, and we will come in to dinner.

LAUN.   For the table, sir, it shall be served in; for the meat, sir, it shall
be covered; for your coming in to dinner, sir, why, let it be as
humours and conceits shall govern.   [*Exit.*]

LOR.   O dear discretion, how his words are suited!
The fool hath planted in his memory
An army of good words; and I do know
A many fools, that stand in better place,
Garnish'd like him, that for a tricksy word

---

4. *cover*] The clown quibbles on the use of the word "cover" in the two senses of laying the
table and wearing one's hat.

Defy the matter. How cheer'st thou, Jessica?
And now, good sweet, say thy opinion,
How dost thou like the Lord Bassanio's wife?

JES. Past all expressing. It is very meet
The Lord Bassanio live an upright life;
For, having such a blessing in his lady,
He finds the joys of heaven here on earth;
And if on earth he do not mean it, then
In reason he should never come to heaven.
Why, if two gods should play some heavenly match
And on the wager lay two earthly women,
And Portia one, there must be something else
Pawn'd with the other; for the poor rude world
Hath not her fellow.

LOR.   Even such a husband
Hast thou of me as she is for a wife.

JES. Nay, but ask my opinion too of that.

LOR. I will anon: first, let us go to dinner.

JES. Nay, let me praise you while I have a stomach.

LOR. No, pray thee, let it serve for table-talk;
Then, howsoe'er thou speak'st, 'mong other things
I shall digest it.

JES. Well, I 'll set you forth.   [*Exeunt.*]

ACT IV.

SCENE I. *Venice. A Court of Justice.*

Enter the DUKE, *the* Magnificoes, ANTONIO, BASSANIO, GRATIANO, SALERIO, *and others*

DUKE.   What, is Antonio here?

ANT.   Ready, so please your Grace.

DUKE.   I am sorry for thee: thou art come to answer
  A stony adversary, an inhuman wretch
  Uncapable of pity, void and empty
  From any dram of mercy.

ANT.   I have heard
  Your Grace hath ta'en great pains to qualify
  His rigorous course; but since he stands obdurate,
  And that no lawful means can carry me
  Out of his envy's reach, I do oppose
  My patience to his fury; and am arm'd
  To suffer, with a quietness of spirit,
  The very tyranny and rage of his.

DUKE.   Go one, and call the Jew into the court.

SALER.   He is ready at the door: he comes, my lord.

Enter SHYLOCK

DUKE.   Make room, and let him stand before our face.
  Shylock, the world thinks, and I think so too,
  That thou but lead'st this fashion of thy malice
  To the last hour of act; and then 't is thought
  Thou 'lt show thy mercy and remorse more strange

Than is thy strange apparent cruelty;
And where thou now exact'st the penalty,
Which is a pound of this poor merchant's flesh,
Thou wilt not only loose the forfeiture,
But, touch'd with human gentleness and love,
Forgive a moiety of the principal;
Glancing an eye of pity on his losses,
That have of late so huddled on his back,
Enow to press a royal merchant down,
And pluck commiseration of his state
From brassy bosoms and rough hearts of flint,
From stubborn Turks and Tartars, never train'd
To offices of tender courtesy.
We all expect a gentle answer, Jew.

SHY.   I have possess'd your Grace of what I purpose;
And by our holy Sabbath have I sworn
To have the due and forfeit of my bond:
If you deny it, let the danger light
Upon your charter and your city's freedom.
You 'll ask me, why I rather choose to have
A weight of carrion-flesh than to receive
Three thousand ducats: I 'll not answer that:
But, say, it is my humour: is it answer'd?
What if my house be troubled with a rat,
And I be pleased to give ten thousand ducats
To have it baned? What, are you answer'd yet?
Some men there are love not a gaping pig;[1]
Some, that are mad if they behold a cat;
And others, when the bagpipe sings i' the nose,
Cannot contain their urine: for affection,
Mistress of passion, sways it to the mood
Of what it likes or loathes. Now, for your answer:
As there is no firm reason to be render'd,
Why he cannot abide a gaping pig;
Why he, a harmless necessary cat;

---

1. *gaping pig*] a pig prepared for the table with a lemon in its mouth.

Why he, a woollen bag-pipe; but of force
Must yield to such inevitable shame
As to offend, himself being offended;
So can I give no reason, nor I will not,
More than a lodged hate and a certain loathing
I bear Antonio, that I follow thus
A losing suit against him. Are you answer'd?

BASS.   This is no answer, thou unfeeling man,
To excuse the current of thy cruelty.

SHY.   I am not bound to please thee with my answer.

BASS.   Do all men kill the things they do not love?

SHY.   Hates any man the thing he would not kill?

BASS.   Every offence is not a hate at first.

SHY.   What, wouldst thou have a serpent sting thee twice?

ANT.   I pray you, think you question with the Jew:[2]
You may as well go stand upon the beach,
And bid the main flood bate his usual height;
You may as well use question with the wolf,
Why he hath made the ewe bleat for the lamb;
You may as well forbid the mountain pines
To wag their high tops, and to make no noise,
When they are fretten with the gusts of heaven;
You may as well do any thing most hard,
As seek to soften that — than which what 's harder? —
His Jewish heart: therefore, I do beseech you,
Make no more offers, use no farther means,
But with all brief and plain conveniency
Let me have judgement and the Jew his will.

BASS.   For thy three thousand ducats here is six.

SHY.   If every ducat in six thousand ducats
Were in six parts and every part a ducat,
I would not draw them; I would have my bond.

DUKE.   How shalt thou hope for mercy, rendering none?

SHY.   What judgement shall I dread, doing no wrong?

---

2. *think you . . . Jew*] remember you are conversing with, seeking to move the inflexible
Jew.

You have among you many a purchased slave,
Which, like your asses and your dogs and mules,
You use in abject and in slavish parts,
Because you bought them: shall I say to you,
Let them be free, marry them to your heirs?
Why sweat they under burthens? let their beds
Be made as soft as yours, and let their palates
Be season'd with such viands? You will answer
"The slaves are ours:" so do I answer you:
The pound of flesh, which I demand of him,
Is dearly bought; 't is mine and I will have it.
If you deny me, fie upon your law!
There is no force in the decrees of Venice.
I stand for judgement: answer; shall I have it?

DUKE.   Upon my power I may dismiss this court,
Unless Bellario, a learned doctor,
Whom I have sent for to determine this,
Come here to-day.

SALER.   My lord, here stays without
A messenger with letters from the doctor,
New come from Padua.

DUKE.   Bring us the letters; call the messenger.

BASS.   Good cheer, Antonio! What, man, courage yet!
The Jew shall have my flesh, blood, bones, and all,
Ere thou shalt lose for me one drop of blood.

ANT.   I am a tainted wether[3] of the flock,
Meetest for death: the weakest kind of fruit
Drops earliest to the ground; and so let me:
You cannot better be employ'd, Bassanio,
Than to live still, and write mine epitaph.

Enter NERISSA, *dressed like a lawyer's clerk*

DUKE.   Came you from Padua, from Bellario?
NER.   From both, my lord. Bellario greets your Grace.

[*Presenting a letter.*]

---

3. *wether*] castrated ram.

BASS.   Why dost thou whet thy knife so earnestly?

SHY.   To cut the forfeiture from that bankrupt there.

GRA.   Not on thy sole, but on thy soul, harsh Jew,
Thou makest thy knife keen; but no metal can,
No, not the hangman's axe, bear half the keenness
Of thy sharp envy. Can no prayers pierce thee?

SHY.   No, none that thou hast wit enough to make.

GRA.   O, be thou damn'd, inexecrable dog!
And for thy life let justice be accused.
Thou almost makest me waver in my faith,
To hold opinion with Pythagoras,
That souls of animals infuse themselves
Into the trunks of men: thy currish spirit
Govern'd a wolf, who hang'd for human slaughter,
Even from the gallows did his fell soul fleet,
And, whilst thou lay'st in thy unhallow'd dam,
Infused itself in thee; for thy desires
Are wolvish, bloody, starved and ravenous.

SHY.   Till thou canst rail the seal from off my bond,
Thou but offend'st thy lungs to speak so loud:
Repair thy wit, good youth, or it will fall
To cureless ruin. I stand here for law.

DUKE.   This letter from Bellario doth commend
A young and learned doctor to our court.
Where is he?

NER.   He attendeth here hard by,
To know your answer, whether you 'll admit him.

DUKE.   With all my heart. Some three or four of you
Go give him courteous conduct to this place.
Meantime the court shall hear Bellario's letter.

CLERK.   [Reads] Your Grace shall understand that at the receipt of your letter
I am very sick: but in the instant that your messenger came, in loving
visitation was with me a young doctor of Rome; his name is Balthasar. I
acquainted him with the cause in controversy between the Jew and
Antonio the merchant: we turned o'er many books together: he is
furnished with my opinion; which, bettered with his own learning, —
the greatness whereof I cannot enough commend, — comes with him,
at my importunity, to fill up your Grace's request in my stead. I beseech
you, let his lack of years be no impediment to let him lack a reverend

estimation; for I never knew so young a body with so old a head. I leave him to your gracious acceptance, whose trial shall better publish his commendation.

DUKE. You hear the learn'd Bellario, what he writes:
And here, I take it, is the doctor come.

Enter PORTIA *for* BALTHASAR

Give me your hand. Come you from old Bellario?
POR. I did, my lord.
DUKE. You are welcome: take your place.
Are you acquainted with the difference
That holds this present question in the court?
POR. I am informed throughly of the cause.
Which is the merchant here, and which the Jew?
DUKE. Antonio and old Shylock, both stand forth.
POR. Is your name Shylock?
SHY. Shylock is my name.
POR. Of a strange nature is the suit you follow;
Yet in such rule that the Venetian law
Cannot impugn you as you do proceed.
You stand within his danger,[4] do you not?
ANT. Ay, so he says.
POR. Do you confess the bond?
ANT. I do.
POR. Then must the Jew be merciful.
SHY. On what compulsion must I? tell me that.
POR. The quality of mercy is not strain'd,[5]
It droppeth as the gentle rain from heaven
Upon the place beneath: it is twice blest;
It blesseth him that gives, and him that takes:

---

4. *within his danger*] in his power. The original meaning of danger was not, as in modern times, "peril," but "dominion," including the power to hurt or harm.
5. *strain'd*] compelled, moved by force or compulsion. Portia takes up the challenge conveyed in Shylock's query, "On what compulsion must I?"

    'T is mightiest in the mightiest: it becomes
    The throned monarch better than his crown;
    His sceptre shows the force of temporal power,
    The attribute to awe and majesty,
    Wherein doth sit the dread and fear of kings;
    But mercy is above this sceptred sway;
    It is enthroned in the hearts of kings,
    It is an attribute to God himself;
    And earthly power doth then show likest God's
    When mercy seasons justice. Therefore, Jew,
    Though justice be thy plea, consider this,
    That, in the course of justice, none of us
    Should see salvation: we do pray for mercy;
    And that same prayer doth teach us all to render
    The deeds of mercy. I have spoke thus much
    To mitigate the justice of thy plea;
    Which if thou follow, this strict court of Venice
    Must needs give sentence 'gainst the merchant there.
SHY.   My deeds upon my head! I crave the law,
    The penalty and forfeit of my bond.
POR.   Is he not able to discharge the money?
BASS.   Yes, here I tender it for him in the court;
    Yea, twice the sum: if that will not suffice,
    I will be bound to pay it ten times o'er,
    On forfeit of my hands, my head, my heart:
    If this will not suffice, it must appear
    That malice bears down truth. And I beseech you,
    Wrest once the law to your authority:
    To do a great right, do a little wrong,
    And curb this cruel devil of his will.
POR.   It must not be; there is no power in Venice
    Can alter a decree established:
    'T will be recorded for a precedent,
    And many an error, by the same example,
    Will rush into the state: it cannot be.
SHY.   A Daniel come to judgement! yea, a Daniel!

O wise young judge,[6] how I do honour thee!

POR. I pray you, let me look upon the bond.

SHY. Here 't is, most reverend doctor, here it is.

POR. Shylock, there 's thrice thy money offer'd thee.

SHY. An oath, an oath, I have an oath in heaven:
Shall I lay perjury upon my soul?
No, not for Venice.

POR.   Why, this bond is forfeit;
And lawfully by this the Jew may claim
A pound of flesh, to be by him cut off
Nearest the merchant's heart. Be merciful:
Take thrice thy money; bid me tear the bond.

SHY. When it is paid according to the tenour.
It doth appear you are a worthy judge;
You know the law, your exposition
Hath been most sound: I charge you by the law,
Whereof you are a well-deserving pillar,
Proceed to judgement: by my soul I swear
There is no power in the tongue of man
To alter me: I stay here on my bond.

ANT. Most heartily I do beseech the court
To give the judgement.

POR.   Why then, thus it is:
You must prepare your bosom for his knife.

SHY. O noble judge! O excellent young man!

POR. For the intent and purpose of the law
Hath full relation to the penalty,
Which here appeareth due upon the bond.

SHY. 'T is very true: O wise and upright judge!
How much more elder art thou than thy looks!

POR. Therefore lay bare your bosom.

SHY.   Ay, his breast:
So says the bond: — doth it not, noble judge? —

---

6. A *Daniel . . . young judge*] The allusion is to the "History of Susannah" in the *Apocrypha*, where Daniel, "a young youth" (v. 45) convicted the elders "of false witness by their own mouth" (v. 61), and "from that day forth was had in great reputation in the sight of the people" (v. 64).

"Nearest his heart:" those are the very words.

POR.   It is so. Are there balance[7] here to weigh
The flesh?

SHY.   I have them ready.

POR.   Have by some surgeon, Shylock, on your charge,
To stop his wounds, lest he do bleed to death.

SHY.   Is it so nominated in the bond?

POR.   It is not so express'd: but what of that?
'T were good you do so much for charity.

SHY.   I cannot find it; 't is not in the bond.

POR.   You, merchant, have you any thing to say?

ANT.   But little: I am arm'd and well prepared.
Give me your hand, Bassanio: fare you well!
Grieve not that I am fallen to this for you;
For herein Fortune shows herself more kind
Than is her custom: it is still her use
To let the wretched man outlive his wealth,
To view with hollow eye and wrinkled brow
An age of poverty; from which lingering penance
Of such misery doth she cut me off.
Commend me to your honourable wife:
Tell her the process of Antonio's end;
Say how I loved you, speak me fair in death;
And, when the tale is told, bid her be judge
Whether Bassanio had not once a love.
Repent but you that you shall lose your friend,
And he repents not that he pays your debt;
For if the Jew do cut but deep enough,
I 'll pay it presently with all my heart.

BASS.   Antonio, I am married to a wife
Which is as dear to me as life itself;
But life itself, my wife, and all the world,
Are not with me esteem'd above thy life:
I would lose all, ay, sacrifice them all
Here to this devil, to deliver you.

---

7. *balance*] commonly treated as a plural noun with the sense of "scales."

POR.   Your wife would give you little thanks for that,
    If she were by, to hear you make the offer.
GRA.   I have a wife, whom, I protest, I love:
    I would she were in heaven, so she could
    Entreat some power to change this currish Jew.
NER.   'T is well you offer it behind her back;
    The wish would make else an unquiet house.
SHY.   These be the Christian husbands. I have a daughter;
    Would any of the stock of Barrabas[8]
    Had been her husband rather than a Christian!   [*Aside.*]
    We trifle time: I pray thee, pursue sentence.
POR.   A pound of that same merchant's flesh is thine:
    The court awards it, and the law doth give it.
SHY.   Most rightful judge!
POR.   And you must cut this flesh from off his breast:
    The law allows it, and the court awards it.
SHY.   Most learned judge! A sentence! Come, prepare!
POR.   Tarry a little; there is something else.
    This bond doth give thee here no jot of blood;
    The words expressly are "a pound of flesh:"
    Take then thy bond, take thou thy pound of flesh:
    But, in the cutting it, if thou dost shed
    One drop of Christian blood, thy lands and goods
    Are, by the laws of Venice, confiscate
    Unto the state of Venice.
GRA.   O upright judge! Mark, Jew: O learned judge!
SHY.   Is that the law?
POR.   Thyself shalt see the act:
    For, as thou urgest justice, be assured
    Thou shalt have justice, more than thou desirest.
GRA.   O learned judge! Mark, Jew: a learned judge!
SHY.   I take this offer, then; pay the bond thrice,
    And let the Christian go.
BASS.   Here is the money.

---

8. *Barrabas*] In New Testament accounts, when Pilate allowed the people of Jerusalem to choose a prisoner to be released in honor of the Passover they chose Barrabas rather than Jesus.

POR.   Soft!
  The Jew shall have all justice; soft! no haste:
  He shall have nothing but the penalty.
GRA.   O Jew! an upright judge, a learned judge!
POR.   Therefore prepare thee to cut off the flesh.
  Shed thou no blood; nor cut thou less nor more
  But just a pound of flesh: if thou cut'st more
  Or less than a just pound, be it but so much
  As makes it light or heavy in the substance,
  Or the division of the twentieth part
  Of one poor scruple, nay, if the scale do turn
  But in the estimation of a hair,
  Thou diest and all thy goods are confiscate.
GRA.   A second Daniel, a Daniel, Jew!
  Now, infidel, I have you on the hip.
POR.   Why doth the Jew pause? take thy forfeiture.
SHY.   Give me my principal, and let me go.
BASS.   I have it ready for thee; here it is.
POR.   He hath refused it in the open court:
  He shall have merely justice and his bond.
GRA.   A Daniel, still say I, a second Daniel!
  I thank thee, Jew, for teaching me that word.
SHY.   Shall I not have barely my principal?
POR.   Thou shalt have nothing but the forfeiture,
  To be so taken at thy peril, Jew.
SHY.   Why, then the devil give him good of it!
  I 'll stay no longer question.
POR.   Tarry, Jew:
  The law hath yet another hold on you.
  It is enacted in the laws of Venice,
  If it be proved against an alien
  That by direct or indirect attempts
  He seek the life of any citizen,
  The party 'gainst the which he doth contrive
  Shall seize one half his goods; the other half
  Comes to the privy coffer of the state;
  And the offender's life lies in the mercy

Of the Duke only, 'gainst all other voice.
In which predicament, I say, thou stand'st;
For it appears, by manifest proceeding,
That indirectly, and directly too,
Thou hast contrived against the very life
Of the defendant; and thou hast incurr'd
The danger formerly by me rehearsed.
Down, therefore, and beg mercy of the Duke.

GRA.   Beg that thou mayst have leave to hang thyself:
And yet, thy wealth being forfeit to the state,
Thou hast not left the value of a cord;
Therefore thou must be hang'd at the state's charge.

DUKE.   That thou shall see the difference of our spirits,
I pardon thee thy life before thou ask it:
For half thy wealth, it is Antonio's;
The other half comes to the general state,
Which humbleness may drive unto a fine.

POR.   Ay, for the state, not for Antonio.

SHY.   Nay, take my life and all; pardon not that:
You take my house, when you do take the prop
That doth sustain my house; you take my life,
When you do take the means whereby I live.

POR.   What mercy can you render him, Antonio?

GRA.   A halter gratis; nothing else, for God's sake.

ANT.   So please my lord the Duke and all the court
To quit the fine for one half of his goods,
I am content; so he will let me have
The other half in use,[9] to render it,
Upon his death, unto the gentleman
That lately stole his daughter:
Two things provided more, that, for this favour,
He presently become a Christian;
The other, that he do record a gift,
Here in the court, of all he dies possess'd,
Unto his son Lorenzo and his daughter.

---

9. *in use*] in trust.

DUKE.   He shall do this, or else I do recant
    The pardon that I late pronounced here.
POR.   Art thou contented, Jew? what dost thou say?
SHY.   I am content.
POR.   Clerk, draw a deed of gift.
SHY.   I pray you, give me leave to go from hence;
    I am not well: send the deed after me,
    And I will sign it.
DUKE.   Get thee gone, but do it.
GRA.   In christening shalt thou have two godfathers:
    Had I been judge, thou shouldst have had ten more,[10]
    To bring thee to the gallows, not the font.   [*Exit* SHYLOCK.]
DUKE.   Sir, I entreat you home with me to dinner.
POR.   I humbly do desire your Grace of pardon:
    I must away this night toward Padua,
    And it is meet I presently set forth.
DUKE.   I am sorry that your leisure serves you not.
    Antonio, gratify this gentleman,
    For, in my mind, you are much bound to him.
                  [*Exeunt* DUKE *and his train.*]
BASS.   Most worthy gentleman, I and my friend
    Have by your wisdom been this day acquitted
    Of grievous penalties; in lieu whereof,
    Three thousand ducats, due unto the Jew,
    We freely cope[11] your courteous pains withal.
ANT.   And stand indebted, over and above,
    In love and service to you evermore.
POR.   He is well paid that is well satisfied;
    And I, delivering you, am satisfied,
    And therein do account myself well paid:
    My mind was never yet more mercenary.
    I pray you, know me when we meet again:
    I wish you well, and so I take my leave.

---

10. *ten more*] a jury of twelve men.
11. *cope*] requite, give the equivalent of.

BASS.   Dear sir, of force I must attempt you further:
Take some remembrance of us, as a tribute,
Not as a fee: grant me two things, I pray you,
Not to deny me, and to pardon me.

POR.   You press me far, and therefore I will yield.
Give me your gloves, I 'll wear them for your sake; [*To* ANTONIO.]
And, for your love I 'll take this ring from you: [*To* BASSANIO.]
Do not draw back your hand; I 'll take no more;
And you in love shall not deny me this.

BASS.   This ring, good sir, alas, it is a trifle!
I will not shame myself to give you this.

POR.   I will have nothing else but only this;
And now methinks I have a mind to it.

BASS.   There 's more depends on this than on the value.
The dearest ring in Venice will I give you,
And find it out by proclamation:
Only for this, I pray you, pardon me.

POR.   I see, sir, you are liberal in offers:
You taught me first to beg; and now methinks
You teach me how a beggar should be answer'd.

BASS.   Good sir, this ring was given me by my wife;
And when she put it on, she made me vow
That I should neither sell nor give nor lose it.

POR.   That 'scuse serves many men to save their gifts.
An if your wife be not a mad-woman,
And know how well I have deserved the ring,
She would not hold out enemy for ever,
For giving it to me. Well, peace be with you!
[*Exeunt* PORTIA *and* NERISSA.]

ANT.   My Lord Bassanio, let him have the ring:
Let his deservings and my love withal
Be valued 'gainst your wife's commandment.

BASS.   Go, Gratiano, run and overtake him;
Give him the ring; and bring him, if thou canst,
Unto Antonio's house: away! make haste.   [*Exit* GRATIANO.]
Come, you and I will thither presently;
And in the morning early will we both
Fly toward Belmont: come, Antonio.   [*Exeunt.*]

SCENE II. *The same. A street.*

Enter PORTIA *and* NERISSA

POR.   Inquire the Jew's house out, give him this deed
And let him sign it: we 'll away to-night
And be a day before our husbands home:
This deed will be well welcome to Lorenzo.

Enter GRATIANO

GRA.   Fair sir, you are well o'erta'en:
My Lord Bassanio upon more advice
Hath sent you here this ring, and doth entreat
Your company at dinner.
POR.   That cannot be:
His ring I do accept most thankfully:
And so, I pray you, tell him: furthermore,
I pray you, show my youth old Shylock's house.
GRA.   That will I do.
NER.   Sir, I would speak with you.
I 'll see if I can get my husband's ring,   [*Aside to* PORTIA.]
Which I did make him swear to keep for ever.
POR.   [*Aside to* NERISSA.] Thou mayst, I warrant. We shall have old[1]
swearing
That they did give the rings away to men;
But we 'll outface them, and outswear them too.
[*Aloud*] Away! make haste: thou know'st where I will tarry!
NER.   Come, good sir, will you show me to this house?

                                                            [*Exeunt.*]

---

1. *old*] any amount of.

ACT V.

SCENE I. *Belmont. Avenue to* PORTIA'S *house.*

Enter LORENZO *and* JESSICA

LOR.   The moon shines bright: in such a night as this,
     When the sweet wind did gently kiss the trees
     And they did make no noise, in such a night
     Troilus methinks mounted the Troyan walls,
     And sighed his soul toward the Grecian tents,
     Where Cressid lay that night.
JES.   In such a night
     Did Thisbe fearfully o'ertrip the dew,
     And saw the lion's shadow ere himself,
     And ran dismay'd away.
LOR.   In such a night
     Stood Dido with a willow in her hand
     Upon the wild sea banks, and waft her love
     To come again to Carthage.
JES.   In such a night
     Medea gather'd the enchanted herbs
     That did renew old Æson.[1]
LOR.   In such a night
     Did Jessica steal from the wealthy Jew,

---

1. *Troilus . . . Æson*]. The allusions to Troilus and Cressid probably refer to Chaucer's *Troylus and Cresseide*; Thisbe is Chaucer's second subject in his *Legend of Good Women* and the tale of Dido is the third, followed by the legend of Medea and Æson (Jason).

79

And with an unthrift love did run from Venice
As far as Belmont.
JES.   In such a night
Did young Lorenzo swear he loved her well,
Stealing her soul with many vows of faith
And ne'er a true one.
LOR.   In such a night
Did pretty Jessica, like a little shrew,
Slander her love, and he forgave it her.
JES.   I would out-night you, did no body come;
But, hark, I hear the footing of a man.

Enter STEPHANO

LOR.   Who comes so fast in silence of the night?
STEPH.   A friend.
LOR.   A friend! what friend? your name, I pray you, friend?
STEPH.   Stephano is my name; and I bring word
My mistress will before the break of day
Be here at Belmont: she doth stray about
By holy crosses, where she kneels and prays
For happy wedlock hours.
LOR.   Who comes with her?
STEPH.   None but a holy hermit and her maid.
I pray you, is my master yet return'd?
LOR.   He is not, nor we have not heard from him.
But go we in, I pray thee, Jessica,
And ceremoniously let us prepare
Some welcome for the mistress of the house.

Enter LAUNCELOT

LAUN.   Sola, sola! wo ha, ho! sola, sola!
LOR.   Who calls?
LAUN.   Sola! did you see Master Lorenzo? Master Lorenzo, sola, sola!
LOR.   Leave hollaing, man: here.
LAUN.   Sola! where? where?
LOR.   Here.

LAUN.   Tell him there's a post come from my master, with his horn full
    of good news: my master will be here ere morning.   [*Exit.*]
LOR.   Sweet soul, let's in, and there expect their coming.
    And yet no matter: why should we go in?
    My friend Stephano, signify, I pray you,
    Within the house, your mistress is at hand;
    And bring your music forth into the air.   [*Exit* STEPHANO.]
    How sweet the moonlight sleeps upon this bank!
    Here will we sit, and let the sounds of music
    Creep in our ears: soft stillness and the night
    Become the touches of sweet harmony.
    Sit, Jessica. Look how the floor of heaven
    Is thick inlaid with patines of bright gold:
    There's not the smallest orb which thou behold'st
    But in his motion like an angel sings,
    Still quiring[2] to the young-eyed cherubins;
    Such harmony is in immortal souls;
    But whilst this muddy vesture of decay
    Doth grossly close it in, we cannot hear it.

Enter Musicians

    Come, ho, and wake Diana with a hymn!
    With sweetest touches pierce your mistress' ear,
    And draw her home with music.   [*Music.*]
JES.   I am never merry when I hear sweet music.
LOR.   The reason is, your spirits are attentive:
    For do but note a wild and wanton herd,
    Or race of youthful and unhandled colts,
    Fetching mad bounds, bellowing and neighing loud,
    Which is the hot condition of their blood;
    If they but hear perchance a trumpet sound,
    Or any air of music touch their ears,
    You shall perceive them make a mutual stand,
    Their savage eyes turn'd to a modest gaze
    By the sweet power of music: therefore the poet

---

2. *quiring*] singing in concert.

Did feign that Orpheus drew trees, stones and floods;
Since nought so stockish, hard and full of rage,
But music for the time doth change his nature.
The man that hath no music in himself,
Nor is not moved with concord of sweet sounds,
Is fit for treasons, stratagems and spoils;
The motions of his spirit are dull as night,
And his affections dark as Erebus:[3]
Let no such man be trusted. Mark the music.

Enter PORTIA *and* NERISSA

POR. That light we see is burning in my hall.
How far that little candle throws his beams!
So shines a good deed in a naughty world.
NER. When the moon shone, we did not see the candle.
POR. So doth the greater glory dim the less:
A substitute shines brightly as a king,
Until a king be by; and then his state
Empties itself, as doth an inland brook
Into the main of waters. Music! hark!
NER. It is your music, madam, of the house.
POR. Nothing is good, I see, without respect:[4]
Methinks it sounds much sweeter than by day.
NER. Silence bestows that virtue on it, madam.
POR. The crow doth sing as sweetly as the lark,
When neither is attended; and I think
The nightingale, if she should sing by day,
When every goose is cackling, would be thought
No better a musician than the wren.
How many things by season season'd are
To their right praise and true perfection!
Peace, ho! the moon sleeps with Endymion,[5]
And would not be awaked.   [*Music ceases.*]

---

3. *Erebus*] Tartarus, hell.
4. *without respect*] without consideration of circumstances.
5. *Endymion*] a youth loved by the goddess of the moon.

LOR.   That is the voice,
  Or I am much deceived, of Portia.
POR.   He knows me as the blind man knows the cuckoo,
  By the bad voice.
LOR.   Dear lady, welcome home.
POR.   We have been praying for our husbands' healths,
  Which speed, we hope, the better for our words.
  Are they return'd?
LOR.   Madam, they are not yet;
  But there is come a messenger before,
  To signify their coming.
POR.   Go in, Nerissa;
  Give order to my servants that they take
  No note at all of our being absent hence;
  Nor you, Lorenzo; Jessica, nor you.   [A *tucket sounds.*]
LOR.   Your husband is at hand; I hear his trumpet:
  We are no tell-tales, madam; fear you not.
POR.   This night methinks is but the daylight sick;
  It looks a little paler: 't is a day,
  Such as the day is when the sun is hid.

Enter BASSANIO, ANTONIO, GRATIANO, *and their followers*

BASS.   We should hold day with the Antipodes,[6]
  If you would walk in absence of the sun.
POR.   Let me give light, but let me not be light;
  For a light wife doth make a heavy husband,
  And never be Bassanio so for me:
  But God sort all! You are welcome home, my lord.
BASS.   I thank you, madam. Give welcome to my friend.
  This is the man, this is Antonio,
  To whom I am so infinitely bound.
POR.   You should in all sense be much bound to him,
  For, as I hear, he was much bound for you.
ANT.   No more than I am well acquitted of.
POR.   Sir, you are very welcome to our house:

---

6. *the Antipodes*] the people living on the opposite side of the globe.

It must appear in other ways than words,
Therefore I scant this breathing courtesy.

GRA.   [*To* NERISSA] By yonder moon I swear you do me wrong;
In faith, I gave it to the judge's clerk:
Would he were gelt[7] that had it, for my part,
Since you do take it, love, so much at heart.

POR.   A quarrel, ho, already! what 's the matter?

GRA.   About a hoop of gold, a paltry ring
That she did give me, whose posy[8] was
For all the world like cutler's poetry
Upon a knife, "Love me, and leave me not."

NER.   What talk you of the posy or the value?
You swore to me, when I did give it you,
That you would wear it till your hour of death,
And that it should lie with you in your grave:
Though not for me, yet for your vehement oaths,
You should have been respective, and have kept it.
Gave it a judge's clerk! no, God's my judge,
The clerk will ne'er wear hair on 's face that had it.

GRA.   He will, an if he live to be a man.

NER.   Ay, if a woman live to be a man.

GRA.   Now, by this hand, I gave it to a youth,
A kind of boy, a little scrubbed[9] boy,
No higher than thyself, the judge's clerk,
A prating boy, that begg'd it as a fee:
I could not for my heart deny it him.

POR.   You were to blame, I must be plain with you,
To part so slightly with your wife's first gift;
A thing stuck on with oaths upon your finger
And so riveted with faith unto your flesh.
I gave my love a ring, and made him swear
Never to part with it; and here he stands;

---

7. *gelt*] castrated.
8. *posy*] inscription on a ring.
9. *scrubbed*] a contemptuous epithet implying both repulsiveness and insignificance.

I dare be sworn for him he would not leave it
Nor pluck it from his finger, for the wealth
That the world masters. Now, in faith, Gratiano,
You give your wife too unkind a cause of grief:
An 't were to me, I should be mad at it.

BASS.   [Aside] Why, I were best to cut my left hand off,
And swear I lost the ring defending it.

GRA.   My Lord Bassanio gave his ring away
Unto the judge that begg'd it, and indeed
Deserved it too; and then the boy, his clerk,
That took some pains in writing, he begg'd mine;
And neither man nor master would take aught
But the two rings.

POR.   What ring gave you, my lord?
Not that, I hope, which you received of me.

BASS.   If I could add a lie unto a fault,
I would deny it; but you see my finger
Hath not the ring upon it, it is gone.

POR.   Even so void is your false heart of truth.
By heaven, I will ne'er come in your bed
Until I see the ring.

NER.   Nor I in yours
Till I again see mine.

BASS.   Sweet Portia,
If you did know to whom I gave the ring,
If you did know for whom I gave the ring,
And would conceive[10] for what I gave the ring,
And how unwillingly I left the ring,
When nought would be accepted but the ring,
You would abate the strength of your displeasure.

POR.   If you had known the virtue of the ring,
Or half her worthiness that gave the ring,
Or your own honour to contain[11] the ring,
You would not then have parted with the ring.

---

10. *conceive*] form an idea, imagine.
11. *contain*] retain.

What man is there so much unreasonable,
If you had pleased to have defended it
With any terms of zeal, wanted the modesty
To urge the thing held as a ceremony?[12]
Nerissa teaches me what to believe:
I 'll die for 't but some woman had the ring.

BASS.   No, by my honour, madam, by my soul,
No woman had it, but a civil doctor,
Which did refuse three thousand ducats of me,
And begg'd the ring; the which I did deny him,
And suffer'd him to go displeased away;
Even he that did uphold the very life
Of my dear friend. What should I say, sweet lady?
I was enforced to send it after him;
I was beset with shame and courtesy;
My honour would not let ingratitude
So much besmear it. Pardon me, good lady;
For, by these blessed candles of the night,
Had you been there, I think you would have begg'd
The ring of me to give the worthy doctor.

POR.   Let not that doctor e'er come near my house:
Since he hath got the jewel that I loved,
And that which you did swear to keep for me,
I will become as liberal as you;
I 'll not deny him anything I have,
No, not my body nor my husband's bed:
Know him I shall, I am well sure of it:
Lie not a night from home; watch me like Argus:[13]
If you do not, if I be left alone,
Now, by mine honour, which is yet mine own,
I 'll have that doctor for my bedfellow.

NER.   And I his clerk; therefore be well advised
How you do leave me to mine own protection.

GRA.   Well, do you so: let not me take him, then;
For if I do, I 'll mar the young clerk's pen.

---

12. *ceremony*] an ornament of sacred import; a solemn trophy.
13. *Argus*] Io's keeper, who had 100 eyes.

ANT.   I am the unhappy subject of these quarrels.

POR.   Sir, grieve not you; you are welcome notwithstanding.

BASS.   Portia, forgive me this enforced wrong;
    And, in the hearing of these many friends,
    I swear to thee, even by thine own fair eyes,
    Wherein I see myself, —

POR.   Mark you but that!
    In both my eyes he doubly sees himself;
    In each eye, one: swear by your double self,
    And there 's an oath of credit.

BASS.   Nay, but hear me:
    Pardon this fault, and by my soul I swear
    I never more will break an oath with thee.

ANT.   I once did lend my body for his wealth;
    Which, but for him that had your husband's ring,
    Had quite miscarried: I dare be bound again,
    My soul upon the forfeit, that your lord
    Will never more break faith advisedly.

POR.   Then you shall be his surety. Give him this,
    And bid him keep it better than the other.

ANT.   Here, Lord Bassanio; swear to keep this ring.

BASS.   By heaven, it is the same I gave the doctor!

POR.   I had it of him: pardon me, Bassanio;
    For, by this ring, the doctor lay with me.

NER.   And pardon me, my gentle Gratiano;
    For that same scrubbed boy, the doctor's clerk,
    In lieu of this last night did lie with me.

GRA.   Why, this is like the mending of highways
    In summer, where the ways are fair enough:
    What, are we cuckolds ere we have deserved it?

POR.   Speak not so grossly. You are all amazed:
    Here is a letter; read it at your leisure;
    It comes from Padua, from Bellario:
    There you shall find that Portia was the doctor,
    Nerissa there her clerk: Lorenzo here
    Shall witness I set forth as soon as you,
    And even but now return'd; I have not yet
    Enter'd my house. Antonio, you are welcome;

And I have better news in store for you
Than you expect: unseal this letter soon;
There you shall find three of your argosies
Are richly come to harbour suddenly:
You shall not know by what strange accident
I chanced on this letter.

ANT.   I am dumb.

BASS.   Were you the doctor and I knew you not?

GRA.   Were you the clerk that is to make me cuckold?

NER.   Ay, but the clerk that never means to do it,
Unless he live until he be a man.

BASS.   Sweet doctor, you shall be my bedfellow:
When I am absent, then lie with my wife.

ANT.   Sweet lady, you have given me life and living;
For here I read for certain that my ships
Are safely come to road.

POR.   How now, Lorenzo!
My clerk hath some good comforts too for you.

NER.   Ay, and I 'll give them him without a fee.
There do I give to you and Jessica,
From the rich Jew, a special deed of gift,
After his death, of all he dies possess'd of.

LOR.   Fair ladies, you drop manna in the way
Of starved people.

POR.   It is almost morning,
And yet I am sure you are not satisfied
Of these events at full. Let us go in;
And charge us there upon inter'gatories,
And we will answer all things faithfully.

GRA.   Let it be so: the first inter'gatory
That my Nerissa shall be sworn on is,
Whether till the next night she had rather stay,
Or go to bed now, being two hours to day:
But were the day come, I should wish it dark,
That I were couching with the doctor's clerk.
Well, while I live I 'll fear no other thing
So sore as keeping safe Nerissa's ring.   [*Exeunt.*]

Study Guide

Text by

Garrett T. Caples
Instructor of English
University of California at Berkeley,
Berkeley, California

Contents

**Each scene includes List of Characters,
Summary, Analysis, Study Questions and
Answers, and Suggested Essay Topics.**

SECTION ONE

Introduction

The Life and Work of William Shakespeare

The details of William Shakespeare's life are sketchy, mostly mere surmise based upon court or other clerical records. His parents, John and Mary (Arden), were married about 1557; she was of the landed gentry, and he was a yeoman—a glover and commodities merchant. By 1568, John had risen through the ranks of town government and held the position of high bailiff, which was a position similar to a mayor. William, the eldest son and the third of eight children, was born in 1564, probably on April 23, several days before his baptism on April 26 in Stratford-upon-Avon. Shakespeare is also believed to have died on the same date-April 23-in 1616.

It is believed that William attended the local grammar school in Stratford where his parents lived, and that he studied primarily Latin, rhetoric, logic, and literature. Shakespeare probably left school at age 15, which was the norm, to take a job, especially since this was the period of his father's financial difficulty. At age 18 (1582), William married Anne Hathaway, a local farmer's daughter who was eight years his senior. Their first daughter (Susanna) was born six months later (1583), and twins Judith and Hamnet were born in 1585.

Shakespeare's life can be divided into three periods: the first 20 years in Stratford, which include his schooling, early marriage, and fatherhood; the next 25 years as an actor and playwright in London; and the last five in retirement in Stratford where he enjoyed the moderate wealth gained from his theatrical successes. The years linking the first two periods are marked by a lack of information about Shakespeare and are often referred to as the "dark years."

At some point during the "dark years," Shakespeare began his career with a London theatrical company, perhaps in 1589, for he was already an actor and playwright of some note by 1592. Shakespeare apparently wrote and acted for numerous theatrical companies, including Pembroke's Men, and Strange's Men, which later became the Chamberlain's Men, with whom he remained for the rest of his career.

In 1592, the Plague closed the theaters for about two years, and Shakespeare turned to writing book-length narrative poetry. Most notable were "Venus and Adonis" and "The Rape of Lucrece," both of which were dedicated to the Earl of Southampton, whom scholars accept as Shakespeare's friend and benefactor despite a lack of documentation. During this same period, Shakespeare was writing his sonnets, which are more likely signs of the time's fashion rather than actual love poems detailing any particular relationship. He returned to playwriting when theaters reopened in 1594, and did not continue to write poetry. His sonnets were published without his consent in 1609, shortly before his retirement.

Amid all of his success, Shakespeare suffered the loss of his only son, Hamnet, who died in 1596 at the age of 11. But Shakespeare's career continued unabated, and in London in 1599, he became one of the partners in the new Globe Theater, which was built by the Chamberlain's Men.

Shakespeare wrote very little after 1612, which was the year he completed *Henry VIII*. It was during a performance of this play in 1613 that the Globe caught fire and burned to the ground. Sometime between 1610 and 1613, Shakespeare returned to Stratford, where he owned a large house and property, to spend his remaining years with his family.

William Shakespeare died on April 23, 1616, and was buried two days later in the chancel of Holy Trinity Church where he had been baptized exactly 52 years earlier. His literary legacy included 37 plays, 154 sonnets and five major poems.

Incredibly, most of Shakespeare's plays had never been published in anything except pamphlet form and were simply extant as acting scripts stored at the Globe. Theater scripts were not regarded as literary works of art, but only the basis for the performance. Plays were simply a popular form of entertainment for all layers of society in Shakespeare's time. Only the efforts of two of Shakespeare's company, John Heminges and Henry Condell, preserved his 36 plays (minus *Pericles*, the thirty-seventh).

Historical Background

There may not be a play more misnamed in Shakespeare's entire canon than *The Merchant of Venice*. Though he is certainly an important character, Antonio—the merchant in question—merits, at best, fourth billing. The main lovers in the play, Portia and Bassanio, command a great deal more attention, and, as most commentators suggest, Shylock is ultimately the main attraction. Although the Jewish moneylender "appears in only five of the play's twenty scenes, and not at all in the fifth act, everyone agrees that the play belongs to Shylock" (Barnet 193-4). His dominance is such that, in certain productions (particularly in the nineteenth century), the last act has been "omitted entirely" (Myrick, "Introduction" xxii). Yet, despite his somewhat lesser role, Antonio proves crucial to both main plots of *The Merchant of Venice*. His agreement to serve as collateral for Shylock's loan to Bassanio facilitates the latter's courtship of Portia, and the risk to his life which results from this arrangement generates much of the plot's complications. Shakespeare's decision to make him the title character perhaps stems from an acknowledgment of Antonio's structural importance to all the various story lines, as well as from an effort—perhaps unsuccessful—to balance the audience's attention equally between Shylock's thirst for revenge and the romance of Portia and Bassanio.

Antonio's importance as the hinge between the play's two main plots may reflect the fact that Shakespeare had no one particular inspiration for *The Merchant*, but rather drew primarily on two different sources. Both the story of the three caskets and the story of a usurer's demand of a pound of human flesh apparently derive from Oriental folk-tales (Myrick, "Sources" 142-3; Barton 250), though it is likely that Shakespeare encountered them from Italian and Latin sources. A collection of Italian stories,

Il Pecorone, is usually suggested as Shakespeare's source for the pound of flesh, while *Gesta Romanorum*, a book of medieval Latin stories (first translated into English in 1577), was very likely his introduction to the three caskets (Myrick, "Sources" 142-3). As with most of Shakespeare's plays, the exact date of composition is unknown, but contemporary references prove that it had been performed at least by 1598. "In 1598 and in 1600 the play was entered in the Stationers' Register. It was first published in a quarto (Q1) in 1600" (Myrick, "Textual Note" 139).

The most prominent cultural issues in *The Merchant*, both embodied in the character of Shylock, are the Elizabethan attitudes toward Jews and usury (moneylending). Although "[e]laborate arguments have been mounted to demonstrate that *The Merchant of Venice* is not anti-Semitic"—presumably stemming from critics' desire to defend the ethics of the man many consider to be the greatest poet of the English language—"it is no good to try to discard the hate that energizes the play" (Charney 47). "Jews had been officially banished from England for three centuries" by the time Shakespeare was writing, and there was a lingering hatred of the Jewish race and religion among Christian societies (Barton 250). Such a Christian grudge against Jews allegedly stemmed from the latter group's rejection of Christ, and this sad mixture of racial and religious prejudice is by no means absent from the play. The anti-Semitic mood of England was further fueled by the trial and execution of Roderigo Lopez—a Portuguese Jew and physician to Queen Elizabeth—who was accused of attempting to poison his employer in 1594, a few years before Shakespeare's play was written (Barton 250). The association of Jews with usury is a stereotype unfortunately still familiar to us today; apart from such racial animosity, however, the Elizabethans despised moneylending for interest in and of itself. The practice was technically illegal in England at the time, although there were various ways—some officially-sanctioned—around the law (Myrick, "Introduction" xxvii-iii). The possibility of Antonio's death as a result of his financial dealings with Shylock no doubt reflects the contemporary fear about the exorbitant interest rates usurers sometimes charged.

The stage history of *The Merchant of Venice* has largely been the history of the interpretation of Shylock. How Shakespeare staged the play and the part is unknown; the absence of extensive reference to it throughout the 1600s suggests it wasn't originally one of the author's most popular works (Barnet 194). George Granville staged a notable adaptation of it in 1701, featuring a bumbling, comic Shylock, and this interpretation appears to have been the standard one until 1741, when Charles Macklin radically transformed the character into a terrifying, almost monstrous villain (Barnet 194-6). The next major revision in the acting of the role occurred in 1814, when Edmund Kean presented a Shylock who "evoked not simply terror but pity"; Shylock was seen as justified in his rage, due to his ill-treatment at the hands of the Christians (Barnet 196-7). The evolution of a kinder, gentler Shylock culminated in 1879, when Henry Irving played the character as "a sympathetic and tragic figure," a heroic victim of the increasingly unseemly Christians (Barnet 119). As the dominant Christian culture in England and America has gradually mollified its attitudes toward Jews, Shylock has been portrayed in an increasingly sympathetic light, and subsequent interpretations have oscillated between the various elements of horror and pity, comedy and tragedy, available to the role.

Perhaps the most important aspect of Shakespeare's writing—one which no study guide can presume to replace—is his linguistic style. Indeed, though this may be an obvious point, it is Shakespeare's language (rather than, say, his characters or plots) which has earned him his reputation as the pre-eminent English poet. The large number of expressions or sayings from his plays that have found their way into everyday speech, testifies to the English-speaking world's fascination with Shakespeare as an architect of language. Ironically, however, it is the very strangeness or poetic quality of Shakespeare's language that many beginning students find to be the chief difficulty in coming to terms with his plays, and a few remarks on this subject may serve to clarify some of the peculiarities of Shakespeare's version of English.

It is important to note at the outset that the English of Shakespeare's time and that of our own are relatively the same. That is, both fall under what is broadly designated "Modern English," as opposed to "Old English" (such as one might find in the epic poem

Beowulf) or "Middle English," (as in Chaucer's *The Canterbury Tales*). Be that as it may, some mitigating factors tend to estrange the present-day reader or audience member from Shakespeare's language. The most obvious of these is age. *The Merchant of Venice*, for example, is roughly four hundred years old, and while its language may be substantially the same as ours, a great many words, phrases, and even whole syntaxes have altered over the course of time. This can be shown in the following example:

In Act II, scene I, when the Prince of Morocco attempts to persuade Portia of the value of his dark skin, he remarks, "I tell thee, lady, this aspect of mine/ Hath feared the valiant." There are a number of minor differences easily dispensed with; most English speakers will know "thee" and "hath" are the equivalents of "you" and "has" respectively. The word "aspect" may seem a somewhat unusual or archaic way to refer to "complexion" or "face," but presents no serious difficulty. What is strangest about this sentence is that, for the present-day reader, it seems to say the opposite of what it means. In current usage, to say that someone "feared the valiant" would be to indicate that the person was "afraid of" valiant people. In Shakespeare's time, however, the verb "fear" could also be used to indicate "make afraid" or "cause to fear," a usage which has since died out in our everyday speech. The sense of Morocco's utterance is apparent only in the context of his whole speech, where "afraid of the valiant" wouldn't fit into a list of his complexion's attributes. Such moments may cause a reader confusion in certain passages, but a little detective work usually clears the matter up. A good edition of the play will most likely footnote such passages and explain the disparity.

Not all of the differences between Shakespeare's English and our own are strictly chronological, however. *The Merchant of Venice*, like all of Shakespeare's plays, is written largely in verse, and as such, is estranged from any variety of spoken English. (Although we can make very educated conjectures, we can't, in any case, be positively sure of how English was spoken in Shakespeare's day based on written documents alone. This is, of course, the only evidence available.) Much of what a present-day reader might find estranging in Shakespeare's language is simply due to his poetic techniques. A reader must be prepared to grant Shakespeare a great deal of leeway in his use of language; otherwise the encounter will end in frustration. Sometimes, for example, Shakespeare will concoct a usage of a word different from, but related to, its previous senses. Shylock, in Act II, scene VI complains of the laziness of his former servant, Launcelot Gobbo, with the remark "Drones hive not with me;/ Therefore I part with him…" A present-day reader is probably not used to seeing "hive" as a verb at all; although it has such uses in Shakespeare's time, he seems to have invented this particular one. According to the Oxford English Dictionary, the earliest recorded usage of "hive" in the sense of "To live together as bees in a hive" is this same example from *The Merchant of Venice* (Compact Edition OED 1312). Shakespeare frequently bends previous senses of his words to accommodate his poetic desires, sometimes initiating new trends in the word's employment.

Shakespeare is at his best (though for the new student most difficult) when he makes words perform tasks they ordinarily don't do, and this is often manifested in more subtle and complicated ways than merely inventing a new-but-related sense for a word. The final example is from the same scene as the previous one and is also spoken by Shylock. In cautioning his daughter Jessica to ignore the Christian revelries taking place on the street below, Shylock says:

> *Lock up my doors; and when you hear the drum*
> *And the vile squealing of the wry-necked fife,*
> *Clamber not you up to the casements then…"*

The phrase in question here is "wry-necked fife," which—strictly speaking—doesn't make sense. A fife is one cylinder-shaped piece; nothing on it could be called its "neck." The phrase might thus be taken to refer to the fife-player, whose neck would be so twisted in order to play the instrument. "Fife" would then be a synecdoche for "fife-player," much as one can refer to a king by saying "the crown." The trouble with this reading is that it doesn't fit with "vile squealing," which would refer to the sound of the fife not the player, and a reader may also be inclined to take "fife" as the instrument in parallel with the reference to "drum." The best solution to this dilemma is to say not that "fife" must refer either to the player or the instrument, but rather that Shakespeare accesses both with his grammatical violation. Both player and instrument are needed to fill out the sense of the sentence, which, though perhaps difficult for new readers, can hardly be construed as a flaw since the poet manages to say two things for the price of one, in a remarkable feat of "verbal economy." Such moments, once the reader is familiar and comfortable enough with the language, become transformed from the poet's greatest difficulty to his chief attraction.

A twentieth-century philosopher, attempting to grasp the significance of and his own difficulty with the most renowned of English poets, once wrote: "I do not believe that Shakespeare can be set along side any other poet. Was he perhaps a *creator of language* rather than a poet?" (Wittgenstein 84). This is perhaps a useful way to conceive of Shakespeare, inasmuch as his plays often create their own rules for language usage and readers must be willing to loosen their hold on their sense of "correct English" in order to partake of them. If anything justifies Shakespeare's reputation as the greatest of English poets, it is such "creative power," the poet's ability to fashion linguistic objects which are not only unprecedented in our language but which subsequently become part of that language.

Master List of Characters

Antonio—*a merchant of Venice and intimate friend of Bassanio.*

Salerio—*friend to both Antonio and Bassanio.*

Solanio—*friend to both Antonio and Bassanio.*

Bassanio—*a young gentleman of Venice in financial difficulty; suitor to Portia and intimate friend of Antonio.*

Lorenzo—*friend of Bassanio and Antonio; Christian lover of the Jewish woman, Jessica.*

Gratiano—*friend of Bassanio and Antonio; joins Bassanio's expedition to Belmont; romancer of Nerissa.*

Portia—*a wealthy heiress of Belmont; she approves of Bassanio's suit to her.*

Nerissa—*Portia's waiting woman and confidante; approves Gratiano's advances.*

Shylock—*a Jewish moneylender of Venice.*

Morocco—*an African Prince and suitor to Portia.*

Launcelot Gobbo—*a clown (comical member of the lower class); ex-servant of Shylock who enters into Bassanio's service.*

Old Gobbo—*Launcelot's father; nearly blind from age.*

Leonardo—*servant of Bassanio.*

Jessica—*daughter of Shylock; Jewish lover of the Christian man, Lorenzo.*

Aragon—*a prince; suitor to Portia.*

Tubal—*a friend of Shylock; a Jew of Venice.*

Jailer—*holds Antonio prisoner.*

Balthasar—*a servant of Portia.*

The Duke of Venice—*the highest authority in Venice.*

Stephano—*a messenger sent by Portia to Lorenzo and Jessica.*

Various Magnificoes of Venice, Officers of the Court, Musicians, Servants, Messengers, *and* **Attendants**

Summary of the Play

Bassanio, a Venetian nobleman with financial difficulties, wishes to compete for the hand of Portia, a wealthy heiress of Belmont, in order to restore his fortune. He asks his friend Antonio, a successful merchant of Venice, to loan him the money necessary to undertake such an attempt. Antonio agrees, but, as all of his assets are tied up at sea, he will have to use his credit in order to obtain the money for his friend. They go to Shylock, a Jewish moneylender and enemy of Antonio's. Shylock agrees to lend them 3000 ducats, but only if Antonio will sign a bond offering the usurer a pound of his flesh if the loan is not repaid in three months' time. Despite Bassanio's misgivings, Antonio assents to the arrangement.

Meanwhile, in Belmont, Portia laments to her serving woman, Nerissa, the terms of her late father's will. They state that whoever seeks to marry Portia must solve the riddle of the three caskets—one gold, one silver, one lead, each with an inscription—or, failing in the attempt, agree to remain a bachelor for the rest of his days. Various suitors attempt the test and fail, until Bassanio arrives. Portia favors him and is delighted when he succeeds. His man, Gratiano, also proposes to Nerissa. She accepts.

But all is not well in Venice. Lorenzo, a friend of Bassanio and Antonio, elopes with Shylock's daughter, Jessica. This enrages Shylock, who vows to show no mercy should Antonio be unable to repay the loan. Much to the usurer's delight, Antonio's ships become lost at sea, placing him in financial jeopardy. Shylock has him arrested and waits eagerly to make good on the bond.

After Bassanio succeeds at the challenge of the caskets, Jessica and Lorenzo arrive in Belmont seeking refuge. Bassanio simultaneously receives a letter from Antonio, revealing his predicament. Having no time to perform the wedding services, Bassanio and Gratiano depart for Venice, promising to return. Leaving Jessica and Lorenzo in charge of her household, Portia, accompanied by Nerissa, secretly leaves for Venice.

In court before the parties concerned, Shylock appeals to the Duke of Venice for the fulfillment of his bond. The Duke is reluctant, but sees no legal way to prevent Shylock's claim. Portia and Nerissa, disguised as a doctor of law and his clerk, arrive to help decide the case. Portia initially rules in favor of Shylock; before he can begin to cut, however, she points out that he is not entitled to spill any of Antonio's blood. She finds him guilty, furthermore, of attempting to take the life of a Venetian citizen. At the mercy of the court, Shylock loses half of his possessions and is forced to convert to Christianity. He leaves in defeat.

In payment for her services, the disguised Portia asks Bassanio for a ring she had given him in Belmont on the condition that he would never part with it. He refuses, and she storms off in pretended anger. Antonio, however, prevails upon his friend to send the ring after the doctor for "his" services to them; Bassanio sends Gratiano, who also gives up the ring Nerissa gave him with the same stipulation, to the clerk.

Portia and Nerissa arrive in Belmont. Pretending they never left, the two woman demand to see the rings they gave their future husbands and feign outrage when they cannot produce them. Portia finally lets everyone off the hook and admits her and Nerissa's roles in the events in Venice. She also gives Antonio a letter informing him that three of his ships have arrived safely in port, restoring his wealth. The group go to Portia's house to celebrate.

Estimated Reading Time

As a rule, students should equip themselves with a well-annotated edition of the play, in order to smooth some of the friction between Elizabethan English and our own variety of the language. One hour per act is a rough guideline for the first read-through. This will vary, of course: Act V, which consists of only one scene, is obviously a great deal shorter than the rest; Acts II and III are longer than average. Certain scenes, such as Act IV, Scene I, will command more attention than others, given their length and importance. Use your own discretion, and realize that reading Shakespearean English—like encountering any rich and complicated variety of language—becomes easier the more one is exposed to it.

SECTION TWO

Act I

Act I, Scene I (pages 1–7)

New Characters:

Antonio: *a merchant of Venice*

Salerio and Solanio: *friends to Bassanio and Antonio*

Bassanio: *a young gentleman of Venice, friend of Antonio*

Lorenzo: *friend of Bassanio and Antonio, loves Jessica*

Gratiano: *friend of Bassanio and Antonio*

Summary

In Venice, Antonio is depressed, though he is uncertain why. Salerio and Solanio try to account for his sadness by suggesting he is worried about his merchant ships sailing in dangerous waters. Antonio denies this, but can suggest nothing in its place. Salerio and Solanio leave as Bassanio, Lorenzo, and Gratiano enter. Gratiano and Lorenzo jest with Antonio, lifting his spirits slightly, before departing.

Left alone, Bassanio apologizes to Antonio for owing him a great deal of money. Antonio tells him not to worry about it. Bassanio then informs Antonio of a wealthy heiress in Belmont whom he wishes to court. The trouble is, he needs to borrow more money from Antonio to outfit himself properly, in order to compete with the many wealthier suitors. Bassanio suggests that, with a little more money, he will improve his chances of repaying his debt to his friend. Marrying the heiress will solve all of Bassanio's financial problems. Antonio readily agrees to this plan; however, as all of his capital is tied up at the moment with his ships, he will be unable to lend money directly. Bassanio instead can use Antonio's name to obtain credit.

Analysis

This scene is primarily exposition, conversation made to fill the audience in on the various circumstances leading up to the events of the play. The audience learns about Antonio's generosity and successful business standing, Bassanio's present financial embarrassments, and the prospect of Portia's wealth as the solution to the latter's problems. Crucial financial information about Antonio—which will account for his future predicament—is revealed. His ships are out to sea, tying up his available assets, and this will lead him to seek a loan from Shylock. The news that his ships have been wrecked will make Antonio unable to repay the money.

Act I, Scene II (pages 7–10)

New Characters:
Portia: *the wealthy heiress of Belmont*
Nerissa: *her waiting woman*

Summary

In Belmont, Portia confides to Nerissa her distaste for the provisions of her father's will. Portia's father devised a test for anyone seeking her hand in marriage. A would-be suitor must choose among three caskets (ornamental boxes)—one gold, one silver, one lead—one of which contains permission to marry Portia. The suitor must agree, however, that if he makes a wrong choice, he will spend the rest of his days single. This situation is aggravated by Portia's complete distaste for any of her potential husbands. Nerissa names them all, while Portia enumerates her particular dislikes of each. She takes heart in the news that each has announced he will return home, fearing the strict consequences of her father's test. The two women suddenly remember Bassanio, whom they find more appealing; however, they are interrupted in their praise by a messenger who declares that her suitors seek an audience with her, and that a new contestant, the Prince of Morocco, will arrive soon.

Analysis

This short scene primarily serves as the audience's introduction to the plot of the three caskets, which determines who may marry Portia. The test of the caskets will be performed three times in the play, by Morocco in Act II, Scene VIII, Aragon in Act II, Scene IX, and Bassanio in Act III, Scene II. The audience learns here of Portia's inclination toward Bassanio. Her resentment of her father's will is also significant; Portia is too independent to be told what to do, as becomes clear when, later in the play, she takes matters into her own hands to resolve Antonio's plight. Apart from these important introductions, the substance of the scene is largely comic, a series of jokes based on various prevailing national and ethnic stereotypes as Portia disdains each suitor in turn. As is the case with much of Shakespeare, this scene is an excuse for the playwright to exercise his linguistic ingenuity in constructing clever sentences, such as "when he is best he is a little worse than a man; and when he is worst, he is little better than a beast" (p. 9).

Act I, Scene III (pages 10–16)

New Character:

Shylock: *a Jewish moneylender of Venice*

Summary

In Venice, Bassanio negotiates with Shylock to borrow three thousand ducats (monetary units) for three months, for which "Antonio shall be bound." Shylock doesn't agree immediately, but wishes to speak to Antonio first. Antonio enters, provoking Shylock to vent his hatred of him in an aside. Shylock claims to hate Antonio for being a Christian, for loaning money to people in need without charging interest, and for publicly slandering Shylock's own business practices. Antonio, despite his customary scruples against usury (moneylending for interest), personally asks Shylock to loan Bassanio the money. Still Shylock hesitates, reminding Antonio of the merchant's past ill-treatment of him and suggesting Antonio's hypocrisy in now coming to him for a favor. Antonio is unrepentant, however, claiming that they needn't be friends in order to do business together.

Shylock then turns the tables on his adversaries, suddenly announcing his intention to loan Bassanio the money out of "kindness," i.e., without charging interest. There is one catch, however: Antonio must go with Shylock to a notary and sign an agreement stating that if he fails to repay the loan on time, he must allow Shylock to cut off a pound of his flesh. Shylock claims this is "merry sport," and Antonio readily agrees, treating the whole affair as a gag. Bassanio, however, is alarmed at this arrangement and insists Antonio not enter into the bargain. Antonio is not convinced of any real danger, however, and agrees to meet with Shylock "forthwith" to sign the bond.

Analysis

This is the most complicated scene thus far in the play. Its function is to establish the second major complication of the plot, the bond for a pound of Antonio's flesh. It also introduces the audience to Shylock, possibly the most engaging character in the play. Beyond these plot considerations, however, the ramifications of this scene are immense.

The appearance of Shylock announces two of the play's central issues: the relationship between Jews and Christians, and the Venetian—and by association, the Elizabethan—attitude toward usury. The animosity between Christians and Jews is almost immediately established as the scene unfolds, and, although it is Shylock who first calls these matters to the audience's attention, Antonio confirms that the hostility is mutual. The fact that Shylock is referred to as "the Jew" by the others suggests that their contempt for him is more than merely personal; to them, Shylock represents a group whom they are compelled to dislike for religious and even racial reasons.

It is perhaps impossible for us to decide how much of the animosity between the two Christians and Shylock is personal and how much is based on group identity. Indeed, the characters move between both sets of reasons as if there were no distinction between them, or as if their identities guaranteed the nature of their personal relations. Shylock initiates hostilities in this scene, informing Bassanio that, although he will transact business with him, "I will not eat with you, drink with you, nor pray with you" (p. 11). Shylock makes it clear in his speech—with the reference to "pork," a food many Jewish sects forbid its members to consume—that even their culinary differences are religious. His initial expression of disgust for Antonio is explicitly religion-oriented: "I hate him for he is a Christian" (p. 12).

Shylock's bitterness, however, next becomes a business matter; Antonio's interest-free loans to the needy "[bring] down/ The rate of usance" in Venice, affecting the usurer's profits. His complaint against Antonio then takes a personal turn, as Shylock recalls, "he rails/ Even there where merchants most do congregate,/ On me, my bargains, and my well-won thrift,/ Which he calls interest" (p. 12). The personal tenor of Shylock's hatred is magnified in a later speech, when he confronts Antonio: "You call me misbeliever, cutthroat dog,/ And spit upon my Jewish gaberdine,/ And all for use of that which is mine own" (p. 14). Clearly the religious dispute has moved to the level of personal insult, even to mild scuffling. Antonio shows no remorse in the face of such accusations, however, justifying his behavior on moral principles.

The issue of usury seems inextricable from the religious bickering. Antonio equally despises Shylock for his moneylending practices as for his religion and race. It is as if commerce and religion are the same; Antonio's contempt for Shylock's usury may stem from his Christian faith, while for Shylock, there is no contradiction between his profession and his religious convictions. There is, obviously, no one interpretation of this scene which can satisfy all of its possibilities. The Elizabethan distaste for usury no doubt inclined the play's original audience to side with Antonio on this matter. If this is the case, however, we might, along with Shylock, detect a certain hypocrisy in Antonio's coming to him for a loan in a time of need. His principles bend to practical considerations, much like Elizabethan law, which made usury illegal but left provisions that it wouldn't be punished if the interest rate was less than 10%. An audience's feelings about Shylock matter a great deal in this scene, for either he will appear as justifiably resentful of Antonio's seemingly-unprovoked treatment of him, or else as deserving such treatment for his beliefs and practices.

One final aspect of this scene that has been a source of contention among critics concerns the agreement of a pound of flesh as collateral for the loan. Shylock twice refers to the arrangement as "merry," as though the whole affair is in no way a serious one. Some readers of the play have taken him at his word; they believe that he only becomes serious in his demand after Lorenzo, Antonio's friend, runs off with Shylock's daughter Jessica, who in turn steals some of her father's money and possessions. Others argue that the entire arrangement is from start to finish motivated by Shylock's desire for revenge against Antonio.

Study Questions

1. What causes do Salerio and Solanio suggest for Antonio's melancholy?

2. What humorous advice does Gratiano offer Antonio?

3. Why does Bassanio want Antonio to loan him more money?

4. Why is Portia angry with her deceased father?

5. Why does Nerissa tell Portia she "need not fear" her unwelcome suitors?

6. What do Portia and Nerissa think of Bassanio?

7. According to Shylock, why does he hate Antonio?

8. Why is Shylock indignant over Antonio's request?

9. What is Antonio's response to Shylock's accusation?

10. In exchange for what does Shylock agree to lend Antonio and Bassanio the money?

Answers

1. Salerio and Solanio think Antonio is distracted because his money is tied up in his ships, which are sailing on dangerous seas. When he denies this suggestion, Solanio guesses that he's in love, an answer Antonio also rejects.

2. Gratiano tells Antonio not to be so grave about worldly affairs, but rather "With mirth and laughter let old wrinkles come,/ ...Why should a man whose blood is warm within/ Sit like his grandsire.../ ...And creep into the jaundice/ By being peevish?" In other words, he suggests Antonio is acting old before his time.

3. Bassanio tells Antonio that "had [he] but the means" to compete with Portia's suitors, he would "questionless be fortunate," i.e., win the wealthy heiress's hand, thus solving his financial difficulties.

4. Because of the provisions of her father's will—the challenge of the three caskets—Portia cannot choose her own husband. As she says, "I may neither choose who I would nor refuse who I dislike, so is the will of a living daughter curbed by the will of a dead father."

5. Nerissa tells Portia she "need not fear" marrying any of the undesirable suitors because "[t]hey have acquainted [Nerissa] with their determinations; which is indeed to return to their home, and trouble [Portia] with no more suit..."

6. Nerissa claims that Bassanio, "of all the men that ever [her] foolish eyes looked upon, was the best deserving a fair lady." Portia agrees and "remember[s] him worthy of [Nerissa's] praise."

7. Shylock claims to hate Antonio because "he is a Christian;/ But more, for in that low simplicity/ He lends out money gratis, and brings down/ The rate of usance here with us in Venice." He also remembers being personally insulted by Antonio.

8. Shylock suggests that Antonio is a hypocrite, having first spurned him for being a usurer and now asking him for a loan. As Shylock taunts him, "You come to me and you say,/ 'Shylock, we would have moneys'—you say so,/ You that did void your rheum upon my beard..."

9. Antonio insists their mutual hatred is a proper business relationship, telling Shylock, "If thou wilt lend this money, lend it not/ As to thy friends.../ But lend it rather to thine enemy,/ Who if he break, thou mayst with better face/ Exact the penalty."

10. Shylock asks Antonio to sign a bond stating that, if he doesn't repay Shylock within the allotted time, he must sacrifice "an equal pound/ Of [his] fair flesh, to be cut off and taken/ In what part of [his] body pleaseth [Shylock]."

Suggested Essay Topics

1. Compare and contrast Antonio's situation in signing the agreement with Shylock, with Portia's situation of being held bound to her father's will.

2. Contrast Antonio's loans to Bassanio with Shylock's loan to Antonio and Bassanio.

SECTION THREE

Act II

Act II, Scene I (pages 17–18)

New Character:

Morocco: *an African prince, suitor to Portia*

Summary

The Prince of Morocco arrives at Portia's house in Belmont, seeking her hand in marriage. He asks Portia to disregard their racial difference and judge him instead by his personal merits. Portia reminds Morocco that the choice is not hers to make; he, like the other suitors, must face her father's challenge of the three caskets. She assures him, however, that she regards him "as fair/ As any comer I have look'd on yet/ For my affection" (p. 17). Morocco laments that, in spite of his valor, mere chance may deprive him of Portia. Portia refers him to the terms of her father's will, which he accepts. They agree to perform the test after dinner.

Analysis

This short scene introduces the audience to the Prince of Morocco, who will make the first unsuccessful attempt to pass the test designed by Portia's father to determine who will marry her. In terms of the play's themes, its chief interest is its explorations of racial animosity, which we have seen earlier in the encounter between Shylock and the two Christians. Morocco requests that Portia "Mislike me not for my complexion" (p. 17) but rather consider him for his personal worth. Although Portia claims that this is her policy, the sincerity of her claim is later called into question at the close of Act II Scene VII. After Morocco fails the test and departs, Portia says in relief "A gentle riddance... / Let all of his complexion choose me so" (p. 34). Unlike Shakespeare's contemporaries, who may have endorsed such sentiments, more modern audiences might perhaps have an ugly impression of the attitudes of the Christians in the play. Though Morocco is a minor character, such scenes may inform the audience's feeling about Shylock and his indictments of Christian hypocrisy.

Act II, Scene II (pages 19–24)

New Characters:

Launcelot Gobbo: *ex-servant of Shylock*

Old Gobbo: *Launcelot's father*

Leonardo: *servant of Bassanio*

Summary

This scene opens with Launcelot Gobbo debating whether or not to leave Shylock's service. Just as he decides to quit, his near-blind father, Old Gobbo, arrives with a gift for Shylock. Since his father doesn't recognize him, Launcelot toys with him for a time before revealing his identity. He asks his father to give the gift instead to Bassanio—who subsequently enters with Leonardo—as a means of begging a position in his household. The Gobbos make their pitch and Bassanio accepts, hiring Launcelot on the spot. Bassanio then dispatches Leonardo to prepare his household to receive Antonio for dinner. Gratiano enters and asks Bassanio if he may attend him on his journey to Belmont. Bassanio agrees, but not before cautioning Gratiano to curtail his ribaldry.

Analysis

Little of this scene actually bears much relation to the plot of the play, save the establishment of Gratiano as Bassanio's attendant. It is more or less an excuse for Shakespeare to indulge his audience with a bit of linguistic comedy, in the form of the Three Stooges-like double-talk spoken by the Gobbos. We should note, however, that even in a scene as light as this one, Shakespeare keeps the issue of racial hostility before his audience. Launcelot's desire to leave Shylock's employ stems largely from the fact that his boss is Jewish, coupled with his belief that the Jew "is a kind of devil" (p. 19). Significantly, Shylock is never referred to in this scene by name, but simply as "the Jew."

Act II, Scene III (page 25)

New Character:

Jessica: *daughter of Shylock*

Summary

At Shylock's house, Jessica, his daughter, bids farewell to Launcelot as he prepares to leave her father's service. She entreats him to deliver a message to Lorenzo. After he departs, she expresses her desire to marry Lorenzo and become a Christian.

Analysis

This scene sets in motion another important subplot—the romance between Shylock's daughter and Bassanio's and Antonio's friend. Some critics speculate that it is Jessica's departure with Lorenzo, coupled with her theft of her father's money and jewels, that pushes Shylock over the edge and provokes him to pursue the pound of Antonio's flesh in earnest. (Others, of course, claim that this was Shylock's intention all along.) The anti-Semitism of the play is fueled here by Jessica's own self-loathing, i.e., her desire to shed her own religion and become a Christian.

Act II, Scene IV (pages 26–27)

Summary

Gratiano, Lorenzo, Salerio, and Solanio prepare for an evening of street festivities. Launcelot arrives to deliver Jessica's message to Lorenzo. Lorenzo sends Launcelot back with the reply "I will not fail her," and instructs the messenger to "Speak it privately." Lorenzo explains to Gratiano Jessica's plan to flee her father.

Analysis

This is essentially a development of the subplot begun in Act II, Scene 3, confirming the plan on Lorenzo's end. Lorenzo magnifies the Christians' dislike of "Jew-for-Jews sake" in the following lines: "And never dare misfortune cross her foot,/ Unless she do it under this excuse,/ That she is issue to a faithless Jew" (p. 27). In other words, Lorenzo perceives the "flaw" of Jessica's Jewishness as potentially outweighing her personal merits.

Act II, Scene V (pages 27–29)

Summary

Launcelot has come to Shylock's house to deliver the invitation for the usurer to dine with Bassanio and Antonio. Shylock apparently overcomes his earlier religious scruple against dining with the Christians and accepts. He cautions his daughter against the Christian masquers (street-revelers); she is instructed to keep the house shut tight. Before departing, Launcelot secretly informs Jessica that Lorenzo will come by that night. Shylock quizzes his daughter on what just passed between her and Launcelot, but she throws him off the scent. He expresses satisfaction at having Launcelot leave his employ, and then exits to dine at Bassanio's house. Jessica prepares to flee.

Analysis

Like the two preceding scenes and the scene to follow, Act II, Scene V sets up the circumstances under which Jessica can rob her father and escape with Lorenzo. This scene perhaps fuels the interpretation that only after Jessica's flight does Shylock become serious in his desire to kill Antonio, as we might well imagine Shylock's feeling duped by the Christians (as though Bassanio lured him away with the invitation to dinner so Lorenzo and Jessica could elope).

Act II, Scene VI (pages 29–31)

Summary

Gratiano and Salerio, dressed for the street festivities, stand before Shylock's house, awaiting Lorenzo. As soon as he arrives, Jessica appears "above" (i.e. on the second level of the Elizabethan stage, presumably the second floor of Shylock's residence), disguised as a boy. Lorenzo recognizes her and identifies himself. He asks her to come down and be his torchbearer for the revelry, although she is embarrassed at her present appearance. Lorenzo persuades her to descend; on her way out, Jessica pilfers more ducats from her father. Lorenzo, Jessica, and Salerio depart as Antonio arrives. He detains Gratiano, informing him that the masque is canceled and Bassanio shall sail that evening. This suits Gratiano, and the two men exit to prepare.

Analysis

This scene more or less wraps up the subplot of Jessica's and Lorenzo's elopement, though its consequences—primarily consisting of Shylock's rage—will continue to be felt throughout the play. Jessica and Lorenzo will flee to Belmont, Portia's region, and will mind her household in her absence.

In many of Shakespeare's comedies, there are two separate locales, the court, where normal business occurs according to fairly rigid codes, and a more magical realm where rules are suspended and transformation is possible. In such plays, characters from the first realm visit the second and, on their return to the first, feel renewed. It may be Jessica's and Lorenzo's flight to Belmont and the play's romantic final act which have encouraged some critics to fit The *Merchant of Venice* into this structural pattern. According to such an outline, Venice would be the narrow rule-bound court while Belmont serves as the enchanted land, just like the forest of Arden in *As You Like It* or the woods outside Athens in *A Midsummer Night's Dream*. But this is an oversimplification of *The Merchant*, a critical attempt to force it into a pre-ordained pattern rather than attend to the play's particulars. It ignores, for one, the circumstance of Portia's father's will and the challenge of the three caskets. Belmont seems to be as strictly bound by legality and technicality as Venice, and much of the play is devoted to subverting or accommodating the letter of the law in both cities. If anything, *The Merchant of Venice* might fore-shadow Shakespeare's later, so-called "problem comedies," such as *Measure for Measure,* in which the levity is tempered by threats of danger. The possibility exists that Portia could end up with an undesirable husband, and the threat to Antonio's life according to the terms of Shylock's bond casts an even darker shadow.

Act II, Scene VII (pages 32–34)

Summary

Meanwhile, back in Belmont, Morocco prepares to undergo the challenge of the three caskets in order to win Portia's hand, while the lady in question looks on. The prince surveys each casket and its inscription. The first is made of gold and bears the message "Who chooseth me shall gain what many men desire." The second, of silver, reads "Who chooseth me shall get as much as he deserves." The third, finally, is made of lead and warns "Who chooseth me must give and hazard all he hath." Portia informs Morocco that the correct casket contains her picture, signifying success. The prince then deliberates for some time, weighing both factors: the material of each casket and the message on it. By a process of elimination, he chooses the gold one. Much to his chagrin, it contains a death's head and a scroll informing him of his error. Upset, the prince makes a gracious but hasty exit, and Portia expresses her relief at his lack of success.

Analysis

This is the first of three scenes (Act II, Scene VII, Act II, Scene IX, and Act III, Scene II) displaying the challenge of the three caskets in action. The interest these scenes generate is, in some respects, *not* a dramatic one, for although the fear of an undesir-able marriage is a very real one for Portia, it is a great deal less of one for her audience. Indeed, the progressive workings of these scenes are so formulaic that they are almost without any drama at all. Each of the three caskets is successively chosen by each of the three suitors, no choice is repeated, and, of course, the winning casket is the last one picked. By the time Bassanio arrives in Belmont, the audience is well aware of which choice is correct and is simply waiting for him to make it. This contrived inevitability need not be considered a flaw, however; unlike, say, the final scene of a detective drama, where plot and plausibility are of extreme importance, one doesn't read Shakespearean comedy with such demands. The spirit of comedy here suspends issues of realistic plausibility.

The question then becomes, what is the interest these scenes hold for an audience? (Remember, Shakespeare was a successful and popular showman. He wouldn't have dropped *three* such scenes into his play unless they had other, non-dramatic attractions.) The value of these scenes, perhaps, lies in the issues of reading and interpretation which they bring to the foreground. Indeed, the bulk of Act II, Scene VII (p. 32) is devoted to the reasoning process by which Morocco arrives at his choice of the gold casket. What the challenge of the caskets reveals is the flexibility and ambiguity of language, and in this revelation, a reader or theater-goer may find an analogy to his or her own experience of the play. As the need or desire to analyze Shakespeare's plays has already made us aware, certain displays of language require interpretation in order for someone to be able to act on them or even to decide what to think about them. The suitors of Portia engage in a task not terribly different from the audience's own, or from the director's own when he or she decides, for example, how the part of Shylock ought to be acted.

It is important to remember that the choice of the lead casket is only obvious and inevitable in hindsight; Morocco is not to be deemed a fool for his incorrect choice. We might even say that, of all of Portia's suitors, the Prince is the one most unfairly duped by the process of casket selection. His interpretation of the inscription "Who chooseth me shall gain what many men desire" as signifying Portia is a sound one, for as he points out, "all the world desires her;/ From the four corners of the earth they come/ To kiss this shrine, this mortal–breathing saint" (p. 33). The courting of Portia is central to *The Merchant of Venice*; it sets the entire plot in motion, as Bassanio's need of additional capital to outfit himself is the reason Antonio becomes indebted to Shylock in the first place. Perpetual chastity—the penalty for choosing the wrong casket—is a highly improbable interpretation of "what many men desire." It is, indeed, the opposite of desire. Whereas it is relatively easy to imagine the silver casket's inscription as the wrong choice (i.e., the man in question may not "deserve" Portia and may rather deserve the punishment for his presumptuousness), an audience may very well feel that Morocco has been lied to.

The underhandedness with which Morocco is treated might be, however, in keeping with the racial hostilities permeating the play. As Shylock is automatically excluded by the others for his Jewishness, the Prince is disliked, among other reasons perhaps, for his skin color. Morocco's first utterance in the play (line 1) is a plea for racial tolerance; he is on the defensive at the outset. Although Portia assures him in Act II, Scene I that his race is not a factor in her acceptance—and we must assume this is true, insofar as, by the rules of her father's will, Portia must marry whoever makes the right choice—her tolerance is called into question at the end of this scene. After Morocco departs, Portia breathes a sigh of relief and says "Let all of his complexion choose me so" (p. 34), continuing the theme in the play that one is automatically included or excluded from the circle of favorable people in Christian society according to one's religion or race. Portia can't even imagine meeting a black man who could satisfy her and dismisses "all" of them in one sentence.

Act II, Scene VIII (pages 34–36)

Summary

This scene consists entirely of a brief conversation between Salerio and Solanio, aimed at informing the audience of a variety of events which have occurred while the scene in Belmont was taking place. The audience learns that Shylock has discovered his deception, that his daughter has run off with his money and

Lorenzo. Shylock is white with rage, much to the amusement of Christian Venice. Salerio reveals that Bassanio's ship is underway for Belmont. He also reports the news that a Venetian vessel has been wrecked in the English Channel, and worries that it might be Antonio's. Solanio recalls witnessing Bassanio's departure, and Antonio's melancholy at their separation. Salerio and Solanio resolve to seek Antonio out to attempt to cheer him.

Analysis

This is another scene of pure exposition, providing the audience with information crucial to advancing various strains of the plot as they currently stand. Some critics have made much of Shylock's confused lamentation concerning his daughter and his ducats, ascribing various aspects to his character based upon his equating of the two. One ought to keep in mind, however, that this is a reported speech; the audience doesn't witness Shylock making such a spectacle, which mitigates the speech's effect on the audience.

Other critics have suggested the possibility of a homosexual relationship between Bassanio and Antonio, or at least a strong homosexual attachment to his friend on Antonio's part. It could be argued that Antonio's general sadness throughout the play stems from the prospect of his intimate friend turning away from their love by entering a heterosexual partnership with Portia. While the evidence of a sexual friendship between Bassanio and Antonio is too scant to insist on, it is clear that the latter's attachment for the former extends beyond the bounds of simple friendship. Not only does Antonio loan Bassanio money with only a shaky prospect of repayment, but he freely and willingly risks his life for his friend's happiness. Clearly Bassanio is Antonio's primary attachment, which makes it no surprise that, in a play that ends with three marriages, Antonio remains conspicuously single.

Act II, Scene IX (pages 36–39)

New Character:

Aragon: *a prince, suitor to Portia*

Summary

The Prince of Aragon undertakes the challenge of the caskets to win Portia's hand, agreeing to abide by the rules of her father's will. He dismisses the lead casket immediately, not thinking it worth the "hazard." He next considers the golden chest, reading its inscription of "what many men desire" as implying a lack of discrimination. Finally, he selects the silver, believing he must "deserve" that which he seeks. Much to his dismay, however, the silver casket contains a fool's head and a scroll informing him of his error. Aragon leaves. A messenger then arrives, informing Portia that a Venetian lord is on his way to try to win her. Nerissa hopes aloud that it is Bassanio.

Analysis

This is the second of the three casket selecting scenes. Aragon is a bolder, less-subtle reasoner than Morocco and makes his incorrect choice quickly, firm in his belief of his own merit. Yet for that, his justification for choosing the silver casket is an eloquent one and may arouse an audience's admiration. The casket's own interpretation of what its selector "deserves" (i.e. the presumptuous man is a fool and deserves to be treated to a fool's head) is, however, a more justifiable one than that of the gold casket.

Study Questions

1. Why does Morocco fear Portia will reject him at the outset?

2. What is Bassanio's reservation about Gratiano accompanying him to Belmont?

3. What is Jessica's dilemma concerning her father, Shylock?

4. How does Lorenzo plan to disguise Jessica in order for her to escape from her father?

5. Before going to dine with Antonio and Bassanio, what advice does Shylock give his daughter?

6. Why does Jessica not want Lorenzo to see her when he arrives at Shylock's house?

7. What is Morocco's rationale for choosing the gold casket?

8. What news has Salerio heard, making him anxious?

9. How does Solanio interpret Antonio's sadness at Bassanio's departure?

10. Which casket does Aragon choose, and why?

Answers

1. Morocco fears Portia would not want to marry someone of his race. Upon entering the play, he pleads: "Mislike not for my complexion/ The shadowed livery of the burnished sun..."

2. Bassanio suspects that Gratiano will appear "too wild, too rude, and bold of voice" for the people of Belmont. "[W] here thou art not known," Bassanio warns, such traits "show/ Something too liberal."

3. Jessica believes it is a "heinous sin... / To be ashamed to be [her] father's child!" Although she is Shylock's daughter by "blood," she claims not to be by "manners" and hopes to become a Christian by marrying Lorenzo.

4. Jessica will be dressed as Lorenzo's torchbearer for the street festivities.

5. Shylock tells Jessica that if she hears commotion outside, she should "Clamber not...up to the casements then,/ Nor thrust [her] head into the public street/ To gaze on Christian fools... / But... / [she should] Let not the sound of shallow fopp'ry enter/ [his] sober house."

6. Jessica is ashamed because she has been "transformed to a boy," i.e. is dressed in men's clothing in order to make her escape.

7. The gold casket is engraved "Who chooseth me shall gain what many men desire." As Morocco points out, "All the world desires [Portia];/ From the four corners of the earth they come/ To kiss this shrine, this mortal breathing saint."

8. A Frenchman informed him that a Venetian ship has been wrecked in the English Channel, and Salerio fears it may be one of Antonio's.

9. Solanio believes that Antonio "only loves the world for [Bassanio]." In other words, his friendship with Bassanio is the one thing which keeps Antonio from being overwhelmed by melancholy.

10. Aragon selects the silver casket, engraved "Who chooseth me shall get as much as he deserves," because, he asks, "who shall go about/ To cozen fortune, and be honorable/ Without the stamp of merit? Let none presume/ To wear an undeserved dignity," Aragon feels whoever wins Portia had better be deserving of her.

Suggested Essay Topics

1. What is the relationship—both structurally and thematically—of the Jessica/Lorenzo subplot to the main plots of The Merchant of Venice ?

2. Compare and contrast Morocco's reasoning during the selection of caskets with Aragon's speech during the same test.

3. Aside from the obvious one of comic relief, what function might Launcelot Gobbo be seen to have in the play?

SECTION FOUR

Act III

Act III, Scene I (pages 41–44)

New Character:

Tubal: *a Jewish friend of Shylock*

Summary

In Venice, Salerio and Solanio discuss Antonio's financial state. Salerio has received confirmation that one of Antonio's merchant vessels was wrecked in the English channel. As the two lament this ill news, Shylock enters. He is bitter with both men for their knowledge of Jessica's elopement before the fact, but they simply mock him in return. The conversation turns to Antonio, on whom Shylock is intent on wreaking his revenge according to the terms of the bond. Salerio asks Shylock what good a pound of Antonio's flesh will do him, but Shylock dismisses this line of questioning as irrelevant. He is after vengeance, not reimbursement.

Salerio and Solanio learn from a messenger that Antonio awaits them at his house. As they leave, a friend of Shylock's, Tubal, arrives with news concerning both Jessica and Antonio. In Genoa, Tubal learned that another of Antonio's ships was lost coming away from Tripoli. Shylock rejoices at the news, but this is soon tempered by the knowledge that Jessica has been frivolously spending his money. He is dismayed to find that she has traded (for a monkey) a ring given him by his wife, but Tubal comforts him by reminding him of Antonio's bad luck. Shylock asks Tubal

ACT III, SCENE I

to arrange to have an officer arrest Antonio, and they part, making plans to meet later at their synagogue.

Analysis

The plot thickens for Antonio, threatening to make him a pound thinner. Not one, but two, of his ships, the audience learns, have come to ruin, throwing his finances into chaos and bankruptcy. Shylock already feels he has grounds to detain the merchant, in order to insure his adherence to the terms of their bond. The next time Antonio appears on stage (Act III, Scene III), he will be in the custody of a jailer.

As is the case in most scenes in which he appears, however, Shylock steals the show here. He utters one of the most famous speeches of the play, if not of Shakespeare generally, the "Hath not a Jew eyes?" monologue (pages 42–43). This speech may initially strike a reader or audience member as an eloquent plea for racial and religious harmony, climaxing in the dramatic lines, "If you prick us, do we not bleed? If you tickle us, do we not laugh? If you poison us, do we not die?". There is, however, a sinister undercurrent running throughout the speech; Shylock follows the above lines with "And if you wrong us, shall we not revenge?". In this line, the plea for harmony explicitly spills over into the harsher "eye-for-an-eye" sentiments of Mosaic Law. Keep in mind that the tension in this speech is between its forceful eloquence and its purpose as a justification for performing brutal violence against Antonio. The skilled talkers in Shakespeare's plays—be they as silly as Polonius in *Hamlet* or as repulsive as Caliban in *The Tempest*—always command an audience's attention and consideration. One must acknowledge a certain righteousness in Shylock's position. He has been abused at the hands of the Christians before, and now he has just cause to suspect Antonio's complicity in his daughter's flight.

One interesting detail which perhaps does more than any other to humanize Shylock and enlist audience sympathy is his grief over the loss of a ring given him by his wife (whose absence from Shylock's household throughout the play may indicate that he is a widower). Shylock's outrage over his daughter's theft moves from the economic to the personal, as he wouldn't have parted with this item for any price. The audience may be more perplexed than ever at the end of this scene, as both Shylock's venom and his humanity increase.

Act III, Scene II (pages 44–54)

Summary

Act III, Scene II contains the first major climactic moment in the play, as one of its two main plots—Bassanio's quest for Portia and the challenge of the three caskets—comes to a resolution. The scene opens with Bassanio and his attendants at Portia's house in Belmont. For the first time in The *Merchant of Venice*, Portia exhibits enthusiasm for her potential suitor. She bids Bassanio to delay his choice, so that, in the event of his failure, they will still have had a chance to spend time together. Bassanio refuses, however, impatient to get the trial over with. Portia makes a speech praising him and wishing him success. A song is sung while Bassanio deliberates in silence.

After the song, Bassanio reasons aloud over the caskets. Unlike his predecessors, Bassanio primarily concentrates on the material of the caskets rather than the descriptions. Distrusting the lure of appearance, he chooses the leaden one, which contains a picture of Portia and a congratulatory note. Bassanio kisses Portia, according to the instructions. Portia proclaims her unworthiness, before giving herself and all of her possessions over to Bassanio. She offers him a ring, with the proviso that if he take it from his finger or lose it, he indicates the end of his love for her. Bassanio swears to keep the ring, till death do them part.

In the mirth which ensues, Gratiano suddenly reveals that he and Nerissa are to be wed and receives permission to do so at Bassanio's and Portia's wedding. At that moment, Salerio arrives from Venice, accompanied by the fugitives, Jessica and Lorenzo. Salerio delivers a letter from Antonio to Bassanio. As Bassanio reads, Portia observes that he loses his gaiety, and she demands to know the message. Bassanio reveals to her his indebtedness to Antonio and the fact that all of the latter's ventures at sea have failed. Salerio informs his friends of Shylock's absolute refusal to settle for anything less than the terms of his bond (i.e., the pound of Antonio's flesh).

Perceiving the closeness between her future husband and his friend, Portia offers to pay the debt to Shylock twelve times over. All she requests is that Bassanio marry her before setting out. When she discovers that Antonio's life is at stake and that he begs to see Bassanio one last time before dying, however, Portia dispatches Bassanio immediately. He promises to return as soon as possible.

Analysis

Act III, Scene II is one of the longest and most important scenes in the entire play. Its primary purpose is to show how Bassanio solves the riddle of the caskets and win Portia. Beyond that, it sets up or continues the other storylines which will lead to the resolution of the pound of flesh plot.

The first item of significance in the scene is the fact of Portia's enthusiasm for Bassanio's attempt to win her hand. This is unprecedented in the play and, true to the spirit of comedy, Portia obtains her choice even though the terms of her father's will allow her no choice.

The next major aspect of the scene is Bassanio's solution to the challenge of the caskets. He announces his logic at the very beginning of his attempt: "So may the outward shows be least themselves;/ The world is still deceived with ornament" (p. 47). In other words, he knows the lure of the surface may be misleading and refuses to be taken in by mere appearances. Interestingly, Bassanio eschews the inscriptions of the caskets entirely and this, the audience might feel, is wise. Already we have seen how the same words can be bent to virtually opposite ends. Although it could be argued that the legend on the gold casket is misleading, the silver and lead caskets' inscriptions could easily be read as invitations or as warnings. This is not to say that Bassanio avoids linguistic matters entirely; far from it. He instead balances his distrust of appearances against the cultural significance of all three metals. By his rationale, the least worthy casket by outward appearances—lead, a metal of no cultural worth—becomes the correct choice. And so it is.

Bassanio's future marriage to Portia guarantees him financial security and the wherewithal to pay his debts to Antonio. This, we might recall, was ostensibly his motive for seeking Portia's hand in the first place, though it appears that he and Portia, at this point in the play, are genuinely in love. Paying off Antonio becomes a largely irrelevant concern, in any case. Portia seems to have more money than she knows what to do with; Antonio discharges his friend from his debts as long as Bassanio returns to Venice before his execution; Shylock will never collect on his 3,000 ducat loan in skin or cash. After all these complications, the audience may feel, Bassanio and Portia had better be in love!

As one plot is resolved, another more minor plot is introduced in the form of the ring Portia gives Bassanio to seal their love. Portia ends up generating the remaining portion of the play beyond Act IV, Scene I with her mischievous shenanigans involving the ring. Otherwise the play would end after Act IV, Scene I, once the pound of flesh plot is concluded. The reason for this extra plot perhaps stems from a desire on Shakespeare's part to thicken the mix of his play with some pure comedy. Though the threat against Antonio's life ends happily, it may have been deemed too grim a scenario to end the comedy on.

Act III, Scene III (pages 55–56)

New Character:

The Jailer: *holds Antonio on Shylock's behalf*

Summary

Meanwhile, back in Venice, Shylock encounters Antonio on the streets, albeit in the custody of the Jailer hired to guard him and accompanied by Solanio. Antonio begs a word with the usurer, but Shylock won't even listen to him. "I'll have no speaking; I will have my bond" (p. 55) he cries before departing. Solanio tries to encourage Antonio, saying the Duke will not permit the fulfilling of the bond, but Antonio is resigned to his death. He knows it is important to law and order (as well as the economy) in Venice that the Duke uphold Shylock's legal right to have his bond fulfilled. Antonio seems to have reconciled himself to his impending doom, so long as Bassanio returns to Venice to see him one last time.

Analysis

For the most part, this scene serves to put us back in touch with Venice after the previous long scene in Belmont, to assure the audience that things are indeed going as badly as Bassanio and company think they are. Aside from this, it advances the image of an unyielding, bitter Shylock and a melancholy, resigned merchant of Venice. Antonio's last lines are interesting, however: "Pray God Bassanio come/ To see me pay his debt, and then I care not!" (p. 56). After his magnanimous, even passionate displays towards Bassanio, these lines ring with an almost spiteful bitterness. Perhaps there is some sexual jealousy on Antonio's part, the way he recalls Bassanio from his future bride's side in order to tell him, "I would die for you."

Act III, Scene IV (pages 56–58)

New Character:

Balthasar: *a servant of Portia*

Summary

Portia begins this scene in discussion with Lorenzo, during which she commits the management of her household to his and Jessica's hands. She informs him that she and Nerissa are going to a monastery to pray until her husband comes home. After Jessica and Lorenzo exit, however, Portia instructs her servant Balthasar to deliver a letter to her cousin Dr. Bellario (a lawyer) and bring whatever clothes and instructions he offers to the ferry, where she will be waiting. He goes, and Portia informs Nerissa that they are to travel to Venice disguised as men, for purposes she will explain shortly.

Analysis

From this point in the play onward, Portia takes a central and commanding role. It's as if, freed from the strictures of her father's will after Bassanio's triumph, Portia now seeks to make up for lost time by solving Antonio's dilemma. Not only is she convinced of Antonio's worth on the basis of his friendship with Bassanio (as she informs Lorenzo), but also, one might speculate, she feels indebted to him for enabling his friend's trip to Belmont.

Portia acknowledges the fact that being a woman has kept her sidelined from the action thus far, in a speech which the Elizabethan audience probably would have found humorous, but which more liberal-minded audiences today would no doubt receive with more sympathy. The play is fraught with images of women's servitude, and their problematic positions as second-class citizens. Clearly, Portia is submissive to her father even after his death, and her wealth and power are transferred to her husband immediately following her marriage. It is important to note that these constraints are placed upon and accepted by the most powerful woman in the play. In even more subtle terms, as the couples pair off in Act III, Scene II, they wager about who will be the first to have a male child, underscoring the desirability of males over females to the Elizabethans. In an exercise of what little power she has, Portia camps it up with some swagger at the expense of the men in her society, poking fun at their self-aggrandizing bluster and making bawdy references to their anatomy. What Portia and Nerissa are about to do, as the audience will learn shortly (in Act IV, Scene I), is disguise themselves as a lawyer and his clerk, in order to arbitrate the bond between Antonio and Shylock, in another subtle way showing that in order to move in the Venetian circles of power, they must disguise their gender.

Act III, Scene V (pages 59–61)

Summary

Launcelot teases Jessica about her genealogy, claiming that being a Jew, she is damned. On the subject of genealogy, Lorenzo walks in and announces that Launcelot has gotten "the Moor" (i.e., a black woman) pregnant. Launcelot and Lorenzo match wits good-naturedly for a time, before the former departs. Lorenzo and Jessica flirt for a few lines before departing for dinner.

Analysis

This is a gratuitous scene, thrown in solely for laughs rather than plot. It does, however, flirt comically with two of the play's themes. Jessica's Jewish ancestry is mocked here, although in a purely light-hearted way. It seems that suddenly, no one takes Jessica's ethnicity seriously anymore, which is quite a reversal from previous scenes. Keep in mind that, even for Lorenzo—who is in love with Jessica—the issue of her race at one point threatened to outweigh any of her particular behavioral characteristics.

Also invoked here is the trouble with words, which previously had manifested itself in relation to the challenge of the three caskets. Lorenzo, exasperated with the linguistic displays of Launcelot, laments "How every fool can play upon the word!" Lorenzo's plea to Launcelot—"I pray thee understand a plain man in his plain meaning" (p. 60)—is a humorous and perhaps nostalgic wish for language to be fixed in its meaning and not available to multiple interpretations.

Study Questions

1. Why, since it won't result in any financial gain, does Shylock insist on the terms of his bond with Antonio?

2. What news does Tubal bring Shylock?

3. Why does Portia want Bassanio to wait before facing the challenge of the three caskets?

4. Why does Bassanio select the lead casket?

5. What does the lead casket contain?

6. What does Portia claim will occur if Bassanio gives up the ring she gives him?

7. What does Gratiano reveal after Bassanio solves the riddle of the three caskets?

8. Why does Portia allow Bassanio to leave before they get married?

9. According to Antonio, why won't the Duke be able to intercede on his behalf?

10.   What does Portia decide to do at the end of Act III?

Answers

1.   Shylock wishes to cut off Antonio's flesh in order to "feed [his] revenge. [Antonio] hath disgraced [him]…laughed at [his] losses…scorned [his] nation, [and] thwarted [his] bargains" out of (so Shylock claims) pure racial hostility.

2.   Tubal tells Shylock that one of Antonio's ships has been wrecked "coming from Tripolis" and that Jessica has spent a great deal of his money.

3.   Afraid that Bassanio will fail, but desirous of his company, Portia wishes to spend as much time with him as possible.

4.   Bassanio distrusts attractive surfaces, for fear they contain corrupt things. As he addresses his choice, "But thou, thou meager lead/ Which rather threaten'st than dost promise ought,/ Thy paleness moves me more to eloquence;/ And here choose I."

5.   Inside the lead casket, Bassanio finds a picture of Portia— signifying his success—and a scroll instructing him to kiss her.

6.   If Bassanio does "part from, lose, or give away [Portia's ring],/ …it [will] presage the ruins of [his] love."

7.   Gratiano announces that he and Nerissa intend to marry.

8.   Portia discovers, while reading Antonio's letter, that he fears "it is impossible [he] should live" and wishes to see Bassanio before he is killed.

9.   "The Duke cannot deny the course of the law;/ For the commodity that strangers have/ …in Venice, if it be denied,/ Will much impede the justice of the state." In other words, the Duke must uphold the law for non-citizens, so that Venice may maintain its good standing in international business affairs.

10.   Portia decides that she and Nerissa must go to Venice disguised as men, to help resolve the situation there.

Suggested Essay Topics

1. Compare and contrast Bassanio's deliberations over the three caskets with those of his rivals.

2. Discuss Shylock's "Hath not a Jew eyes?" speech in relation to the various attitudes toward race demonstrated throughout the play.

3. How does Portia's character develop over the course of Act III?

Act IV

Act IV, Scene I (pages 63–76)

New Character:

The Duke of Venice: *highest authority in Venice*

Summary

Bassanio and his attendants are back in Venice and wait with Antonio in the presence of the Duke to discover the fate of the merchant of Venice. Shylock enters the court, and the Duke makes a personal appeal to him to not only spare Antonio's life but also, in light of the merchant's recent losses at sea, to reduce the amount of the debt. But Shylock will have none of it, demanding that the bond be executed. When questioned on his motives, Shylock responds that he simply hates Antonio and is not obliged to have any particular justification. Bassanio offers Shylock twice the amount of Antonio's debt, but the latter remains firm. Shylock reminds the Duke that it is necessary to uphold the law in order to maintain Venice's good standing in international trade.

The Duke declares that he will make no decision until he hears from Bellario of Padua, who he has asked to come decide the matter. Nerissa enters, dressed in men's clothes, posing as a messenger from Bellario. She gives the Duke a letter, which he reads while Gratiano and Shylock bicker. The Duke reveals that the letter recommends a young doctor (lawyer) to the Venetians to help decide the case. The Duke sends for the man while the letter is read to the court.

This "man" is actually Portia, disguised as a lawyer. She questions Shylock and Antonio on the particularities of their case, and asks Shylock if he would be merciful. He refuses, of course. Bassanio, offering to pay the debt twice over, asks the disguised Portia if they might bend the law in this particular case. Much to Shylock's delight, however, she declares this cannot be, for it would set a dangerous legal precedent in Venetian law. Portia asks Shylock if he'll take three times the amount of the debt and spare Antonio's life, but he refuses to budge. She decrees that the bond must be adhered to. Antonio thus steels himself for death.

Before Shylock can start slicing away, however, Portia points out that although he is perfectly entitled to Antonio's flesh, he has no claim to spill any of the merchant's blood. Moreover, should he do so, his "land and goods/ Are, by the laws of Venice, confiscate/ Unto the state of Venice" (p. 72). Shylock is dismayed by this news and seeing no way to obtain Antonio's flesh without bloodshed, asks for the money instead. Portia prevents Bassanio from handing over the money, however, insisting that justice must be served. She points out, however, that Shylock will be subject to execution if he takes more or less than a pound of flesh.

Realizing that his sinister jig is up, Shylock attempts to slink away with only the original 3,000 ducats. Portia won't allow this, however, as he has already "refused it in open court." Shylock sees he is trapped and is prepared to leave court empty-handed. But Portia produces another law, decreeing that if any foreigner "by direct or indirect attempts/ ... seek[s] the life of a citizen," he loses half his goods to the citizen, the other half to the state, and his "life lies in the mercy/ Of the Duke..." The Christians take great delight in this, and the Duke spares Shylock's life though confiscates his wealth.

Embittered, Shylock asks that he be killed, as he cannot sustain himself without his goods. Antonio intercedes, however, and asks the Duke to pardon the state's portion of the fine, in exchange for the following conditions: Antonio must receive half of Shylock's goods to use in trust for Lorenzo and Jessica; Shylock must become a Christian; and he must will all his possessions upon his death to Jessica and Lorenzo. The Duke agrees to this arrangement, as does Shylock, who has little choice. Shylock then pleads illness and hobbles away from the scene a broken man.

The Duke requests that Portia dine with him, but she begs off, claiming she must return to Padua. The Duke leaves. Bassanio and Antonio offer to pay the disguised Portia the 3,000 ducats earmarked for Shylock, but she refuses, claiming satisfaction in justice. Bassanio presses, so Portia asks for his gloves, which he gives her, and his ring, which he holds back. He pleads first the ring's worthlessness, and then his sentimental attachment to it. Portia scorns him in pretended outrage, and she and Nerissa depart. Antonio then persuades Bassanio to let the lawyer have the ring, for the service "he" rendered. Bassanio relents and sends Gratiano with his ring to find the pair.

Analysis

This scene marks the resolution of the second major plot complication of *The Merchant of Venice*, namely the pound of flesh scenario. There doesn't seem much point in denying that the play climaxes with this particular scene, and that the remaining scenes constitute little more than some good-natured dénouement. It is also the last scene of which Shylock is part, and so central is he deemed to the play that several productions have ended here, omitting the rest altogether. This is perhaps appropriate, for with Shylock go all the issues which have been preoccupying the audience for the length of the play. The sole remaining concern is the subplot of the rings, which was only introduced into the plot in the preceding scene and is quite extraneous to the major business on stage.

Shylock enters the scene well past the point of reconciliation; he wants Antonio dead, and will accept no amount of money in exchange for foregoing the terms of his bond. The issue of Jewishness comes to a head at this point, as the Christians attribute Shylock's stubbornness to an inbred racial/religious sensibility. Antonio even asks his friends not to try to change Shylock's mind, for, he feels, "You may as well forbid the mountain pines/ To wag their high tops, and to make no noise/ When they are fretten with the gusts of heaven;/ You may as well do any thing most hard/ As seek to soften.../ His Jewish heart" (p. 65). Shylock's rigidity is seen to stem from his constitution. The usurer himself, however, belies this claim, for, we may recall from Act III, Scene I, Shylock insists he learned this behavior from "Christian example."

The Christian animosity towards Shylock's Jewishness is made most apparent, however, in the terms of Shylock's punishment. The most conspicuous of Antonio's three conditions for Shylock is the demand that he must convert to Christianity. Some stage productions of The Merchant have given a great deal of weight to this detail, representing it as the crushing blow to the usurer. This is a convincing interpretation, insofar as Shylock appears to take his religion very seriously throughout the play. Moreover, shortly after the demand has been made and agreed to, Shylock must leave the court, pleading illness. It's as if the idea of conversion is physically repugnant to him. Given his treatment at the hands of the Christians, it may very well be.

An issue somewhat related to these religious matters is the traditional opposition between the letter and the spirit of the law. Some critics have suggested that the dispute between the Christians and Shylock boils down to the latter's stubborn insistence on formally codified laws as opposed to the spirit in which such laws were written. They further insist that this trait is in keeping with the Elizabethan conception of Jews as cold-hearted exploiters of legal language, a sensibility expressed today in the stereotypes of the lawyer as a shrewd manipulator of language against truth and justice, and as typically Jewish. This binary opposition between Jew/letter and Christian/spirit seems forced, however, when held against the background of Act IV, Scene I. The Christians, especially Portia, are brutally clever manipulators of the law, as evinced through their juxtaposing of various laws to transform Shylock from a violated creditor waiting to receive his due, to an impoverished supplicant of the Duke, suing for mercy. Portia proves particularly adept at pulling laws out of her assumed hat of "Doctor." It is difficult to say how convincing an audience might find her reasoning that the bond doesn't entitle Shylock to spill any of Antonio's blood; one could argue that the bond doesn't exclude it either, or that the idea of spilling blood is presumed in the idea of cutting off a pound of flesh. (The bond doesn't specifically entitle Shylock to hold the knife with his hand, but it would be difficult to imagine arguing on such grounds.) In any case, it seems petty to fault Shylock for adhering to the letter of the law because, as a Jew in a Christian society, what else does he have to protect him? The "spirit" in Venice is not very friendly to him. The Christians clearly don't want Shylock to have his way and continue to maneuver until they succeed at circumventing his legal claims, however brutal.

The theme of Antonio's possible homosexual love for Bassanio perhaps attains its loudest crescendo here. The morbidity and melancholy which Antonio has from time to time exhibited throughout the play reaches new depths, as throughout the scene he demonstrates a peculiar willingness to die. This eagerness might be accounted for if, as Solanio insists in Act II, Scene VIII Antonio "only loves the world" for Bassanio's presence. Perhaps Antonio feels he has already lost his friend to the world of heterosexual love and would just as soon be killed by Shylock as not. As Antonio steels himself for slaughter, he tells Bassanio, "Commend me to your honourable wife./ Tell her the process of Antonio's end,/ Say how I loved you, speak me fair in death;/ And when the tale is told, bid her be judge/ Whether Bassanio had not once a love" (p. 71). An actor could deliver these lines with a great deal of spite, as if to suggest Bassanio had a love and, upon Antonio's death, would no longer have one. In other words, Antonio suggests, no heterosexual relationship could supplant, replace, or even compare with the love he and Bassanio shared.

The last item one might note about Act IV, Scene I is the continuance of the subplot of Portia's ring. Upon Shylock's quitting the court, there's no particular reason for Portia and Nerissa to maintain their secret identities. But rather than reveal themselves, the women instead embark upon some gratuitous tomfoolery at the expense of their future husbands. Portia creates the new conflict out of thin air. It's as if, freed from her father's will and armed with a new sense of subjective agency, Portia is reluctant to relinquish her new-found power. Perhaps she is sowing her wild oats, given that, according to the custom of the time, all of Portia's property and possessions will become Bassanio's upon their marriage, and he will be her lord and master. Rather than go directly from one guardian to another, Portia wishes to prolong her freedom and express herself through her own action. This is offset, however, by the fact that her action remains hidden by her disguise, and at its boldest, remains all in fun; she offers no challenge to this social order, especially in light of the fact that her actions are, in the end, a service to her husband.

It should be noted, finally, that Bassanio initially passes Portia's test of his devotion by refusing to part with the ring. But rather than reveal herself then, she storms off in pretended anger, giving Bassanio time to cave in. Portia is determined to have her fun, it seems.

Act IV, Scene II (page 77)

Summary

Gratiano overtakes Portia and Nerissa as they seek Shylock's house in order to have the usurer sign the deed willing his properties to Lorenzo. Gratiano offers Portia the ring and an invitation to dinner. She accepts the former and declines the latter. Nerissa, meanwhile, determines to lure Gratiano into the same trap Portia laid for Bassanio, and sets off with Gratiano, ostensibly in search of Shylock's house, in order to obtain her future husband's ring.

Analysis

This scene simply serves to advance the ring plot by giving Portia the chance to obtain Bassanio's ring and allowing Nerissa the same opportunity with Gratiano, in order to complete the comic symmetry.

Study Questions

1. What does the Duke request of Shylock?
2. What reason does Shylock give for his wanting the pound of Antonio's flesh?
3. Why does Antonio advise his friends to give up attempting to dissuade Shylock?
4. Why does Shylock believe the Duke must enforce the terms of the bond?

5. Why does Portia, disguised as the lawyer, initially conclude that Shylock's bond must be adhered to?

6. Although she acknowledges Shylock's right to a pound of Antonio's flesh, how does Portia prevent the usurer from acting on it?

7. Why is Shylock stripped of his possessions?

8. Apart from the financial conditions, what does Antonio's new arrangement demand of Shylock?

9. What does the disguised Portia demand from Bassanio for her services?

10. Why is Bassanio reluctant to give up the ring?

Answers

1. The Duke asks Shylock if he will "not only loose the forfeiture,/ But touched with human gentleness and love,/ Forgive a moiety of the principle,/ Glancing an eye of pity on [Antonio's] losses." In other words, he asks Shylock to consider Antonio's financial predicament and not only accept money in place of the pound of flesh, but also reduce the amount of the debt.

2. Shylock claims he can "give no reason, nor will [he] not,/ More than a lodged hate and a certain loathing/ [He] bear[s] Antonio…"

3. Antonio believes that Shylock cannot be reasoned with, due to a racially-determined stubbornness within him. He claims, "You may as well do any thing most hard/ As seek to soften that—than which what's harder?—/ His Jewish heart."

4. Shylock thinks that the Duke must uphold the terms of the bond, otherwise all Venetian law will be held up to scorn and ridicule.

5. Portia insists that there is "no power in Venice/ Can alter a device established," i.e., Shylock's bond can't be changed after its terms have already been violated.

6. Portia points out that, although it allows Shylock to cut away a pound of Antonio's flesh, "This bond doth give [Shylock] here no jot of blood..."

7. Shylock's goods are confiscated because Venetian law decrees such a penalty to a foreigner who "by direct or indirect attempts...seek[s] the life of any citizen..."

8. Shylock must convert from Judaism to Christianity.

9. Portia asks for Bassanio's gloves and his ring.

10. Bassanio promised Portia that he'd take it off only when he'd stopped loving her.

Suggested Essay Topics

1. What factors motivate Antonio's resignation in Act IV, Scene I? Discuss this in relation to his ambiguous position of both envying his friend's new relationship and yet sacrificing himself to make it possible.

2. How does the plot of the rings relate to the other contractual obligations dramatized in the play?

3. Consider and discuss the process by which Portia turns the situation in the court from Shylock's advantage to Antonio's.

SECTION SIX

Act V

Act V, Scene I (pages 79–88)

New Character:

Stephano: *a messenger*

Summary

Lorenzo and Jessica are in the garden in front of Portia's house in Belmont, whispering sweet nothings in each other's ears. Stephano, a messenger, enters and announces that Portia will soon return. Launcelot Gobbo arrives and makes the same announcement with respect to Bassanio. Lorenzo dispatches Stephano to ready the household for Portia's return. Lorenzo babbles for a time about the moon and music.

Portia and Nerissa enter and encounter the two mooning lovers, who welcome them home. Portia orders that no one in her household mention her and Nerissa's absence. Bassanio, Antonio, Gratiano, and their followers arrive. Portia welcomes them home to Belmont and is introduced to Antonio.

The company notice Gratiano and Nerissa quarreling. Portia inquires why, and it is revealed that Gratiano gave away the ring Nerissa had given him, which he promised never to remove from his hand. Portia chastises Gratiano, claiming that her betrothed, Bassanio, would never do such a thing. Gratiano reveals that Bassanio too gave his ring away and pleads that they both sacrificed their rings to the judge and clerk, who would take no other payment. Portia and Nerissa feign disbelief, insisting the men must have given the rings away during some tawdry sexual encounter and vowing never to sleep with their future husbands until the rings are recovered.

Antonio attempts to intercede on his friends' behalf, promising that never again will Bassanio break his oath. To seal the bargain, Portia produces a ring, which turns out to be the same as the one she gave him in the first place. She claims to have recovered it by sleeping with the doctor. Nerissa also insists that she regained her ring from the clerk using a similar method. Having thoroughly bewildered all parties concerned, Portia reveals that she and Nerissa were the doctor and the clerk. She also gives Antonio a letter, informing him that three of his ships have in fact returned and are laden with riches. Nerissa tells Lorenzo of Shylock's new will, naming him heir of the usurer's estate. There is general merriment, and the company goes inside Portia's house.

Analysis

Act V, Scene I is the final scene of the play, and its primary purpose seems to be to restore the comic mood threatened by Shylock's attempt on Antonio's life. The frivolous final subplot is resolved here; Portia reveals that she and Nerissa were the doctor and the clerk, and thus that Bassanio and Gratiano simply gave the rings back to their original owners. Clearing away any remaining ill residue from the previous scenes, Portia also reveals that some of Antonio's ships have returned safe, thus restoring his previous good fortune as a businessman. The spirit of comedy wins the day.

Shakespeare's primary agenda in this scene, as in so many, is a linguistic one; in other words, much of the dialogue here is aimed at displaying his wit and ingenuity, with a barrage of puns, double-entendres, and metaphors. Lorenzo's sole purpose in this scene, for example, is to make long decorous speeches, which advance nothing in the play, save its poetry. In particular, Shakespeare milks the humorous potential in Portia's and Nerissa's secret activities for as many double meanings as possible. Nerissa's accusation, that "The clerk will ne'er wear hair on's face that had [the ring from Gratiano]," for example, has two main senses, one for most of the characters—i.e., Nerissa claims to suspect

Gratiano of giving his ring not to a clerk but to another woman—and an extra one for Nerissa, Portia, and the audience—i.e., the clerk, who was actually Nerissa, therefore a woman, will indeed never grow a beard. The chief interest and delight in this scene, one might argue, is the sight of Bassanio and Gratiano squirming, while Portia and Nerissa rattle off string after string of accusations which the women know are both false and true, depending on how one interprets the words. This ties the last scene into the recurring theme of multiple interpretations of words which runs throughout the play. The difference here is that unlike the scenes involving the three caskets, in which much was at stake depending on how one reads the words in question, the final scene offers us this linguistic play for its own sake—just for laughs, as it were—in a spirit of comedy where several interpretations are available and no one—audience and cast alike—is obliged to settle on a single reading to the exclusion of all others. And such is perhaps the ultimate attraction of Shakespearean comedy.

Study Questions

1. What message does Stephano deliver to Lorenzo and Jessica?

2. What opinion does Lorenzo hold of men who don't like music?

3. What does Portia order her household not to do?

4. To whom does Nerissa claim to believe Gratiano gave his ring?

5. What does Portia threaten when Bassanio admits he gave the ring away?

6. What does Portia claim she will do if she encounters the doctor to whom Bassanio gave the ring?

7. How does Antonio attempt to placate Portia?

8. What does Portia offer Bassanio to seal the new promise?

9. What secret does Portia reveal to the company?

10. What good news does Portia tell Antonio?

Answers

1. Stephano announces that Portia "will before the break of day/ Be here at Belmont. She doth stray about/ By holy crosses where she kneels and prays/ For happy wedlock hours."

2. Lorenzo claims that "The man that hath no music in himself,/ Nor is not moved with concord of sweet sounds,/ Is fit for treasons, stratagems, and spoils" and is thus not to be trusted.

3. Portia insists that no one reveal that she and Nerissa have been away from home.

4. Nerissa claims whoever has the ring "will ne'er wear hair on's face..." In other words, she says she suspects him of giving it to a woman.

5. Portia swears that she "will ne'er come in [Bassanio's] bed/ Until [she] see[s] the ring!"

6. Portia says to Bassanio, "Since [the Doctor] hath got the jewel that I loved,/ And that which you did swear to keep for me,/ I will become as liberal as you,/ I'll not deny him anything I have,/ No, not my body nor my husband's bed."

7. Antonio promises Portia that "[his] soul upon the forfeit... [Bassanio]/ Will never more break faith advisedly."

8. Portia offers the same ring she initially gave Bassanio, claiming she recovered it by sleeping with the doctor.

9. Portia reveals that she and Nerissa were in fact the doctor and his clerk.

10. Portia gives Antonio a letter in which it is revealed that "three of [his] argosies [i.e., ships]/ Are richly come to harbor suddenly."

Suggested Essay Topics

1. Trace the development of Portia from a daughter bound by her father's will to a behind-the-scenes manipulator of events.

The Merchant of Venice

2. How do Lorenzo's speeches concerning the moon and music suggest other themes previously explored in The Merchant of Venice?

3. What purpose does the parallel romance of Gratiano and Nerissa serve in terms of an audience's evaluation of the relationship between Bassanio and Portia?

Bibliography

Barnet, Sylvan. "*The Merchant of Venice on the Stage.*" Shakespeare 192-205.

Barton, Anne. "Introduction to *The Merchant of Venice.*" *The Riverside Shakespeare*. By William Shakespeare. Eds. G. Blakemore Evans, et al. Boston: Houghton Mifflin Co., 1974. 250-253.

Charney, Maurice. *All of Shakespeare*. New York: Columbia University Press, 1993.

Compact Edition of the Oxford English Dictionary, The Oxford: Oxford University Press, 1971.

Myrick, Kenneth. Introduction. Shakespeare xxi-xxxviii.

—. "Textual Note." Shakespeare 139-141.

—. "A Note on the Sources of *The Merchant of Venice.*" Shakespeare 142-144.

Shakespeare, William. *The Merchant of Venice*. Ed. Kenneth Myrick. Rev. ed. New York: Signet Classic, 1987.

Wittgenstein, Ludwig. *Culture And Value*. Eds. G.H. Von Wright and Heikki Nyman. Trans. Peter Winch. Chicago: University of Chicago Press, 1980.

12/2/98

BRIDAL SHOWERS

50
Great Ideas
for a
Perfect Shower

Sharon E. Dlugosch
and
Florence E. Nelson

A PERIGEE BOOK

A Perigee Book
Published by The Berkley Publishing Group
200 Madison Avenue
New York, NY 10016

First published in a limited edition by Brighton Publications, Inc.
Illustrations by Sandra T. Knuth

First Perigee edition: April 1987

The Putnam Berkley World Wide Web site address is
http://www.berkley.com

Library of Congress Cataloging-in-Publication Data

Dlugosch, Sharon.
Bridal showers.
Rev. ed. of: Wedding shower fun. © 1984
"A Perigee book."
Includes index.
1. Showers (Parties) 2. Weddings I. Dlugosch,
Sharon. Wedding shower fun. II. Nelson,
Florence E. III. Title.
GV1472.7.S5D55   1987   793.2   86-30387
ISBN: 0-399-51344-2

Cover photograph copyright by the estate of Alex Gotfryd.

Printed in the United States of America

30   29   28   27   26   25   24   23   22   21

Contents

Introduction

This book was written because neither of us particularly liked showers. For years, each of us kept this fact hidden under our umbrellas. Then, on a bright, sunny day, one of us said it out loud: "I hate showers!" We can't tell you who voiced it because it was such a shock.

Well, we reasoned, if we each hate showers, that makes two. And if there are two, there must be more closet shower-haters. And indeed there were.

So why a book? Because in talking with many women and reviewing the results of a shower survey we mailed to individuals and gift stores around the country, we found an interesting phenomenon. Even though there seemed to be a general, yet uneasy dislike for giving and going to showers, no one really wanted to banish the custom forever. (That presented a real dilemma, because before the results of the survey started to come in, we began preparing "Down with Showers" posters.) The survey showed that the problem was not showers as a gesture of love toward the bride, but busy schedules, limited funds, wanting to include men and families, and, in general, not knowing just how to put on a shower to be remembered.

The problem was not showers. They had pretty much stayed the same. It was us—our busy lives, our love of activity, our new relationships with men. We had changed. No wonder we'd gotten too big for our umbrellas! So many of us are working outside the home now, there just isn't as much time available. And we do love sports and other activities, and that increases the time pinch even more. And how about the unsettling influence of the sixties? People began to look at the rituals surrounding the wedding in an entirely different way. There's a whole generation of young people who don't even know how to put on a shower.

Most of us do want to join with family and friends at this very special moment in our lives, when fond memories are being formed. And one occasion that adds to this wonderful collection of memories is the wedding shower.

We had done our homework. The survey sent to women around the country brought back a lot of good information and ideas, and opened up a whole new shower world.

So we agreed to act. We were determined to turn all these obstacles around and use them to create a fun and easy party for ourselves as well as for our guests. With what we learned about showers from the results of our survey, and what we already knew about love and romance, we knew we could write a book that would make our next shower a knockout!

—Sharon E. Dlugosch

—Florence E. Nelson

BRIDAL
SHOWERS

50
Great Ideas
for a
Perfect Shower

ONE

Shower Questions
Everybody Asks

Y ou shower givers and goers around the country came up with some party problems worth sharing. It didn't take us long to jot down every question we'd heard from people around the country. Here they are, and the best part is you get answers, too!

Q: Every shower's the same: games, food, and chatter. Isn't there anything new under the sun?
—Bored

Dear Bored:
    You can turn any shower into sunshine if you're willing to do something a bit different. For instance, in one part of the country, there's a new idea that's really taking hold— Wine- and Cheese-Tasting showers. In another, Show Me showers are gaining in popularity. One thing's for sure.

You're not alone in your boredom. So check out Chapter 2, Showerwise Themes, for details of these two showers and for other ideas that may get you and your friends out of the shower blahs!

Q: I know I should, but how can I possibly give a shower for a close friend? My calendar is full.
—Too Busy

Dear Busy:
You won't have to miss a step! If you're too busy, it probably means you're involved in many activities. Chances are at least one of these must include your close friend, or you wouldn't be close for long . . . you'd never see each other! One of these activities could be the germ of a shower theme. Read our No Sweat, Tie-a-Quilt, and Calorie Counter showers for openers. These are all examples of bringing the shower to the group instead of the other way around. Or to put it another way, they make the shower part of your life, not your life part of the shower.

Q: I'd really like to see my whole family take part in the shower custom. Do you have any idea how we can pull it off?
—Family Lover

Dear Family Lover:
Why not? We find children especially love these occasions and will treasure such memories for a long time. If you're part of a religious community, our Sunday-Go-to-Meeting Shower may be what you're looking for. Alternative choices might be our Open-Door or Dollar-Disco-Dance showers. And if you're not into disco dancing, use the same theme idea around polka or ballroom dancing. Ah-one and ah-two!

Q: This is a second marriage for both of us—and really, we have all we need. It would be nice just to celebrate with our friends.

—Second Time Around

Dear Second Time:
   A new start very often makes us want to create entirely different memory patterns. Our Second-Time-Around Shower was meant for couples like you. It's based on an actual shower we attended and really enjoyed. We think you'll enjoy it too.

Q: Between all our different college class schedules and tight budgets, how can I possibly give a shower for my roommate?

—Student

Dear Student:
   We deserve an A for coming up with this one! Now here's your chance to make the grade. What's the one time of day you're all together, no matter what? You've got it! . . . during your favorite soap opera, and that's what we've named this theme. For a quieter, more tender time, see our Tie-a-Quilt Shower, too. Homemakers take note. Instead of a soap opera coffee break, shift the scene and make it a College Soap Opera Shower break.

Q: Everything must be just right. My guests have to leave believing they never have attended—and never again will attend—a shower like the one I host.

—Elegant

Dear Elegant:
   For rave reviews, plan carefully and pay close attention

to detail. Off the top of our brows, we can think of two humdingers—ahem . . . that is, two splendid ideas. The Elegant Shower was created just for you. Do read that theme first. Our Formal Pool Shower is in a class of its own and most impressive.

Q: I want to give a shower for my best friend, but it's a little embarrassing. I find myself with limited funds for such an affair. I'm willing to work . . .
—Time, But No Money

Dear Time:
   Showers do take money, but not necessarily yours. Our Shower on a Shoestring and Co-Hostess Shower are good examples of this, but there are many other ideas. In some places, it's practically a tradition to share the work, time, *and* money. Our College Soap Opera and Tie-a-Quilt showers can also fill the bill when the green stuff is in short supply.

Q: Every shower I've ever attended has been the same old thing. I want to do something *really* different!
—Dramatic

Dear Dramatic:
   Are you ready for us? How about transporting your guests to Gothic times with our Romantic Novel Shower? Or maybe stardom appeals to you. It's all "lights, camera, action!" in our Hollywood Stars Shower. What could be more dramatic than a melodrama or a celebrity hoedown? That's show biz!

Q: Whenever someone in my office is getting married, nobody seems to know what to do about gifting and put

ting on a shower. Another one's coming up soon . . . SOS!
—Need Temporary Office Help

Dear Temporary:
   Back to basics! See Chapter 4, Twelve Steps to a Successful Shower, and also our Shower Planning Sheet (p. 97). Now you didn't say where you are on the office ladder, so we'll give you two helpful ideas. Office Co-Worker and Roast-the-Manager showers should promote your climb to successful showers.

Q: Is there any chance we can get men interested in the traditionally all-female shower?
—Not for Women Only

Dear Not:
   You've hit on the latest trend! Many couples feel the same way and they're doing something about it. In general, you'll find that some kind of activity will hook the male element. Our Wok-on-the-Wild-Side and Apartment/ Condo Pool showers provide that hook. More sneaky ideas in the Showerwise Themes and Showerwise Sprinkles chapters.

Q: There's a bride-to-be in my jazzercise class, and we'd like to give her a shower. Trouble is, we're having a hard time finding a night or weekend we're all free.
—Dancing, But Not on Air

Dear Dancing:
   Believe it or not, you don't have a problem! Keep your leotard on and leap to the locker room right after class. More surprises for you figure-conscious ones in our No Sweat and Calorie Counter showers. Take a peek at our Tailgate Shower in Showerwise Sprinkles, too. See . . . no problem at all!

Q: The bride and groom are moving to another state right after their wedding and won't have room for extra baggage. We thought of sending gifts to their new address, but we'd like to share a shower memory with them before they leave. Any ideas?

—Moving Dilemma

Dear Dilemma:

We'll give you a hint. There's a certain gift that's lightweight, desired by almost everyone, requires no shopping . . . and is definitely portable! Have we stumped you? See our Dollar-Disco-Dance Shower for details. One that may not require gifts at all is our Surprise Friendship Shower. It could mean even more to the couple if the circumstances are right. Either shower will send them off to their new home with happy memories.

Q: I want to have a shower, but everyone I know either hates showers or is too busy. How can I be sure that enough people will come?

—Need Better Odds

Dear Better Odds:

A little bait should do the trick. You can make your shower seem so intriguing that people will forgo other plans and attitudes to attend. Choosing an unusual theme, possibly one that brings the party to the people, is the first step. Then create anticipation with a dramatic invitation. You'll find ideas in our Invitations Guide. Then get ready for a full house!

Q: How can we include men in our next shower? After *their* parties it seems she's mad, her parents are nervous . . . and he's hung over.

—Down with Stag Parties

Dear Down:

Any relationship should have a better start than that. How does our Handy Andy/Hardware Hannah Shower sound? This is one that can also be given by the groom's friends or father, in *place* of the stag party. For couples, we think our Wok-on-the-Wild-Side and Wine- and Cheese-Tasting showers work nicely. Good beginnings are guaranteed.

Q: Most showers are such a mixture of people, you never get a chance to find out who the rich relatives are.
—Poor Relative

Dear Poor:

Delve into our Favors, Name Tag, and Place Card Guide, where you'll find good ideas for name tags. When these are well done, such as Pillow Puff and Rosebud, they also serve as a treasured keepsake. Hence they do double duty: a name tag *and* a favor. As you'll notice, we go a little further than most by also stating the relationship of the guest to the couple on the name tag. We're sure a few discreet inquiries on your part will uncover any rich aunts and uncles!

Q: Gifts are my problem. I never know what to purchase and I'm usually so busy, I can't spend time browsing through stores. I need a good—no, a *great* solution.
—Willing, But Can't Decide

Dear Willing:

Browse no more! Are you familiar with the Wedding Registry (also called the Bridal Registry)? Here's the process: the couple registers their gift preferences at a department or gift store. These can be anything from everyday dishes, decorative items, and linens to china and small appliances. Trained salespeople counsel them in their choices and encourage selections in all price ranges. Gift givers can visit or call these stores to make a speedy selection, and one they know the couple will enjoy and won't return! How's that for *great?*

Q: My parents never had a shower because they eloped. Now some good friends have suddenly decided to marry next month. I know time is short, but I don't want them to miss out on a memory.

—Sentimental

Dear Sentimental:

You're the tender stuff friends are made of. Why not make it easy on the harried couple and plan our Home-from-the-Honeymoon Shower? If conditions are right and you can pull it off, our Surprise Friendship Shower would also be a nice touch. By the way, it's not too late to shower your parents, either. Chances are, the relatives would get a bang out of it, too. Our Dollar-Disco-Dance Shower could give them a second honeymoon.

Q: Why are showers just for women? Leaving men out goes against our philosophy. To us, marriage is a shared endeavor in all ways.

—New Woman and New Man

Dear New:

You're definitely in sync with the future. The truth is, many couples around the country feel as you do and are quietly making changes. Judging from our mail, there's hardly a need to be hush-hush about it anymore. In many places, it's becoming the norm. So go to it! Choose any of our couples' showers for your debut. Wok-on-the-Wild-

Side, Wine- and Cheese-Tasting, and Apartment/Condo Pool are just three you might consider for the togetherness you want.

Q: Showers to me and most of my friends mean just another dose of junk food and adding weight we've so desperately been trying to lose. Why must fun times include so many forbidden foods?
                                    —Health Food/Dieter Nut

Dear Nut:
     You have lots of company! Dieting is very much on people's minds. And when we see the attempt large food companies are making to develop wholesome foods, it has to mean people are becoming conscious of their bodies and what goes into them. Why not look over our Calorie Counter Shower in Showerwise Themes and Health-Food Harvest Shower in Showerwise Sprinkles? Healthy can be fun, too.

Q: When wedding dates fall near a holiday, is it tacky to tie in the shower with the holiday?
                                    —Holiday Hang-up

Dear Hang-up:
     Actually it's a good spot to be in. Decorating is simplified and you've got a ready-made theme. For ideas, see our Be My Valentine Shower in Showerwise Themes and our Christmas Baubles Shower in Showerwise Sprinkles. Hold the shower *before* the holiday, when anticipation is high. There's one exception. The week between Christmas and New Year's Day is still timely. With most other holidays, the thrill and impact are gone . . . like eating yesterday's cold potatoes.

Q: I don't care what it costs! I only have a limited amount of time to plan and give a shower. What have you got for me?

—Money, But No Time

Dear Money:

Lucky you! You can take your pick. All you need is one of our Showerwise Themes and a telephone. Our Elegant and Formal Pool showers can solve your problem. And if you haven't time for phoning, pick a date, hand our plan to your caterer or a professional party service . . . and hand the bills to your accountant!

Q: So many showers are all fluff, and many of the gifts are useless. How can I diplomatically steer guests into purchasing a useful gift?

—Practical

Dear Practical:

Your question reminds us of the bride-to-be who opened a shower gift and exclaimed, "Oh, how lovely" . . . then desperately whispered to her mother, "What *is* it?" The obvious solution is the Wedding Registry Shower (see our Gift Theme Gallery in Showerwise Themes, pp. 77–78). Even if the gift seems ridiculous to you, at least you'll know it was the couple's selection. Some new ideas are our Handy Andy/Hardware Hannah and Pounding Party showers. Strictly useful gifts, fun . . . and no fluff!

Q: Honestly, I don't want to play another dumb shower game! Fill my precious time with something worthwhile.

—No Games

Dear No Games:

Throw away your pencil and dice forever! What you

need are activities, not games. We think our Show Me and Cookie Sampler showers would really appeal to you. Show Me is a capsule version of the how-to classes that are sweeping this country. You might also look over our Activities Guide. Most themes can be adapted for any shower . . . and you'll never have to play another game!

Q: I just love giving showers! We have the best time, but I'm out of fresh ideas. Can you help?
—Showers Forever

Dear Forever:
Hold on to your umbrella! You'll find many fresh and refreshing ideas in our Showerwise Themes. We think you'll especially like our Greenhouse and Show Me showers. Be sure to consider our Share-a-Menu and Tie-a-Quilt showers and look over our Gift Theme Gallery in that section also. Do you know you're an engaged couple's dream?

Q: Don't tell me what to do! Just give me the germ of an idea and let me take it from there.
—Good Imagination

Dear Imagination:
We have a whole section for you. They're not complete showers in themselves . . . just ideas and suggestions you can build on. Actually, they're more like sprinkles. And that's what we've called them . . . Showerwise Sprinkles. Read them through and let your imagination take off. You're on your own!

Q: Because we'll be connected in the future, we'd like both families of the wedding couple to get to know each other a little better. How can we do this without the usual strain and pain involved when "strangers" try to do a social number?

—Families of the Betrothed Couple

Dear Families:

We've got a pretty clever trick up our sleeves for you. It can do more to put everyone at ease on this occasion than a talk show host. Try our Meet-the-Relatives Shower. No strain . . . and definitely no pain!

Q: Our shower has only one requirement: We want it to be the start of many warm and wonderful memories for our favorite wedding couple.

—The Bridal Party

Dear Bridal Party:

We hear you loud and clear! You echo the words of wedding parties around the country who'd all like to honor "their" couple in a very special way. Well, this book is for you! You'll find over fifty workable ideas to choose from. Any one of them will help you give a special shower filled with warm and wonderful memories.

TWO

Showerwise
Themes

S tart with a comfortable theme and one you think will be fun for you and your guests. Casual or formal, traditional or unique—it's all here! But, it's very important to understand that any of the following shower ideas can be blended with others or with your own ideas. So don't feel locked in to following one theme specifically, though you can. Mix and match until you get a fit just right for you. And even though we may say, "This is a good couples shower" for a particular theme, adapt the idea to your own needs: couples, mixed couples, singles, women only, men only, or families.

We've made a distinction between Games, Activities, and Added Attractions. Games have been the mainstay of showers for a long, long time. They give people who may be strangers something to do and can create an element of fun. Several can be found, along with game sheets, in our publication, *Games for Wedding Shower Fun* (New Brighton, MN: Brighton Publications, Inc., 1985), so they won't be repeated here.

Activities are our very own new addition to the shower custom. Rather than separating the shower into sections (food, games, gifts), they tend to pull all the parts together. Besides giving guests something to *do*, they also give them something to focus on, to put them at ease and help conversation flow. In general, they help people with different lives and interests find a common ground to have fun together.

Added Attractions are those special effects that give added sparkle and flair to any event. They may be combined with games or activities, or stand on their own. Added Attractions range from something as simple as background music to a synchronized-swim performance.

Thumb through all our themes and guides to guarantee an exciting and amusing shower you and your guests will enjoy and remember. Just think of the possibilities! But don't think too long. These shower themes are meant to be *used*.

SHOW ME SHOWER

This shower is an outstanding example of an activity theme. It gives people something constructive to *do* and eliminates the need for contrived entertainment. Many people love showers, just as they are. However, in our survey, we noticed a growing number who said, "No more games!" and "Give me something to do!" If this is the case in your area, you may want to try something different.

Do you or one of your friends have a special talent that can easily be shared with your guests? Are there any cake decorators, craftspeople, or gourmet cooks in the group? Holding a short how-to session, with everyone taking part, can be fun for all.

In Minnesota, we held a napkin-folding demonstration that was very successful. This subject lends itself particularly well because instructions are simple, inexpensive paper napkins can be used, and every age group and gender seems to enjoy it. People like joining together for a talking, laughing, and *doing* good time.

Here's how you can make an eye-catching invitation. Fold a paper napkin into an attractive napkin fold, write your invitation on the completed fold, tuck it into your envelope, and mail. A simple napkin fold for this purpose can be found in our Invitations Guide (Chapter 7). Other folds named in this theme can be found in our Activities Guide. See pages 108 to 111 and page 114.

For the actual how-to demonstration, we've chosen four folds that should serve the couple well during their first year: the Cascade for their wedding table, the Cactus for their first breakfast, the Palm Leaf for their first dinner party, and the Rose for their anniversary dinner.

Provide your guests with plenty of variously colored paper napkins so they can work right along with the demonstrator. Allowing time for the usual chatter and laughter you hear when people are having a good time, the demonstration should take about thirty minutes. The completed folds become instant favors for your guests.

Though we've turned the spotlight on napkin folding here, other subjects would work equally well. Some that lend themselves are cake decorating, flower arranging, silk flower making, simple macramé wall hangings, or personal accessories.

If you'd like to bring in someone from the outside to demonstrate, call the community education department at your local high school. They'll be glad to suggest one or two of their instructors. Try your local gift shop, too, especially if that's where the couple's wedding registry is recorded.

And there you have it! Coupled with a simple dessert menu and gift opening, your shower can be the talk of the town . . . or should we say the dinner table!

SHOWER ON A SHOESTRING

This shower is practically a tradition in some parts of the country. It is a cooperative effort, and the emphasis is on food and food-related gifts, with guests very much taking part in the planning. It works especially well for friends who've set an entertaining pattern together or who wish to honor the offspring of a neighbor.

This coordinated potluck activity has each guest bringing a food item in a serving container that will become a gift for the honored guest. After the food is served, everyone joins in to wash and dry the gift pieces. At gift time, each guest tucks a gift card into the appropriate gift, along with the recipe that was used. If additional gifts are desired, baskets to hold the serving dishes, hot pads, serving utensils, or a basic recipe ingredient may be added.

This shower spreads the work, time, and cost around but requires one meeting of all or most of the guests at least three weeks beforehand. At this time, you can plan the entire shower and make all major decisions of date, location, time, menu, decorations, and so on. The rest can be done by telephone. Because of this, invitations are rarely sent.

In creating a festive atmosphere throughout the shower area, don't forget the kitchen. Since it's important to the theme, you may want to do something special here. Aside from that, you'll find good ideas for the table, gift-opening area, and general atmosphere in our Decorations Guide on pages 121–131.

A good activity idea came to us from Arlene Hamernik, a Fridley, Minnesota, home economist. She suggests you make a corsage from ribbon and netting. But instead of using flowers, just fasten small unusual kitchen items to it (strawberry huller, tea infuser, pastry brush, etc.). As you present it to the bride, ask her to explain how each item is used . . . with no coaching from the audience.

Besides the good food and fellowship this shower provides, it's an excellent opportunity to supply the couple with the serving pieces they desire. Of course, gift purchasing is much easier if they've chosen their patterns through a wedding registry at a gift shop. You'll have a choice of china, everyday pieces, glassware, and many other items. If you want to give additional gifts, use your ingenuity to spot pieces that aren't necessarily for table service. Ashtrays can hold celery sticks and olives, while oven mitts can double as utensil packets for an attractive shower buffet.

All in all, this is what we'd call an easygoing occasion. Once the planning and initial work are done, everyone can relax and have a pleasant time.

Other Ideas

(1) Progressive Dinner. This is especially fun in an apartment/condo setting or within a neighborhood. A progressive dinner is a party where the guests/party-givers plan the menu and serve each course at a different home. Guests travel ("progress") to each location. The serving utensils are carried to the dessert location to be washed and dried

by all. (2) Picnic. Arrangements should be made for a place
to wash dishes. National parks and some local parks usually have these facilities.

WINE- AND CHEESE- TASTING SHOWER

A real life-style shower—or something just a bit different—this one adds a little merriment to the occasion. It's
a good way to stock the wedding couple's bar, too. Your
taste buds will ask that you sample no more than five or
six wines . . . for tasting and merriment reasons! Cheeses,
of course, are a different story.

So let's stock the bar and have some fun! Find out if the
couple's preference runs to the red or white wines. Ask
each guest to bring two gift bottles of the same wine. One
is gift-wrapped, with gift card attached. The other is used
for the wine-tasting activity. Since wine is not a lasting
gift, guests may wish to bring an additional, wine-related
item. Good selections are a carafe, a corkscrew, a good
wine book, a wine-making kit, an apron with wine slogan,
or a set of wine glasses inscribed with the couple's names
and wedding date. Visit your local liquor store or one of
the wine shops that have become so popular for gift ideas.

Planning this shower around the cocktail hour should
be enough to lure your guests. But if you feel the need for
more enticement, how about designing a mock wine label
invitation, as illustrated. Choose a favorite label and du-
plicate it, leaving room for date, time, and so on. Or for
a really dramatic effect, write your invitation on plastic
wineglasses! Neatly box them in pillows of tissue paper
and mail . . . or hand deliver.

Wine & Cheese
Tasting Shower
For:
Anne Hill & Jim Smith
Date: _Sat. June 19th_
Time: _8:00 p.m._
Place: _542 Main St._
Please bring 2 bottles of Wine –
One for Tasting – One for Gifting

Now that all the guests are assembled, what's the procedure? You can check with your favorite liquor or wine
store manager, or follow these simple guidelines.

Bring on each wine and cheese selection as a set, one
set at a time. Rinse glasses between tastings. For refreshment variety, also serve crusty french bread or crackers
with fresh fruit slices. Be sure to have club soda and plenty
of water available. These cleanse the palate, rest the taste
buds, and prevent *too* much merriment. As a responsible
host/hostess, see to it that each guest is capable of driving
home safely or that each group has a designated driver.

Before each wine is tested, ask guests to offer a favorite
toast to the wedding couple. Toasting words can be used
for emphasis: *prosit!* (German), *santé!* (French), *salute!* (Italian), *skoal!* (Swedish), *proost!* (Dutch), *salud!* (Spanish)
. . . and *cheers!*

Between wine courses, have the intended couple "test"
their kitchen arts by washing and drying all glasses. Of
course, guests make it a point to stand on the sidelines,

offering suggestions and poking good-natured fun at the couple's cooperative effort.

When you decorate your service table, plan a spot for a wine rack large enough to hold all the wrapped wine bottles. As guests arrive with their gifts, insert them in a slot and your table becomes more and more festive . . . just like magic!

Appropriate for couples, singles, or mixed singles groups, this unusual shower is an alternative. If you've got the life-style, the friends, and the inclination to do something different, chances are before the night is over, they'll be toasting *you!*

SUNDAY-GO-TO-MEETING SHOWER

Here's an open house–type shower for a popular church member or couple. This is a spin-off idea from many Christian churches around the country, but may be adopted by any religious group. It's held right after services and announced at least two weeks before the event in the bulletin or at services. All members' families are invited, so men and children are definitely part of the festivities. You'll be able to enlist lots of person-power for planning, food preparation, and cleaning up . . . a real plus!

In Dallas, Texas, Lynn Wheeler tells us that church members hold showers by sharing the work round-robin style. Eight hostesses serve at each one, with the list rotating. Finger sandwiches, cake, cookies, coffee, and punch are served. They've got it down to a science in Dallas, and their fellowship hall sees lots of action.

Many church communities, especially the smaller ones,

have the same shower custom. If your church already has a system, you may want to incorporate some of our ideas. If it doesn't, maybe you can start this time-honored custom in your area.

One of the nicest activities we've heard of for this shower is a variation of the prayer circle. In this case, guests hold hands, forming a congratulatory circle. The bride and groom stand in the center, and all remarks are addressed to them. A close friend starts with a few words of instruction, to set the tone. The person on his or her right takes it from there and so on around, until everyone has been heard from, even the children. The words are simple: "congratulations," "lots of happiness," "I love you," "I wish you the best," and the like. Once again, it's back to the close friend, who puts a final, tender touch on the bevy of wishes. Then everyone swoops in toward the couple for hand-shaking, hugs, and kisses. Plan this activity as soon as everyone has assembled and before refreshments are served.

In Missouri, selected members of the church choir serenade the couple with appropriate love songs. This is a touching moment for the intended bride and groom and also entertainment for the whole group.

In Washington, guests write a few words of advice in a special blank book. Remarks are both serious and humorous, centered on ways to help the couple keep their religious cool in a secular world.

In New Jersey, Polaroid photos of the occasion are slipped into an album on the spot. This supplies the couple with a special remembrance gift.

In most churches, this shower is an occasion that affirms the marriage contract and provides the couple with gifts to help them enhance their spiritual life. A family Bible, a subscription to a religious magazine or newspaper, a wall plaque, and an anniversary candle are among those that are appropriate.

A buffet lunch served from a nicely decorated table caps the shower. Guests extend their best wishes as the couple circulate around the room, and once again we've brought the shower to the people. Whoever said, "Never on Sunday"?

POUNDING PARTY SHOWER

Here's a shower for the practical-minded. After all, what marriage hasn't been enhanced by a pound of sugar and a pound of nails? Loosely adapted from the custom of welcoming the new preacher into town, it gives the couple a very nice start. When a short, fun-filled verse accompanies each present, gift opening becomes the activity here.

A pound of what? Well, in olden days, any food staple was welcome. The parson and his family most likely arrived in town with a few clothes, some furniture, and very little else. When you think about it, that's the way some couples start their married lives today. This shower changes all that and injects a bit of fun to boot.

We suggest you scour your neighborhood grocery, hardware, drug, and stationery stores. Some unlikely items are sold by the pound. Here are a few we found as we searched. When combined with an obvious gift and a few wise words of advice to the couple, you've got the makings of a laughter-filled and, sometimes, tender shower:

1. A pound of semolina flour with a pasta maker—"Think pasta-tively and have a happy marriage!"
2. A pound of mixed nuts with a nutcracker and dish—"You two nuts have a crackin' good life together!"
3. A pound of note paper with a set of pens—"Always keep in touch with each other!"

Other ideas are coffee with a coffee maker, sugar with a cookie jar, rock salt with an ice cream maker, flour with a baking pan set, a pound loaf of bread with a bread box, and potato chips with a lazy susan.

Get the idea? We've suggested some free verse that you might share with your guests in a pinch. But the fun really begins when remarks are impromptu. So we suggest you wait until gift time to announce the procedure. The rule is: the gift can't be passed around for everyone to see until someone comes up with a few fitting words. Or you might give a prize to the person who creates the best verse for each gift. Let your guests decide the winners.

You'll find that one funny comment leads to another, and you may even have to set a time limit! A mock Laugh-Ah Meter could spur things on . . . a *laugh* side of the meter for the witty ones, and an *ah* side for the tender tidbits. All it takes is a half-circle of cardboard with a dial on it. Then just insert a clasp clip to hold the dial. As remarks are offered, you can move the hand from behind to estimate the group's reaction.

Now, one more consideration. Your invitation must give guests a good idea of what is expected in the way of gifts. As you can see, each present should be paired with a related "pound." The printer-ready copy in our Invitations Guide (pp. 115–120) is designed to get their creative juices flowing. Don't be surprised to find that when your guests leave, they'll either be quoting the great philosophers or rhyming *moon* and *June!* . . . by the pound!

Another Idea

Sheila McGinn-Moorer of Evanston, Illinois, suggests filling a small suitcase with pennies. Guests try to guess the number of coins inside . . . or for our purposes . . . how many pounds the loaded case weighs. This is one time the wedding couple won't mind putting on the pounds. After the guessing is done and a prize awarded, the case and pennies become a surprise gift for them.

FORMAL POOL SHOWER

If you have an outdoor pool, or access to one, the sheer elegance of this shower will captivate your guests. The pool is the focal point, enhanced by the performance of a local synchronized-swim group, who literally decorate the pool during their show . . . right before your eyes! Get ready for oohs, aahs, and bravos!

Plan at least two months ahead so the swim group has time to practice their made-to-order routine. To find such a group, one of these contacts should be successful: swimming coach, local high school; aquatic director, YWCA, YMCA; swimming director, college or university; swimming coach, country club or health spa.

Hire the group to make all props and costumes as well as to perform. Give them a good idea of what you expect, and let them take it from there. Experienced swimmers know many routines. It will simply be a matter of combining various swim strokes, stunts, and graceful maneuvers to decorate your pool and to provide delightful entertainment.

One romantic water sequence we like is performed in the evening, to the song "Some Enchanted Evening." The swimmers appear from the shallow end of the pool carrying a large, heart-shape form (cut from ¾" × 4' × 8' styrofoam). In the center of it is a spray of flowers, with a shower umbrella decoration. Colorful wide ribbons are arranged to come out from underneath the flower centerpiece to the edge of the heart, spoke-style. At the end of each ribbon is a large plastic bowl-type candle holder with candle inside (the kind used in restaurants and available from restaurant supply houses), secured with floral clay.

As the music starts, one swimmer lights the candles, then takes his or her place in the group. The heart is eased into the water, along with the swimmers, and the magic begins. Down the pool they go with graceful strokes, gently taking the shower float with them. In the pool's deep end, they use the heart as a center for all their stunts and strokes, appearing and disappearing, arms and legs in unison. At the climax, they fan out, each having removed a candle holder from the heart in order to place it along the edge of the pool, amid garlands of fresh flowers. In an unexpected move, the heart is swum back to the shallow end, eased out of the pool, and set on a large tabletop. And there you have it—a perfect centerpiece for the refreshment table! As the feast is being laid out, all the swimmers but one dive into the pool and swim back to the edge to retrieve sparklers (as used on the Fourth of July) that were nestled earlier in the flower garlands. They're quickly lighted by the remaining swimmer, and the group executes one more snappy routine for a spectacular ending!

But that's not the end of your shower. Remember, *lovely* is the key word, and the pace has been set with a romantic water dance. Everything else should be in keeping with this tone—formal dress, comfortable seating, dramatically served food, and gracious hosting.

Another Idea

Suppose you don't want to tackle a swim show. You'll still have the makings of a lovely shower setting by following the idea for our heart-shape float. Anchor it in the center of your pool and arrange spot lighting along the edge of the deck, illuminating the float.

HOME-FROM-THE-HONEYMOON SHOWER

Held immediately following the honeymoon, this shower is especially appropriate for the couple who eloped or decided to marry rather quickly. It's a nice way to welcome the couple home while the occasion is still timely. It's also an opportunity for friends and family to get to know the half of the couple they didn't know too well in the hasty preparations (if any) before the wedding.

Besides seeing their families and friends, what do you think the couple would like most? What might they be hankering for after eating in restaurants morning, noon, and night? Right . . . a good home-cooked, cozy, sit-down dinner! We're calling the meal the activity for this shower because everything will revolve around it. Not that the menu has to be elaborate. On the contrary, a light supper is fine, just so it's home-cooked. But this is when most of the conversation will flow, and you should plan around it.

Because this shower works well as a surprise, some good friends or a member of either family can invite the couple over for dinner soon after they return. Encourage them to bring their wedding photo proofs, snapshots taken on their honeymoon, and souvenirs they collected along the way.

Ask the couple's parents to put together some of their baby- and growing-up-years photos, and perhaps some short home movies. Friends can also contribute from their snapshot albums and high school or college yearbooks and pictures they took at the wedding.

As you can see, you'll be reminiscing a great deal. It's a simple way to pull the past together for the couple who has joined in haste. It can help give them a solid base on which to build and let them know they have your support.

So welcome them home in style! When they enter the shower area and hear the shouts of "Surprise!" try to really bowl them over. Hand-lettered Welcome Home! and Just Married! signs can be taped around the party room. Lots of balloons and string confetti will help create the effect you're looking for. And to top off the affair, reserve a place on the serving table for a Welcome Home from the Honeymoon decorated cake with all your guests' names inscribed on it.

Go all-out on decorating. Maria Nelson of St. Paul, Minnesota, suggests buying a large posterboard and printing *Marriage Advice from Your Family and Friends* across the top. Each guest is encouraged to write a few fun phrases on it during the shower. The couple is instructed to "meditate" over it every day. Make them a mock top hat and bridal veil, too (see our Decorations Guide, p. 128).

This shower is liable to be overwhelming for the couple. It would be nice if someone could stay close to give them a bit of behind-the-scenes help, should they need it—refer to our Shower Protocol chapter. Overwhelming or not, we'll bet you'll have just as much fun as they will as you welcome them back to reality!

Another Idea

In Fridley, Minnesota, Judy Simko tells us they include friends, relatives, and their families on a Sunday afternoon for a light supper shower and a few games in which everyone can participate.

COLLEGE
SOAP OPERA SHOWER

Miss seeing your favorite soap to go to a shower? Never! Never! Never! So there's only one thing to do. Switch on the tube and have a bring-your-own-lunch or -snack shower in the student lounge or a dorm room. It's the time of day when you know everyone will be there anyway, so there's no juggling of hours to find a perfect time.

A week or two before your shower event, create excitement by passing the word along via word of mouth, stressing the fact that *no one* has to give up soap opera time to attend. Get as many people as possible in on planning, making decorations, and purchasing the minimal supplies needed. It's a way of sharing the work and the cost . . . and having a good time together.

Decorations can be homemade and simple. One idea is to cut out pictures of soap opera characters from a fan magazine and paste head shots (photos) of the bride and groom over the faces of the stars. Naturally these would adorn the TV set. Another idea is to make a mock top hat and bridal veil from construction paper, foil, and netting (see directions in our Decorations Guide, p. 128).

One goofy, active game after the soap should round out the shower nicely and will probably be all you'll have time for. If you're short on goofy, active games, here's one we think you'll enjoy. It's called the shoe-box shake and comes from Linda Strohbeen of Shoreview, Minnesota. Fill two shoe boxes with clothespins, half of which have been X'd with nail polish or marker. Cut an opening in each box cover, twice the size of a clothespin. Attach ribbon or rope to each end of the shoe boxes, long enough to circle the average hip, and tie. At game time, tie the shoe boxes around two guests at a time, with the boxes resting on their backsides. Turn on the stereo and s-h-a-k-e. The person to empty the most clothespins in 30 seconds gets to keep all of them!

Perhaps goofy is not your bag. Maybe you're the intellectual types. If you put your heads together, we're sure you can create your own soap opera, centered on the courtship, wedding, and happy-life-ever-after of the couple you're showering. Each guest can read a portion of it . . . with proper emoting, of course. Be sure to make a tape recording of your scenario and take plenty of photos. Both are nice remembrances for the couple.

The last activity for your shower is really the best part. It's similar to the custom of throwing rice at the couple after the wedding ceremony. However, you're going to . . . not throw, but blow . . . what else? . . . *soap* bubbles at them. So supply each guest with a child's jar of soap bubbles, pucker up, and give it all you've got for a grand and glorious "soap" finale!

SECOND-TIME-AROUND SHOWER

The thing that makes this shower so romantic is that the couple have gone through life's ups and downs and have found love again. Any one of the shower themes can be adapted for this occasion, but the one we attended was quite simple yet elegant.

Since many second-timers begin their life together with two sets of everything, they don't need "things" to get them started. Some prefer instead to turn the tables, stating in the invitation—"No gifts, please . . . Just loving friends and relatives to share our newfound joy." Rather than a shower of gifts, it becomes a shower of warm wishes. Yes, it's a real departure from the usual shower giving situation.

It's appropriate when a small wedding is planned and most of the shower guests will not be invited. It's also a good way to thank family, friends, and business associates for their past support in whatever circumstances surrounded the couple's first marriages, be it death or divorce.

This event may be held before or after the wedding. The location is determined by the number of guests, and the shower would work equally well in the home, in a country-club setting, or in a hotel meeting room. There isn't much we could say to improve on the affair we attended—it was that good. So we've decided to describe it for you here, down to the last detail.

It was held in a lovely banquet room of a very nice hotel . . . but there was no banquet. Instead, an elaborate hors d'oeuvres table greeted guests as they entered. The centerpiece was an ice-sculpted cupid with hands stretched downward, toward the food. It seemed to be saying, "Behold . . . see the feast prepared for you. Come celebrate!" And, even though it consisted entirely of appetizers, it was indeed a feast: chicken wings, finger sausages, shrimp, tiny barbecued meatballs, cheeses, enormous relish and fruit trays, and an assortment of bread sticks and dinner rolls. It was held during the cocktail hour, so champagne, wine, and soft drinks were served.

In the background, a harpist played and was relieved by two violin players. They alternated during the evening, so there was always soft, unobtrusive music that seemed to carry over to the conversations we heard. Lovely, lilting friendship words and phrases filled the air.

The bride and groom stayed side by side, moving about the room to greet and say a few words to each of their guests. When the room seemed crowded to capacity, the couple asked for quiet by tapping a spoon against a glass. Each said a few words to the group, thanking them for attending and sharing their good fortune. Then they raised their champagne glasses and proposed a very tender, endearing toast to their guests. Believe us, there wasn't a person in the entire room who didn't feel very special!

From the formal, custom-printed invitation requesting no gifts, to the heartwarming toast finale, this shower was a real departure from custom. And yet it worked beautifully. This couple had the courage to fit the custom to the circumstances, and everyone benefited. If your situation is unusual, don't be afraid to try something different. If this couple hadn't, we wouldn't have this five-year-old memory now.

Another Idea

Olga Iacobucci of Newtown Square, Pennsylvania, also departed from custom. Although it's common practice in her area for a member of the family to hold a shower, she went one step further. She invited forty young women . . . and also invited the groom, her son. The wedding couple opened gifts together and all were later joined by other young men for a catered buffet. Why did she invite her son into this traditionally woman's domain? For two reasons. This shower marked the beginning of the marriage festivities, and she wanted him to share in the memories. But more important, the bride's mother was seriously ill and not expected to live. Olga felt her future daughter-in-law needed her son's support at this traumatic time. Did she do the "right" thing? You decide. Following the jwedding reception, she went into her son's old room to pick up a bit and found a note on his bed, addressed to her. It spoke of love and caring and gratitude for her sensitivity at this important time in their lives.

COOKIE SAMPLER SHOWER

Although it is especially nice for a morning coffee klatch shower, the Cookie Sampler can be held almost any time of day. Ask each guest to prepare the dough from a favorite cookie recipe and bring it to the shower on cookie sheets, ready to be popped into the oven. Then simply sample each batch immediately after baking, along with a suitable beverage.

To tie in gifts with this theme, guests might give baking pans, cookie cutters, or other kitchen items. Of course, the recipe for the cookie sampled should also be included with each gift.

Since cookie baking time is usually from eight to twelve minutes, there'll be just enough time between batches for a fresh round of coffee, good conversation, and praise for each cookie chef—and for taste buds to adjust.

This is a very social, easygoing shower and a good way for good friends to celebrate together. In fact, believe it or not, the one we heard about was held for the mother of the bride, without the bride or groom being present (though they can be). A group of Mom's friends and neighbors came together to celebrate *her* emancipation . . . and all gifts and recipes went to the grateful couple.

A shower without the bride or groom? At first glance, that may sound unbelievable, we agree. But when you think about it, it's a perfect way to lend support to the parents who are "losing" a son or daughter . . . or gaining more freedom for themselves.

Best of all, Mom was able to freeze the extra cookies . . . and they came in mighty handy for quick, informal entertaining during hectic prewedding days!

HANDY ANDY/ HARDWARE HANNAH SHOWER

Believe it or not, in some places, the stag party and bachelor bash are phasing out. Instead, friends or family of the groom are throwing a Handy Andy/Hardware Hannah shower for him or for the couple. Besides having a masculine flavor, it's also a tremendous source of practical gift giving.

Hardware stores are gold mines of gadgets and necessities. This one simplifies gift giving like nothing else: scissors, batteries, nails, tacks, hammers, screwdrivers, wrenches, ladders, kerosene lamps, brooms, picture hangers—the list is endless. Such items are a big investment for the couple but barely noticeable when each guest brings one or two. These are the kinds of things the couple won't think about until they're about to hang a picture . . . oops! No hammer.

Your invitation can be on the humorous side, with a cartoon of two inept handy-persons. You might even try writing a four-line verse to get your point across. Not artistic or poetic? That's okay. Just see our Invitations Guide for a printer-ready sample (pp. 116–118). We've combined a cartoon *and* a verse!

In our version, we've suggested that your guests bring their gifts in the original bag, with the hardware motif on the front. These can be tied with colored twine or rope. If the twine is tied around and around several times, the couple has a nice length for future use. Yes, when we get practical, we really outdo ourselves!

Make your decorations as hardware-slanted as possible.

A table centerpiece using flowers, plumber's candles, and pipe joints (sprayed with gold or silver paint) can be created in a jiffy. A flower arrangement encircled by assorted wrenches or with hammers, wrenches, and screwdrivers placed right into the arrangement—all are eye-catching and original. And, of course, there's the good old "plumber's helper." Spray-paint it a color, prop it up in the center of the table, adorn it with flowers held in place with colorful tacks, and in all probability, you'll be labeled *very* original!

The gift-opening area can be worked into this theme in several ways. One big barrel would do the trick. Spiff it up with stain or paint and you've got a great container. Or you can make a circle of wire fencing to corral the presents.

The activity for this theme is simply a "handy hints" session in which each guest gives at least one suggestion. Everyone has at some time been faced with the need to fix something. Your guests will be in all age ranges and will represent many years of experience in fixing . . . or finding the easier way to do a variety of chores. This activity is a sharing of that expertise. Be sure to write down all hints (we suggest 3″ × 5″ cards), so the couple can refer to them in time of need. Another alternative is to ask each guest to write a handy hint beforehand and enclose it with the gift.

So, yes, this shower can replace the old stag party. And, yes, it makes for very practical gift giving. But best of all . . . you may never have to lend the couple one of *your* prized tools!

APARTMENT/CONDO POOL SHOWER

Jump right in . . . the water's fine! This shower's a natural for the active couple with friends who expect an action-packed time. Informality is the key. Guests come in their bathing suits, sports clothes, and pool clogs, and bring along a towel or robe. The only inactive part of this event is gift-opening time. So reserve the pool area on your chosen date and have extra nose and ear plugs available.

To let your guests know this isn't just any shower, how about writing your invitation on an inflated plastic life preserver (the kind children use)? A permanent marking pen works best and will give you vivid colors. Then deflate and insert it into a large envelope. Write a few catchy words on the envelope back, such as:

Put a "ring" around this date.
Instructions: Blow, read . . . and *be there!*
How about a real wet shower?

Balloons will be your mainstay decoration. They'll give the pool a festive air and can also be used in your games and activities. So order plenty. If you plan far enough ahead, they can be personalized with the couple's names and wedding date. Order them through a novelty store or take a permanent marking pen and do it yourself . . . and if any are left intact, they can become keepsakes for the couple and guests.

Make your gifting special, too. Twist two colors of crepe paper streamers together (to resemble rope) and cordon off an area amid the deck chairs. Seat the couple in this spot at gift-opening time.

Place your refreshment table nearby and use general

shower decorations (see our Decorations Guide). Since most apartment/condo pools have kitchen facilities, you can plan hot or cold food. Just be sure to use plastic, paper, or foam glasses, dinnerware, and utensils, for safety reasons.

Now, get your whistle ready because here we go . . . on to the Shower Olympics! You've got people, water, and b-a-l-l-o-o-n-s. So how about a:

1. Water Balloon Fight: Form teams, fill balloons with water, and go to it!

2. Balloon Discus Throw: Half-fill balloons with water. Use a net for the measure and set it higher as players are eliminated. No fair using two hands.

3. Balloon Race: Set up a "racetrack" on deck and line up the players. Guests kick their air-filled balloons down to the finish line . . . no hands allowed.

4. Distance Kick: Measure who can kick an air-filled balloon the farthest.

5. Water Volleyball: Use an air-filled balloon, of course!

These are just a few ideas, but almost any game can be adapted to the pool area. Remember the three-legged race, so popular at picnics? Just loosely bind people together at the ankles, two by two, and line them up in the shallow end. When the whistle blows, they race across the pool (width-wise), patting a balloon back and forth between the two. The first couple across wins.

Plan some "surprise times," too. Explain to guests that you'll blow a party horn (or ring a bell) at certain intervals. One blast means that if they're in the water . . . the first one out wins a prize. Two blasts if they're on deck . . . the first one in gets the goodie. Do this occasionally at first, but at least once during your party, blast them in succession . . . in—out—in!

Make it a rule, please, that no one is allowed to throw, carry, or push anyone else into the pool (tsk, tsk!). In fact, you might consider hiring a lifeguard for this occasion.

The lifeguard can lay the ground rules and you'll rest easy, knowing you've created a safe but fun atmosphere. Find a guard reference by calling any local community or school pool.

We doubt there'll be a dry body in the crowd as this event comes to a close, but just in case, award the escape artist a very special prize—a bouquet of colorful balloons!

Wrap up your party with a wine or juice cheer. Use plastic wineglasses and raise a toast to the showered couple:

"May you always 'pool' together!"

"May your wedded days be filled with joy, and that's no baloony!"

"May you always have time for popping balloons!"

Well, it's time to bid your guests good-bye . . . very wet but invigorated and happy. You can be sure they'll also be water-logged (ahem) with wonderful memories.

Another Idea

From The Personal Touch, a gift store in York, Pennsylvania, that offers ideas and designs—a shower for both the bride- and groom-to-be, rather than just for the bride, is called . . . a drizzle!

ROAST-THE-
MANAGER SHOWER

When it's the boss's turn to say "I do," the shower calls for a little executive ingenuity. After all, the boss is the boss! Chances are you'll want this shower to be something special. A "compliment" roast is a nice touch . . . just a few planned-ahead, pseudocomplimentary, funny remarks from each person, along with attention to menu, decorations, and gift detail, will give you the makings of a shower to be remembered (maybe at raise time!).

Over the lunch hour or immediately after the workday seem to be the most favored times to hold this shower. But we've even heard of roasts held during extended coffee breaks.

Locations vary widely. You can stick to what's usually done in your area or consider these popular options: in the office conference room, over cocktails, at a nice restaurant for a sit-down dinner or buffet, in the company lunchroom, with boxed lunches (see our Co-Worker Shower theme).

In addition to your immediate department, guests may include the spouse-to-be, business friends, the manager's boss, other department heads, and even the president of the company. If you're planning a surprise shower, be sure to clear the date and time with the manager's secretary.

You can hold general decorations to a minimum, but you must do something absolutely crazy for the manager and his or her chair (see No Sweat Shower also, pp. 71–72). Here's what we mean: a Mickey Mouse beanie, a headband with antennae of sparkling stars or hearts, a wild ten-inch bow tie, a superman/woman cape, a grass skirt or a crown with office supplies attached (pens, pencils, rulers, or whatever applies). Decorate the chair of honor with crepe paper or foil streamers and colorful balloons. If you want to do a bit more, try a personalized fun poster (see our Decorations Guide, pp. 122 and 127).

As you plan your roast "digs," plot some fun gifts you can present to the manager after each one. Your remarks need to be personal, so we can't help you there, but these gift ideas may spark your thinking: a T-shirt that says "Who's boss now?" a mock paper ladder (for a quick getaway), a kerosene lamp (for light when the electricity bill hasn't been paid).

In addition to these fun gifts, one large present from the whole department seems to be most popular. Season tickets to an event the couple enjoys, a romantic dinner-for-two gift certificate, and a one-time general house cleaning service are some unusual gift ideas. A briefcase or piece of luggage, an umbrella, a personalized appointment book or brass business card holder are more common but nevertheless much appreciated.

Well, we've had our digs and some good fun besides. It's only fair now that we give the manager the opportunity to respond or to extend thanks to the group. It's a chance for us, also, to get a bit more serious and extend our sincere best wishes and happy marriage salutations. In other words, after the monkey business . . . it's back to business as usual!

BE MY VALENTINE SHOWER

What can be more romantic than a Valentine's Day wedding? You can take full advantage of this ready-made theme and play it to the hilt. There'll be no trouble finding decorations for this natural couples or mixed singles shower. If you stress the romantic, the sentimental, and love, love, love—you'll have cupid tripping over arrows in midair!

Go all-out with a red, pink, and white color scheme and lots of romantic decorations. Red foil hearts and white paper wedding bells; red, white, and pink crepe paper streamers; silver heart-shape balloons; and pink or silver cupids will all give your space the look you want.

Carry your decorations over to the refreshment table, too. A red floral centerpiece on a white tablecloth makes an attractive focal point. Dress it up with pink and white candles and you'll have a perfect setup for dimming the lights! And how about gifting each guest with a red carnation . . . the symbol of love? Present it in the Cascade Napkin Fold to enhance your table even more (see our Activities Guide, p. 110).

Give your foods romantic names, too. Beverages can be "love potions," dinner rolls can be shaped into "love knots," and a casserole might be the "love pot." Consider cherry pie or a heart-shape cake for dessert . . . better known as "sweetie pie" and "heart's desire," respectively. Make small labels and tape them to each food container. Write them in a most romantic script . . . red ink on white paper, of course.

To keep everyone in a love-ly spirit, gather as many romantic ballad records or cassette tapes as possible. Now who wouldn't succumb to "My Funny Valentine" or "Love Makes the World Go 'Round"? Lilting background music can add a very special touch. But if you really want to get mellow, hire a harpist or piano player to softly serenade your guests and the honored couple.

Now how about your invitation? We couldn't find a specific Valentine shower invitation; but you may be able to in your area. Of course, you could purchase a package of children's Valentine cards, so popular at that time of year. All you'd have to do is write your invitation on the reverse side. But if you prefer a tailor-made invitation for a Valentine wedding shower, a short verse would be nice. Turn to our Invitations Guide, pages 115–118 for printer-ready copy. Choose a pink paper and have it printed in red ink. Then, after printing, add a little pizzazz to the envelope with red foil hearts of different sizes. Any drug or gift store carries the self-adhesive kind.

Well, what more can we say? Every shower celebrates

a love story . . . and this theme can make your shower a real labor of love!

Another Idea

If you like this theme but you're not showering a Valentine wedding couple, why not do as Fran Maloney of Fridley, Minnesota, suggests? Simply change it to a Something-to-Go-with-Love shower. Fran also sent us a good favor idea she used with a large guest list. She made small heart-shape pillows trimmed with lace and sewed two silver rings in the center of each. They were numbered on the back and pinned to guests as they arrived. Several nice door prizes were awarded as matching numbers were drawn.

MEET-THE-RELATIVES SHOWER

This event is actually more than a shower. It's a unique opportunity to foster a good relationship between the two families who'll quite possibly be seeing a lot of each other in the future. Many times they're practically strangers, and for this reason, we suggest everyone be invited—mothers, fathers, sisters, brothers, aunts, uncles, and cousins of each family.

So we'll start right off with a name tag or favor that states the guest's name *and* relationship to the bride or groom. Mary McGinn of Roseville, Minnesota, sent us directions for making Pillow Puff—a small rectangle of satin edged with lace and filled with a puff of nylon batting. Then press a white address label to the front and you have a very pretty name tag (see our Favors, Name Tag, and Place Card Guide, p. 137). The point is for everyone to get to know everyone else a little better, and this is a good beginning.

Another way to encourage intermingling is to plan a sit-down dinner or a buffet with enough table groupings to seat everyone. Then use place cards to position one of his relatives next to one of hers, and on around until everyone has a place next to a member of the "other" family. This tactic, along with the name tag, can get the conversational ball rolling very nicely.

Now that you've got people in a position to talk to each other, what can they talk *about?* What's the one thing they all have in common? The wedding couple. So, back to name tags. After these have been distributed, people will try to communicate with each other, but it's liable to be strained.

So take them out of their misery. This will call for lots of special bait . . . hung on the walls and from lamp-shades, on tables and windowsills . . . anywhere. As you can see, we're not going to be subtle.

The bait, of course, is anything graphic that has to do with the couple: scrapbooks, blown-up baby picture posters, photos, home movies, awards, trophies, letters of appreciation, and so on. You should have quite a collection of items dating back to the birth of the two babes.

At shower time, place the collection you've harvested in obvious places. If you've been able to obtain home movies, run these continuously (and off to the side), so those who are interested may watch whenever they like.

The highlight of this shower is the presentation of a special gift to the couple. Ask both families for a copy of their family tree. An artist or a calligrapher can make these look very professional. Place them side by side in an elegant frame and gift wrap them. We suggest that you consider eliminating the usual custom of gift giving. Because our intent in this shower is to cement relations, not to start a gifting competition, the framed family trees serve as a lasting memento from both families.

This shower is one that lends support to the couple and attempts to unite not only two people but two families as well. Make it work for you and the old saying, To know you is to love you, will become a reality.

THE ELEGANT
SHOWER

Strictly elegant, from the chic invitation to the favor each guest takes home, this shower has flair. No expense is spared to add the extraspecial touches that set the mood. The use of satin decorations instead of paper, lavish baskets and garlands of fresh flowers, and an imported champagne toast are just a few of the embellishments. Yes, it's lavish . . . but strictly in good taste.

A gracious home, a country club, a fine supper club, or a patio restaurant are all likely locations. Plan a leisurely luncheon or sit-down dinner to show off this shower to its best advantage.

Personalize your invitation by hiring a balloon-a-gram service to deliver a dozen silver and gold balloons to each guest, with a formal, printed invitation attached. These companies will also compose a persuasive jingle for you. This can be very dramatic, but only if the verse is in good taste. A bouquet of fresh flowers can also create the desired effect.

If you really want to impress the guest of honor, arrange to have her picked up by limousine. If you want to impress your guests, too, send the car for all of them.

Collaborate closely with the maître d' for an elaborate service. A champagne fountain or shower-type sculpture (watering can, umbrella, wedding bells) make eye-catching centerpieces. A small music box favor that plays a romantic melody can also double as a distinctive place card. Or use miniature baskets of silk flowers the same way.

Chances are that all gifts will be brought to the shower splendidly adorned. Should your gift-opening area be anything less? Create an extraspecial temporary home for these beauties with the use of satin props and fresh flower garlands.

Good conversation is the activity here, so provide the opportunity for leisurely chatting among the bride, family members, and other guests. Soft background music, either live or piped in, can help to fashion an effective atmosphere. Allow enough time for this most pleasant interaction and for your guests to take in the beautiful setting you've created.

Top off your party with a sparkling toast, served in fluted champagne glasses, so popular years ago and now making a comeback, perhaps because of their bubble-saving design. Encourage your guests to take part by expressing their warm thoughts and good wishes.

It's too bad this day will soon be over. Then all we'll have left is the magnificent memory. But wait! Not so fast. Why don't we record this lovely time on film? A videotape or an album of still photographs is a lasting keepsake for the bride of this special day she was honored, the splendid way in which she was honored, and the person who honored her—you!

DOLLAR-DISCO-DANCE SHOWER

What do you give the couple who'll be off to another state immediately following the ceremony? Chances are you'll hesitate to burden them with heavy crockery, blankets, or dinnerware. Our solution? Something light, extremely useful, and green . . . money! Although the gifting of money at a shower may not be considered good taste in some parts of the country, when everyone is having such a good time, it seems to soften the mercenary aspect. This is great fun when lots of people take part and solves the gift problem beautifully.

Since you're going for large numbers, invite relatives, friends, business associates, and their families. Children love taking part in these affairs and feel very special when they are invited.

If you live in a small town, your invitation can be extended through an announcement in the local weekly newspaper or by word of mouth. In a larger city, you can form "calling teams"—each person calls from five to ten families. Of course, in either case, you may choose to send out formal invitations.

You'll need a dance floor and seating area large enough to accommodate the group. VFW halls, country clubs, golf clubs, and large meeting rooms in motels and hotels would all be good choices.

Pick an evening that most people will be available. We suggest Friday or Saturday, after dinnertime. Then all you'll have to furnish are snacks: peanuts, pretzels, popcorn, potato chips, punch, and a cash bar.

When you're making rental arrangements, find out what the agent can supply. Most places have at least some appropriate decorations, lighting, and a microphone. Then fill in where you need to. Hire a small dance band with a leader who will also act as master of ceremonies. To keep costs down, you can use records, cassettes, or a jukebox, but we like to economize somewhere else. There's just something special about *live* music!

You'll find a table centerpiece suggestion in our Decorations Guide that would be perfect for this shower called Mirrored Reflection (p. 124). A printed card to inform guests of the dollar-dance procedure can be propped up in this centerpiece.

Enough background "music" . . . let's get on with the dance! We suggest you plan five "cash" dances throughout the evening. Four of them will be $1 dances and one will cost $5 (set your own prices). Although most dances will be free, the cash dance gives guests the opportunity to pay for the privilege of dancing with the bride or groom at a lively, quick-change-partner pace. Your MC should plan two $1 dances in the beginning of the evening and two nearer the end. The $5 dance should start in about the middle of the evening, when latecomers have arrived and earlygoers are still present. These dances should be lively and as long as possible. End the music when all the guests who wanted to have danced with the couple.

All dances should be announced with a drum roll and great fanfare. You'll need several people to help add to the excitement by encouraging "buyers" to form two lines, one to dance with her and the other to dance with him. They'll also act as "cashiers," collecting the dollars in a hat and allowing about thirty to sixty seconds per dance. Then—and here's the surprise—when the music suddenly stops, the two people who are dancing with the bride and groom win a prize! Your prizes can be bought or donated, but they should be displayed throughout the evening. Some suggestions are: photo album, plant, floral arrangement, book ends, magazine rack, two movie tickets. Of course, the most coveted prizes are won during the $5 dance.

Well, to be sure, the engaged couple will never forget

this night . . . and the generosity of everyone. They'll be off to their new home in a new state with very fond memories of all those good dancers they left behind!

Another Idea

Norma Flora of Commack, New York, sent us an easy favor idea that would work well for a large group. Just fill a small square of netting with colored rice and tie it all up with a pretty white ribbon. Pin it to a card and it becomes a name tag. Fold the card and it becomes a place card.

TIE-A-QUILT SHOWER

For the sentimental among you, this shower can be given for the bride-to-be in a religious circle, service group, or any group that meets regularly (bridge, bowling, etc.). The idea is to give the honored guest a tangible, lasting, from-the-heart gift. And that it is, as each member makes a quilt square at home and helps complete the quilt at the shower, amid good cheer and good friends.

We must say, this was one of the most meaningful showers we've attended, and we did actually help make a memory quilt. But the idea is too good; there's no reason it can't be used to create other treasures. How about a wall hanging instead? Just do it up with minisquares. And if you're not into stitchery, how about original, hand-drawn squares, using colorful textile markers for either version?

Each square is stitched or drawn with a symbol or message. They're accompanied by an album of short notes explaining the significance of each piece, and the best wishes and signature of the giver. During the shower, the quilt is tied and hemmed over good conversation. When it's completed, each person reads her own contribution from the album.

It's important to choose an overall theme for the squares, such as state flowers, geometric figures, old quilt patterns, or motifs that are meaningful in the wedding couple's life. We chose marriage advice. This is always a good subject, but your own group should be in on this part of the planning.

We were pleased with our combination of humor and sensitivity. On one square Sue Coldade of Bloomington, Minnesota, had two bears cuddled under a quilt. The album inscription was, "To save energy *and* a marriage—cuddle!" Ours portrayed a pineapple, an old symbol of Southern hospitality. The wish was that "each one would be hospitable to change and growth in the other."

So here you have a ready-made shower activity. About one month before the chosen date, invite members to take part. At this time, distribute instructions for the quilt squares and agree on the type of stitchery everyone should use (appliqué, cross-stitching, embroidery, etc.). Instructions should include the size, color scheme, and type of fabric for the squares. A set fee is collected for the batting and backing material. Finished squares are sent to one person, who will sew them together with edging strips (stitched squares may be alternated with squares of solid-color fabric, also). You should set a deadline for completion.

About half an hour before shower time, members meet to make final preparations. The backing layer is stretched over the quilting frame. Batting is placed over it, and the top layer (the sewn-together squares) is laid over that. A quick basting stitch is taken all around to hold the layers together.

If your secret has been well kept, the bride-to-be will be truly surprised when she arrives. Then all members, along with the bride, tie the quilt and finish the edges as your quilt party progresses. No other arrangements need be made for this shower, except provision for some refreshment. Our meetings are always potluck, and we just carried this through. Since you're all in this together, make it a group decision.

So put your camera on automatic, gather around the handsome quilt, and snap several group photos. Give one to each member and to the bride as a lasting memento.

This shower gives, gives, gives . . . warm feelings—warm memories—*and* a warm bed!

Another Idea

This theme can connect the couple with distant relatives or those who won't be attending the celebration. In this case, send material along with the instructions. Did Haberman of New Brighton, Minnesota, was asked to make a quilt square for her great-niece who lived several states away. She enjoyed being included in the plans for this lasting gift.

Lee Campbell of Penn Wynne, Pennsylvania, suggests supplying each guest with a 3-inch square of Pellon (found in fabric stores) and a marking pen. Ask them to print the one word they think is most important in a marriage. Then glue all squares together for an instant wall hanging gift.

OFFICE CO-WORKER SHOWER

What could be easier than a shower for one of your co-workers? If you think of it as a glorified coffee break, everything can be planned and executed in less time than it takes to write a memo. Well, maybe that's a slight exaggeration, but catered box lunches, simple decorations, and one big gift from the group makes this shower *e-a-s-y!*

Almost any deli has a box lunch containing a sandwich, salad or slaw, pickles, potato chips, and cookies. Call in your order the day before and it will be ready and waiting (maybe even delivered) at the appointed time. However, if your co-workers have the before-payday jitters, perhaps you'll opt for a bring-your-own-bag lunch. Just be sure someone is appointed to bring an extra bag (or order an extra box) for the guest of honor.

You probably already know the best place in your area to hold this type of shower, but we'll mention a few places we've heard of that you might not have considered. Do you have a conference room available? How about a corner of your company lunchroom? Weather permitting, a nearby park area with picnic benches would also be nice. In California, beach showers are "in."

Many co-worker showers are also held in restaurants, where you'll either order from the menu or arrange a group menu beforehand. Don't rule out a corner of your company cafeteria either. It's more public, yes, but for some reason, when people are about to be married, they love the attention. Besides, it won't hurt your company image to be known as a friendly and caring department.

Held indoors or out, your picnic should be a celebration. So be sure to bring along lots of balloons and streamers. Look through our Decorations Guide (pp. 121–131) for more ideas you can use.

But wait—while you're back there, also see our Gift Guide (pp. 142–144) if your co-workers prefer to give their own individual gifts. A lot depends on the area of the country, but most often we've seen the big group gift win out. You can make it special by tying the wrapping in with your department. For instance, computer department—printout paper; finance department—columnar paper; mail room—"Air Mail, Fragile, First Class," and so on rubber stamped all over colorful paper; graphics department—congratulatory messages and illustrations keylined on solid white.

Now about that memo—make it your invitation! Use "Memo" or "From the desk of . . ." note paper. Simply type it up like this:

> Subject: Very Important Occasion—This takes precedence over all other letters, files, reports, meetings, etc., etc., etc.

You'll find a printer-ready copy in our Invitations Guide on page 115 if you'd rather use that. Add your own information using a black thin-line marker. Then have it printed or copy it on the office copy machine, and pass it around.

As you can see, this shower lends itself to several possibilities. Whether you decide to bag it, cater it, dine in, or picnic out, you'll surely add to the happy memories of one of your co-workers.

SHARE-A-MENU SHOWER

How'd you like to have two weeks' worth of breakfasts, lunches, and dinners planned in advance? Sound good? Well, it surely will to the new bride and groom, too. We've taken the popular "recipe" shower one step further. Instead of bringing their favorite recipe, guests donate their most successful menu, complete to the last detail.

Goblet or wineglass? Place mats or tablecloth? Guests

describe how they do it . . . with all recipes for the entire meal included. The intended couple benefits because they'll end up with the cream of the crop. And guests go home with as many new recipes as they care to jot down. Since many more men are becoming adept in the kitchen and at the barbecue grill, don't overlook this one for a couples shower.

Your invitation should give specific instructions so that guests understand they will each compile their own menu booklet. A *booklet?!!!* Yes, a booklet, made with 3-inch-by-5-inch index cards with two punch holes along the top.

The first card lists the menu—appetizer, main course, side dish, salad, dessert—along with a suitable greeting:

FOR SUE & BOB

Our best for two of the very best!

MENU

Golden Dip

Baked Ham California

Red Apple Rings

Golden Gate Salad

Wine

Lemon Tarts

From Aunt Rose & Uncle George.

Subsequent cards contain the recipes for each dish. Special touches are explained on cards following the recipes. After the set is assembled, a pretty colored ribbon can be looped through the holes, tied—and there you have it: a booklet! Or, more accurately, a booklet from each of your guests. Then you supply a recipe box and the couple has a veritable treasure chest!

Include at least six index cards with your invitation. Ask

guests to make their menu gift as unique as possible. They can decorate with markers, photos, magazine pictures, fabric, and the like. Just noting the name of the showered person or couple, the date, and the occasion makes the cards much more personal. And be sure to indicate that they'll have an opportunity to copy any recipes they'd like for their own collection. The more recipe cards you make available at your shower, the fewer games and activities you'll need to plan.

Now, how about a keepsake for each of your guests for doing such a good job? Janis Farrington of the Table Top Shoppe in Lombard, Illinois, sent us a favor suggestion we thought would be a nice addition to this shower. Fill a heart- or bell-shape cookie cutter with candy or nuts. Then tie the whole package together with netting and a pretty bow.

Anyone who loves to cook, loves to swap recipes. And that's what this shower is . . . a glorified swap session.

Another Idea

Guests bring a recipe inserted into the container in which it will be cooked or frozen. An herb or spice needed in preparation may also be added. Or, plan a dessert tasting/ recipe swapping shower.

SURPRISE FRIENDSHIP SHOWER

This shower takes some prearranging, but we promise, it's one that will be remembered long after the wedding fanfare. It was held in Michigan for Jessica Fallon, the person who told us about it. She's been married for fifteen years and still has fond memories.

If good friends and relatives are scattered around the country and are coming in for the wedding, invite them to town a few days early for a shower to be remembered. This must be a surprise, so the wedding couple should merely be told that these guests will try to attend the wedding. As you can see, this shower is held as close as possible to the wedding date.

Chances are everyone will have a lot of catching up to do, but you may have time for one activity. Lucy Oxberry of San Diego, California, suggests a drawing of each guest done with a bright lamp beam. Then guessing which silhouette belongs to each guest brings a small prize to the winner.

To spark recollections, encourage guests to bring along photos from the "old days," yearbooks, pennants, and other paraphernalia from when the group was together. Dig out any remembrances that would be appropriate. You don't actually *need* these, but they'll add just the right flavor.

While you're at it, you might ask your guests to gift the couple with an item their adopted state is known for: from Minnesota—wild rice and casserole dish; from Washington—apples and fruit bowl; from California—wine and wineglasses. On the other hand, being surrounded by far-flung friends can be gift enough.

A nice menu touch is to plan a hometown food that guests have likely been hankering for. Is there a favorite pizza the gang used to order when they got together? How about Mom's fried chicken? Whatever you choose, make sure there's plenty of the favorite to go around two or three times!

After your guests have made this giant effort to be present, a couple of poignant favors would be a nice show of appreciation. Two ideas we like will give them a remembrance of the occasion and a bit of help to stay in touch in the future.

First, take plenty of instant pictures. Be sure each guest is snapped with the couple. Then pose the group as a whole and take as many shots as necessary to give each guest one for the road.

Second, purchase a small address book for each guest. Either enter all names, addresses, and phone numbers in it, or have the guests themselves do it. Be sure to include the current addresses of those who weren't able to attend.

Whether guests pay their own fares or the hostess or parents of the couple choose to do the honors, this shower is like a fairy tale come true.

CALORIE COUNTER SHOWER

Here's a dieter's dream! Guests know beforehand there'll be no frou-frou desserts, extra calories or pounds . . . and no temptation! It's perfect for people who belong to the dieter groups springing up around the country. Since dieting is so popular, you'll find food and gifts a cinch. There's plenty on the market in drugstores, gift shops, and special diet sections in grocery stores.

If you do belong to a dieters' group, read over our No Sweat theme (pp. 71–72). This shower can be held in much the same way, using your meeting location instead of a sports room. Or you can arrange to gather at someone's home afterward. One of the health food restaurants is another possibility.

Of course, any friend or relative may be invited, but this shower is especially for the dieters' support group that wants to shower one of their own. The menu is simple fare. In fact, since diets differ, you may want to suggest that each member bring his or her own diet food or snack.

Any general wedding shower decorations are fine, but incorporating diet slogans can add a personal touch. Some we've seen are:

> Marriage is like dieting—forever!
> Two can live as cheaply as one—but only while dieting!
> Happiness is being a dieter and marrying one!
> Live on love . . . *not* on calories!

These can be made into across-the-chest banners (à la Miss America). Use a marking pen on three-inch-wide colored strips of paper, about two yards in length. A classier version can be made with textile pen on ribbon. Both can be secured in the back with two paper clips or pins. It's a way to make your guests part of the decorations and a good technique when you're short on time or space.

As in the No Sweat theme, you probably won't have time for games or activities. However, if you've decided to hold the shower in a home, you may want to plan a recipe exchange, since you'll have more time. This activity, geared to diet recipes, should be a welcome addition.

We've seen so many dieter gimmicks in our scouting around, we know favors for your guests can easily be found. Dieter slogans decorate refrigerator magnets, aprons, T-shirts, plaques, plates, pins, and so on. If you're handy, you can create mementos by printing the slogans on two-inch-by-two-inch cardboard or painting them on wood (for a more lasting version) and attaching a magnetic square to the back. The self-adhesive magnets can be found in most drug or craft stores. These diet reminders can either shout or subtly tell their messages from refrigerators, auto dashboards, picture frames, or wherever metal can meet metal.

Well, there you have it . . . and we didn't say "gooey dessert" once!

HOLLYWOOD STARS SHOWER

Lights! Camera! Action! Here's a shower you can have lots of fun with. Set it up to resemble a Hollywood premiere. From the moment you greet your guests with a mock microphone to the time they leave with their "Oscars," they'll feel they've really been to a celebrity opening.

Now there's a lot to this shower, so you really have to pay attention. But if you're tired of doing the same old thing, and you have friends who enjoy hamming it up, you could receive an Academy Award for your efforts!

Your invitation should be as intriguing as possible. We suggest you pattern it after a theater program, naming your guests as the star-studded cast. Ask them to be prepared to mimic the mannerisms and speech of a famous star (Bette Davis, Clark Gable, Bette Midler, Zsa Zsa Gabor, Burt Reynolds, Humphrey Bogart, etc.). Be sure to tell them to come and collect their Oscars!

You'll need to gather or make as many theater and movie props as possible: spotlights, marquee lights, film frames, photos of movie stars, take boards, long cigarette holders, director's chairs, a call board. Your props, together with anything that glitters (foil, tinsel, sequined material), should be combined to create your "set." Then if you have or can beg, borrow, steal, or rent a home video camera and recorder, you'll be all set for a great production.

The bride and groom should be the first to arrive. Give them choice seats (decorated director's chairs, of course) so they can watch and contribute to the "filming." Supply them with sunglasses, a cheerleader megaphone, and a pair of berets.

Try to arrange it so that most of your guests arrive at the same time. Start the camera rolling as you usher them in, one couple at a time, just as you've seen TV MCs do at preview showings and premieres. With microphone, or a mock microphone if the real one is in the camera, welcome each couple with a few remarks. Speak to them as the people they've chosen to imitate, but also to them as they really are. Go for a blend of fantasy and reality. For instance, you might say, "Here they are, folks, that ravishing couple from Baker Street in Indiana (real), Burt Reynolds and Bette Midler (fantasy). He's the proud father of the bride (real). I believe Bette is his sixth wife and owner of her own investment firm (fantasy). Hello, you two—do you have a few words of advice for the happy couple?" Greet other guests in the same Hollywood style, leading them to the wedding couple for an exchange of "advice" and impromptu remarks. Try to get all reactions on camera, both from the people speaking and the ones who've already been welcomed and are now watching.

Once everyone is inside, and after the first flow of greetings and conversation, bring on the fresh plaster of Paris. Yes, we said plaster. This should be poured into a container about twenty-four inches square. Have you heard of Grauman's Chinese? That's the place where the prints of the stars are embedded forever in cement. Well, we'll call this your mini Grauman's. Each guest is invited to leave a thumb print along with his or her name, and by so doing, receives an "Oscar" (made of children's Play-Doh) for an outstanding performance as a mother, father, friend, and so on. The plaster plaque becomes a wall hanging for the couple, so be sure to insert a hanger in back before it dries.

Are you still rolling the camera? Fine! For refreshments, appetizers and cocktails should do nicely. Encourage your guests to stay in character throughout the evening. This adds to the fun.

Got your cue cards ready? Good, because now it's gift time. As the couple opens each gift, they must only say what has been written on the cards you hold up. Some comments might be, "Should this be used in the morning or at night?" and "Boy, what we can do with this!" and "Now here's something we can take to bed with us!" and on and on. Know your guests and cue accordingly.

Now it's time to run the film. Settle your guests with bowls of popcorn (what else?) and play back the film of the evening's antics.

As irreverent as this shower may seem, the spoofs are all in good fun. If you think the wedding couple and your guests can make it work, then go to it . . . and on with the show!

CO-HOSTESS SHOWER

Here's a shower idea that's becoming popular around the country. It's for people who lead busy lives and don't have the time needed to host a shower by themselves. Because it's not only enjoyable but divides the work and expenses, the guest list can be substantial. Planning as a team can be more fun, too. No one person has to do it all, and everyone can participate at the level she or he would like.

Liz Joseph of Hopkins, Minnesota, shared this mid-western version of the idea with us: The shower is usually held in a restaurant, over luncheon. After the location and menu have been chosen, calculate the donation each person must make. Be aware of all expenses so no one will be left with more than her share. Invite the bride, her mother, the groom's mother, and all siblings, gratis. Other items, such as gift wrap, flowers, special entertainment, and the like, should be in the budget from the planning stage. Then figure the contribution each guest should make in order for the event to break even. For example, if the luncheon is $10.00 per plate, the gift contribution $12.50, and incidental items $2.50 per person, ask for $25.00. And, of course, if several people wish to donate beyond that— say to supply live background music—that's just dandy. Guests have the option of sending a check for a gift only if they can't attend.

Based on the amount of money you've collected, several lovely gifts can be purchased, wrapped, and delivered. Or you can opt for a single, more "important" offering.

Since your setting will already be quite pleasant, you need only add the finishing touches to the table(s). Fresh flowers and fun-wrapped smaller gifts can be used as attractive centerpieces. Then as the bride-to-be opens each gift, she can interact with guests at that particular table or that section of a larger table.

Extend your invitation via the phone or mail. If you are phoning, round-robin your calls from a list supplied by the couple's parents: Each person reaches five to ten potential guests, explaining the event, time, place, and cost. Many times you'll receive an acceptance on the spot. By written invitation, the same information is given, along with the name and phone number of your RSVP person.

This shower is a timesaver for those who are busy with job, family, and other activities. It's also a reaching out of many friends to honor the bride, and because of that, it creates a special feeling among all who attend.

Another Idea

From the Marble Corner Gift Store in Mattoon, Illinois— "A champagne (or sparkling wine) brunch has been very successful for the past couple of years. No games. It gives guests a chance to visit and is a delightful noontime shower."

NO SWEAT SHOWER

Are you a fitness freak? Chances are, one of your class or teammates will be tying the knot sooner or later. No sweat! Another example of bringing the shower to the group instead of the other way around, it's a nifty idea for after a class session or game. Informal, from its locker room location to the fruit drink you can serve, it's just absolutely no sweat for anyone.

The best part, of course, is this shower's informality. No one has to dress up or even clean house. And whether it's a group effort or the result of the planning of one or two people, no extensive preparations must be made.

The surprise element is crucial here and becomes part of the activity—decorating the bride's (or groom's) chair, mat, or space. Here's how it works. When the class session or game is over, gather around the honored guest and shout "Surprise!" Then blindfold and lead her to the party area amid the usual chatter. Bring out the crepe paper streamers, balloons, bells, and any other noisy props that will pique her curiosity and keep her guessing.

Take two or three minutes to decorate a sitting space where she'll open her gifts. Just fasten balloons to the back of her chair and string bows, plastic flowers, string confetti, or crepe paper streamers from it to reach down to the floor.

While some of the guests are doing the decorating, the others are setting out refreshments. To keep it simple, serve a fruit drink and oatmeal-raisin cookies. If you want to get more elaborate, we suggest a yogurt dip with fresh vegetables.

While all these preparations are in the works, choose one of two strategies: either keep the chatter going or be absolutely quiet, so all that can be heard is the noise of the props.

Then off comes the blindfold to another chorus of "Surprise!" . . . and on with the party. Gift opening and snacking are done simultaneously.

Most often, invitations won't be necessary, especially when the whole group hosts the affair. But if one or two people take charge, consider an invitation card pinned to a clever T-shirt. We found some that would be great— wedding bells, two entwined hearts, and some with appropriate verse. Visit your local T-shirt shop to see what's available. Remind guests to bring them along to the shower. They can be slipped on while the bride is blindfolded. Another clever idea is to make pullover vests out of white plastic garbage bags (see our Decorations Guide, p. 131). It's called decorating your guests when you can't easily decorate your surroundings!

If you'd like to do a little extra something, Zallas Card and Gift Shop in Saugus, Massachusetts, tells us one of their best-selling wedding shower favors is a dry potpourri packet.

This theme may well have been subtitled "The One-Hour Shower" because, from start to finish, that's about how long it should take . . . and that's part of its charm. Most classes and some games are held Monday through Thursday. People are eager to get home, showered, and into bed in preparation for the next workday. They're most willing to spend an extra hour for such an occasion, but not much more. So keep it short, lively, and festive!

ROMANTIC NOVEL SHOWER

"He took her in his arms, pressed her close to him and . . . !" How's that for openers? The popularity of the romantic novel makes this a real fantasy shower. It's especially suited to a couple with dramatic flair. If your group is part of the romantic novel cult, you can let your imagination run wild.

Your decorations should shout, "Romance, romance, romance!" Some novellike settings could be: a magnolia garden; a photographer's studio; a Kentucky horse farm. The trick is to choose a popular novel and to recreate its setting. You may have to hunt up fake grass, magnolia blossoms, or a racetrack, but don't despair. If you're near a retail or theater supply house, you'll be able to buy or rent almost any item used to stage a play or a sale. Try bookstores, too. Many times display posters are discarded for lack of room. Other ideas can be found in our Unusual Locations Guide on pages 149–150.

The activity for this shower focuses on gift opening. So once you have your novel, read through it and select as many juicy parts as there will be gifts.

At gift time, read one scene at a time, using the wedding couple's names in place of the book's characters. The couple themselves must act out what you say and they must read *only* the speaking parts or dialogue. There's *always* a romantic triangle in such stories, so one or two guests can help out.

You'll probably need several "rehearsals," because the guests are also the directors. Anyone can give the couple ideas for trying the scene another way. Show the couple they've got the scene just right by a round of applause. When this happens, one gift can be opened. Repeat until all scenes have been played and all gifts have been opened.

Be sure to record this on audio or video tape. It can be played back over refreshments or during the meal. Then, of course, it's given to the couple as a memento.

Once you've decided on your general atmosphere decorations, you can zero in on specifics. For the refreshment table, the romantic novel paperback you've chosen can stand upright at each place setting. By taping each guest's name over the original author's name, these become place cards and take-home favors. They also serve as the "script" for your gift-opening activity.

Try to do something spectacular for the gift-opening area. One idea is to make a very large replica of the paperback cover, using a folding screen. Stand it up to become an enclosure for gifts and a backdrop for your "scenes" (see our Decorations Guide, p. 127).

Your invitation can be made to look like the cover of the paperback edition of the novel you've chosen, too. In addition to date, time, place, and so on, tell your guests you plan to bring the novel to life at the shower and to come prepared to help direct the action.

This shower is really not for the fainthearted. It's far out. It's fantasy. And it's worth every bit of the extra effort for those determined to do something different.

WOK-ON-THE-WILD-SIDE SHOWER

Here's a surprising variation of the potluck dinner. While guests don't bring the food, they do prepare and cook it . . . with a little help from a wok and you. It's a great idea for a couples or mixed singles shower. Something zany happens to people who cook together, and you won't have to worry about any lulls in conversation. Sipping and munching while the feast is being prepared is a must.

This shower contains two "activities" that are central to the theme. The first is to get your guests busy making their own aprons from white plastic garbage bags (see pattern directions in our Decorations Guide, p. 131). Supply each person with a bright-color permanent marking pen. Instruct them to print a message on their apron, such as: "I wok-ed on the wild side at Joan and Jim's Wedding Shower." Or each apron could have one word on it. When the guests line up (before or after the meal), the aprons reveal the place of a hidden gift or a congratulatory best wishes message for the showered couple. Or, guests can write their own "marriage advice" to the couple. And if they pen their own name in the upper left corner, the apron also serves as a name tag.

Now you're ready for the second activity, which has guests preparing the meal, a stir-fry dinner. Our menu suggestion is shrimp and/or chicken with vegetables. All the jobs—cleaning, peeling, chopping—are easy to do. Naturally you'll want to supervise, because this may be a new experience for some of your guests, but that's part of the fun. If you organize work areas beforehand, people will feel comfortably close but not on top of each other. Then all you'll need to add are fortune cookies and jasmine tea . . . perhaps a bit of Oriental mood music in the background . . . and you have the makings of a delightful and satisfying buffet or sit-down meal.

If this shower appeals to you, be sure to visit a gift shop that sells Oriental items while you're still in the planning stage. We did and found a gold mine of ideas: lanterns and Tientsin kites (for decorations), small origami containers (nut cups), an obi sash and a bamboo straw mat (table runners or wall hanging), brocaded silk pillowcases (place mats), ornate chopsticks (nice touch), tiny jewelry boxes (favors/place cards), and decorated slippers (remember the Oriental custom of removing shoes and donning slippers). But the best idea we found was the inspiration for our invitation—fans! Select a solid-color kind that will slip into a large number 10 business envelope, open the fan, print your invitation on it, fold it again, and mail. You can also attach your invitation, tassel-style, to a patterned fan. Now wouldn't an invitation like that make you sit up and take notice?

All in all, this shower combines many of the ingredients you've asked for. It's a good one for couples or mixed singles. It gives people something to *do*. It helps conversation flow. But most of all, it creates a warm, happy memory for all.

GIFT THEME GALLERY

In some parts of the country, showers have a set pattern that would be very difficult to break. They worked just fine in the past and they'll work just as well in the future. After all, why argue with success? And yet . . . you'd like the next shower you hold to be just a bit different. Nothing wild, mind you. Just something that might leave people with the feeling that you are so-o-o clever.

Well, here's the secret. Do everything else as you've always done, or as custom dictates. Type of food, decorations, invitations, and so on can all stay within the pattern. Only now you'll put the emphasis on the gift-giving portion of your shower. Use our gallery of gift-theme ideas in the Gift Guide (Chapter 12) when you already know the main shower plan. They're a way of adding a little extra something to the occasion, without too much change.

WEDDING REGISTRY SHOWER

Ever been to a shower where one gift was duplicated two, even three times? This one absolutely guarantees that each gift will be unique. Because the couple themselves have chosen each and every piece, guests are assured their present will be very much wanted . . . and no returns will be necessary!

This works well when the couple have a clear idea of their preferences and know what their married life-style will be. They simply choose personal and household items in a variety of price ranges. These are noted on their wedding registry record at a department or gift store. The store keeps tabs of what is bought (sometimes by computer) and checks these items off the list. So you see, the wedding registry not only simplifies gift giving, it makes duplication almost impossible. (For a more detailed description of what a wedding registry is and how it works, see p. 104 in the chapter on Shower Protocol.)

If you want to add a bit of fun to gift opening, inform guests that since the couple already know what they've chosen, there's going to be a little guessing fun. Ask guests to pack the presents in odd-size boxes or to wrap them in unusual ways . . . any disguise that may keep the couple from guessing the contents.

Each gift card should also give a clue to what the package holds. For instance, the gift card for a dinner place setting could say, "Get set for good eating!" An electric mixer's card might proclaim, "There's been a slight mix-up!" Guests can also play the game, and win a small prize if they guess an item before the couple does.

By the way, if the wedding couple's preferences lean in

a specific direction, a wedding registry can be set up in any type store. We heard of a couple in their fifties who planned a honeymoon bike-hike through the northeastern states. A bicycle shop handled their wedding registry. No one was more surprised than the store owner—and, we might add, delighted, as well.

GREENHOUSE SHOWER

Think of this shower as providing a splendid backdrop or decor for the couple's living quarters. Plants, flowers, and greenery of all kinds, and in all shapes and sizes, are most welcome to plant lovers.

Containers are important, too. If you think the couple would enjoy the unusual—goldfish bowls, Mason jars, ice buckets, glass insulators, jewelry boxes, stemmed glassware, mugs, and wicker baskets are a few ideas that can give any plant a delightful permanent home.

Carry the idea over to your refreshment table. You can dress up a flower and candle centerpiece with small garden tools, seed packets, floral clay, tape and wire, watering can, fertilizer sticks, and other related items.

An idea for an activity is one we heard of from Lucy Oxberry of San Diego, California. Guests are asked to think of flower and plant names that are related to love and marriage. Get them started with these: everlasting, bridal wreath, love-in-a-puff, passion flower, silver bell, rose, nosegay, and forget-me-not. Give a small prize for each contribution the group judges to be authentic. Anyone who says *tulips* (two lips) . . . deserves a bonus.

POSTAL SHOWER

When the wedding couple is married in a far-off state and most of the hometown crowd won't be able to attend any of the festivities, a postal shower can be a nice surprise. This is promoted either by written invitation or by telephone.

Here's the process. Set a date for the shower. Write or phone the couple, asking them to be at a given place on a certain day and time. Instruct everyone to mail a present so it will arrive well before that date. The outer wrapping should declare, "Do not open until 6:30 P.M. on September 17!" (whatever day and time you've selected). Plan a gathering in your town for the same time. About half an hour after guests have assembled, telephone the couple long distance for an exchange of greetings and to extend your best wishes.

If you tell friends and family in the other state what you're planning, they may also want to hold a shower for the couple at the same time, in conjunction with yours. Though this shower spans two states, it's perfect for bringing loved ones together in a most surprising way.

CHERISHED GIFT SHOWER

Filled with lighthearted touches, this shower passes down heirlooms from one generation to the next. Family members gather in celebration to hand over antiques, collectibles, mementos, and family treasures to the bride and groom for safekeeping.

As each piece is presented—monogrammed items, cut glass, dinnerware, jewelry—a little of its history is recalled by senior family members. Was the medal of honor really presented to grandfather by the President? Was this the brooch great-grandmother wore at her very own wedding? Every family has memories as well as material possessions. To recall these memories at this time gives special meaning to the gifts and fosters appreciation of them.

This shower works especially well for small families, where descendants are few. A maiden aunt or bachelor uncle of an only child would love this formal opportunity to pass along such heartfelt gifts.

LEND-A-HAND SHOWER

Here's a shower that's built around year-long help for the couple. Guests give "coupons" for services—good anytime during the first year of wedded life—instead of the usual presents.

The range is only limited to the special talents and expertise of your guests. Services might include furniture making or refinishing, budget planning, yard work, appliance repair, auto work, tax help, or simply teaching the couple a decorative or handy skill. Fran Maloney of Fridley, Minnesota, tells us her daughter made coupons good for a car wash, house sitting, window cleaning, and . . . baby-sitting "when the time comes!"

Purchase a file box, index cards, and blank file guides. Print or type the subject headings on the guides in alphabetical order (appliance repair, auto work, budget planning, etc.). This will be the start of a "help in need" filing

COUPON

Service: *Jay Help*

From: *John Doe*

Address: *111 Pleasant St.*

Phone: *800 - 1234*

system for the couple, so give them a good supply of blank guides to list their own contacts for services your guests don't supply.

Decorate enough index cards with a "coupon" border so you can send from one to three to each guest, along with the invitation. These don't have to be fancy. A few squiggly lines and the word *coupon* are fine (as illustrated). This helps the couple immediately identify the shower gift, and brings back memories of helpful and giving friends and family.

GIFTS-AROUND-THE-CLOCK SHOWER

To say this shower is timely may be stretching a point, but timely it is. Sue Norby of Eau Claire, Wisconsin, tells us the idea is to state in your invitation that each guest should bring a gift the couple might use at a certain time of day. Every invitation must specify a different hour. (See? Timely!)

Couple your request with four lines of verse and you'll have an invitation that will bring in both practical and fun gifts (for printer-ready copy, see our Invitations Guide, pp. 115–117). Here's what we have in mind: If you choose any of the following hours, these suggestions can be passed along to guests who may call you for ideas.

> 7:30 A.M. to 8:30 A.M.—coffee pot, bud vase, subscription to morning newspaper
>
> 8:30 A.M. to 9:30 A.M.—breakfast-in-bed trays, toaster, morning-shower towels
>
> noon to 1:00 P.M.—dishes, napkins, place mats
>
> 5:00 P.M. to 6:00 P.M.—blender, electric fry pan, casserole dishes
>
> 7:30 P.M. to 8:30 P.M.—magazine subscription, wineglasses, throw pillows
>
> 9:30 P.M. to 10:30 P.M.—sleepwear, automatic TV selector, blankets

THREE

Showerwise
Sprinkles

N ow that you've got the idea, you're on your own. Here are twenty-four gems that can help you develop your own themes. All have A-1 ratings!

COLLECTIBLES SHOWER

If you know a couple who suffer from acquisition mania, indulge them with a shower of their favorite things. Any addition to their collection—old magazines, coins, dolls, and so on—will bring down their fever.

LAS VEGAS DICE-THROW SHOWER

All those closet gamblers, including bingo addicts, will get into the act on this one. Rent equipment and talk a few friends into providing a little action behind the tables. You'll have the makings of a glamorous Las Vegas night.

CORNUCOPIA SHOWER

Hold a shower of kitchen staples—flour, sugar, vinegar, oil, canned or packaged goods—all giftable and extremely welcome in view of today's grocery prices. Send your invitation in shopping list form, and let guests decide which items will best stock the couple's kitchen shelves.

HERB AND SPICE SHOWER

Here's a good solution when you want the minimum in gifts and the maximum in guests. Ask everyone, by written or casual invitation, to bring a particular herb or spice. Provide a decorated rack or cabinet display at the shower.

It will make a compact carry-home tote for the guest of honor, with all jars neatly nestled inside.

CANDLELIGHT SHOWER

Candlelight and romance go together like love and marriage. Suggest any and all kinds of candles for the gift list, even candle-making kits. Use plenty of candles and low lights at the shower itself. Evening, of course, is best for this romantic party.

SHEET MUSIC SHOWER

Use appropriate piano sheet music, dated from the twenties or thirties, such as "The Wedding of the Painted Doll," and build your theme around the lyrics. For this particular one, you might bring out antique or collectible dolls. Or buy a brand new bridal doll to use as the focal point of your gift table, along with the original sheet music. Very nostalgic.

BIO-RHYTHM SHOWER

If you have access to a home computer, printer, and a bio-rhythm program, you can build a very interesting shower around them. People always like hearing about themselves, so check out everyone's chart for a special day in their lives. And be sure to plot the couple's bio-rhythms for the wedding day! Also, chart everyone's bio-rhythm and send each guest his or her chart for the day of the shower. If any people are to have a bad day, tell them they're invited but they can't come. Just kidding, of course!

FABULOUS FORTIES SHOWER

How's this for a memory jogger: big band sounds—Harry James, Glenn Miller, Benny Goodman; war bonds; "Chattanooga Choo Choo"; and Frank Sinatra at the Paramount? Is it all coming back? A dress-like-the-forties wedding shower can be lots of fun . . . especially if the "older folk" are in on the planning. Send your invitation in the form of a 78 or 45 rpm record. It's important to keep the saddle shoes moving, so plan a surprise jitterbug contest in which all contestants win ribbon awards—for style, for enthusiasm, for persistence, for breath control, and so on and on. And oh yes . . . for just plain guts!

NIFTY FIFTIES SHOWER

Another oldie can be planned along the same lines as the Fabulous Forties Shower. Only this time you can probably get some planning advice from your younger aunts and uncles instead of your parents. Write your invitation on a pair of sunglasses, and here we go: Elvis Presley's rock and roll; cherry Cokes; pink and gray color scheme; poodle skirts worn with yards and yards of crinoline slip underneath; gum, gum, gum . . . *and* a rousing Dick Clark sock hop!

CHRISTMAS BAUBLE SHOWER

Trim their first Christmas tree with gifts of fancy bulbs and other decorations. Handmade and personalized are best, but shiny, satin, and new are also very acceptable. Then if all the guests add a treasured ornament from their own stockpile, it should fill out the couple's first Christmas tree rather nicely.

HEALTH-FOOD HARVEST SHOWER

Ever been invited to a shower by a vitamin? An invitation featuring a vitamin E capsule (for sexy) gets this one off the ground. You can serve anything from a peanut casserole to a veggie-fruit-and-cheese salad bar, along with bran muffins. If the honored couple is into health food as a way of life, this shower's tailor-made, especially when combined with a health food recipe exchange.

OPEN-DOOR SHOWER

Why not transform the popular open-house party into an all day, Open-Door Shower? On arrival, present your guests with our Rosebud name tag (see our Favors Guide, p. 138), and have the wedding couple open each gift on the spot. Lay out an attractive refreshment buffet and help your guests enjoy each other to the tune of soft background music.

LET'S GET CANNED SHOWER

How about showering the wedding couple with gifts that come in cans? Yes, yes, we know—a can of vegetables, a can of fruit, and the like. But what about a can of paint to spruce up a room? Or a can of antifreeze or oil for their car? Or even a can of tennis balls? What's more, there are novelty stores around the country that will do the honors for you. Buy anything you like and have it canned, while you wait!

TAILGATE SHOWER

After the softball, soccer, or football game, how about a little tailgating? Spread out your grub around a motor home or several hatchback cars, get out the lounge chairs, and bring your gifts along. Use the newspaper sports page for wrappings and have yourself a ball . . . in the "private room" you've set up.

FILE-AND-FIND-IT SHOWER

When it's time to pay bills, the wedding couple can be tax-years ahead of the rest of us if you shower them with a filing cabinet, file folders, tabs, paper clips, stapler, and anything else it'll take to get them organized. Be sure to include one of the popular how-to-get-organized books. You'll save them so much time, they'll probably want to spend some of it partying with their farsighted friends.

SCANDINAVIAN SHOWER

Smorgasbord is the key word here. Whether of appetizers, a full meal, or simply desserts, smorgasbord is a must. For an hors d'oeuvres appetizer table, serve hot and cold meats, smoked and pickled fish, sausages, cheeses, salads, and relishes . . . and *lefse,* or flatbread.

MEXICAN SHOWER

Viva Mexico with large, colorful paper flowers and piñatas for decorations, a serape for your table covering, and a menu of tacos, enchiladas, arroz con pollo, and tostada salad for olé refreshment!

GERMAN SHOWER

Toast the *Fräulein* and *Herrn* with German beer and *Gemütlichkeit!* Dress your table with flower-laden beer steins, and if possible, find a pretty cuckoo clock for the centerpiece. Polka music played in the background is a must. Serve bratwurst, German potato salad, and sauerkraut with plenty of beer. Give one great gift from all—a feather comforter from Germany.

ITALIAN SHOWER

Build your shower around a typical leisurely Italian meal with at least five courses. Start with an antipasto tray containing rolled-up slices of salami, ham, prosciutto, Swiss cheese, and provolone, all thinly sliced. Add black olives and roasted peppers to complete the tray. Subsequent courses are minestrone soup, lasagna with meatballs and sausages, salad with oil-and-vinegar dressing, fruit, nuts, and spumoni ice cream or Italian pastries. Serve lots of crusty Italian bread and a good red wine. Rest between courses for hearty conversation and performances by the children. They'll love reciting something learned in school, singing a popular tune, or demonstrating the latest dances, especially when encouraged by applause.

HAWAIIAN SHOWER

Serve a lush luau at the beach or around the pool. Roll out the straw mats and supply pillow seating for this hearty meal. Serve sweet-and-sour dishes, fresh fruit, rum-and-fruit drinks, pineapple sticks, and orange slices. Hire a specialist to teach your guests the hula and another to strum the ukulele with familiar songs everyone can sing together.

ORIENTAL SHOWER

Exchange your guests' shoes for paper slippers and seat them on floor pillows around a low table. Serve a shrimp-and-vegetable stir-fry dinner . . . and don't forget the fortune cookies. Decorate with paper lamps and use Oriental background music. For your table centerpiece, try to find a wooden cricket house (for good luck) or a jolly Buddha (for happiness). Provide chopsticks for your more adept guests.

SONG OF INDIA SHOWER

Plan lots of bright, hot colors for your gift and buffet tables. Use silk scarves as table accents over a bamboo mat. Display brass, carved ivory, or wood accessories. Put on your sari and serve a curry-and-rice dish. Indian music and burning incense will transport you to this gentle world.

ENGLISH TEA SHOWER

Wish the happy couple good health and best wishes with an English tea party. Bring out your collection of assorted china teacups and serve an assortment of teas and finger sandwiches. A vase or bowl of flowers to set off your table would be ver-r-ry English.

ERIN GO BRAGH SHOWER

M-m-m . . . Irish coffee and a rich chocolate dessert give this shower flavor. Plenty of shamrocks, paper elves (better known as the little people), and green and white crepe paper streamers set the tone. Favor each guest with an Irish boast button found in most drug and gift stores. "Thank God I'm Irish" and "Kiss me, I'm Irish" are two of our favorites. Complete the picture with a homemade Blarney Stone and have each guest offer some tongue-in-cheek marriage advice. Faith and begorra . . . what a time we'll have.

FOUR

Twelve Steps to a Successful Shower

To tell you the truth, we got a little nervous when we thought about this part of the book. We knew you'd be counting on us to give you the very best basic advice, in light of all the shower changes taking place.

Well, you needn't worry. We'll walk you through each step until you have a complete plan. All the how-tos are here to help you plan the perfect shower. Right down to protocol for the couple-to-be.

How would you like to reduce preparty panic feelings to just a few minor jitters? It is possible if you have a good plan and get yourself organized in all major areas. The key is organization.

The best way we know to take the pressure off is the checklist system. Make a complete checklist for every detail. If necessary, make a list for each day, and especially for the day before and the day of your shower. When you know you're accomplishing necessary things every day, your enthusiasm will remain high. You won't think—not even for a minute—"Why did I get myself into this?"

With a well-thought-out plan, you'll have ample time to arrange for extra help and to borrow or rent whatever you need. You may even be able to "take five" before your guests arrive, because you've already checked on the ice cubes and coped with last-minute emergencies. Then, if anyone offers to help, you'll be so organized, you can assign things they'll enjoy, and you can relax and enjoy your own party.

Use these steps along with our Shower Planning Sheet (pp. 97–100), themes, and guides to help you plan your party easily and successfully.

1. Guests: Consult with the wedding couple, their parents, the bridal party, and other friends to ensure a complete guest list.

2. Time: Select the day and hour of your shower while you're clearing the guest list. Make sure the principal guests can attend.

3. Theme: Browse through our Showerwise Themes and Showerwise Sprinkles for a plan you think everyone will enjoy.

4. Location: Pick a location that will accommodate the number of potential guests and that will work with your theme (private home, VFW hall, church, pool: See our Unusual Locations Guide).

5. Invitations: Invitations may be purchased or handmade (see our Invitations Guide for ideas). Mail them to arrive at least two weeks before your shower date. Include this information, as well as further directions or instructions:

- For (name of persons being honored)
- Date (before or after the wedding)
- Time (when most convenient for everyone)
- Place (location of shower—home, hall, pool, etc.)
- Kind (kitchen, personal, general, theme, etc.)
- Wedding Registry At (location of store)
- Given By (hostess or host)
- RSVP (name and phone number of person to call for acceptance, or "Regrets Only")

6. Food: Decide who will prepare the food: you; a caterer; a restaurant; your guests; etc. If you engage someone else to do it, have a clear understanding of exactly what will be provided and the cost. If you will be doing it, plan every detail. Make a shopping list from your recipes and do as much as you can ahead of time. Be sure your kitchen facilities can handle everything you've planned to prepare at the time of your shower (enough oven and burner space, ample room in the refrigerator). Plan your silverware, plates, salad bowls, dessert dishes, glasses, cups and saucers, serving dishes, ashtrays, candle holders, etc. (See our Food Table Set-up Guide for how to set up a buffet, a sit-down dinner, and a dessert-only table.)

7. Decorations: Choose decorations that will give your shower area a festive look. Include favors, name tags, and place cards in your thinking—they can help your guests get acquainted. Browse through floral centers and department, novelty, hardware, and gift stores for ideas. Tell salespeople what you're planning and ask for their help (see our Decorations Guide, too). It's customary in some places to provide small corsages for the bride-to-be, her mother, and her future mother-in-law.

8. Games: Plan your games and collect the equipment you'll need (pencils, dice, etc.). Purchase suitable prizes. There are shower game books in gift stores that contain not only ideas but actual game sheets for each guest. Look for our own book, *Games for Wedding Shower Fun* (New

Brighton, MN: Brighton Publications, Inc., 1985), for the latest in shower games.

9. Activities: Buy or make the props you'll need. For example, if you're planning a recipe exchange, have plenty of three-inch-by-five-inch index cards and pens available. Look over our Activities Guide for ideas, too.

10. Added Attractions: Plan or arrange any added attractions. If you're bringing in live entertainment, you'll need to clear your date with them. It's also wise to sign a simple, but specific, contract. Select stereo music, special lighting, and other items beforehand. And look through our Added Attractions Guide for special touches.

11. Helpers: Contact guests you know well to help you run your shower smoothly.

12 Relax and enjoy!

SHOWER PLANNING SHEET

1. Guest list (use separate sheet for additional names)

1 _____

2 _____

3 _____

4 _____

5 _____

6 _____

7 _____

8 _____

9 _____

10 _____

11 _____

12 _____

2. Date _____

   Time: From _____To _____

3. Theme _____

   Special preparations needed _____

   _____

4. Location _____

   Address _____

   Phone # _____Contract signed _____

5. Invitations addressed _____Mailed _____

   RSVP to _____Phone _____

   Wedding Registry at _____

   Gift type preference _____

6. Food (also make a grocery list from your recipes)

   Buffet _____Sit-down _____

   Menu: Brunch   Dinner   Dessert only

   _____   _____   _____

   _____   _____   _____

   _____   _____   _____

   _____   _____   _____

   _____   _____   _____

   _____   _____   _____

7. Decorations (also make a separate list of items you must

   purchase)

Room _____

Serving table _____

Gift-opening area _____

Special chair _____

Guest-of-honor _____

Guests _____

Order corsage for: _____

    Ordered _____   _____

    Picked up _____   _____

Helpers: _____

Favors (keepsake) _____

(Favor may also serve as name tag or place card)

8. Games (if any):

    1 _____

    Prize _____

    Equipment needed _____

    _____

    2 _____

    Prize _____

    Equipment needed _____

    _____

    3 _____

    Prize _____

    Equipment needed _____

    _____

    Game helpers _____

    _____

(Helpers can give directions, distribute and collect equipment, create enthusiasm, and keep things moving.)

9. Activities (if any): _____
   1 _____
   Preparations _____

   _____

   2 _____
   Preparations _____

   _____

   Activities helpers _____

   _____

10. Added attractions (if any):
    1 _____
    Preparations _____

    _____

    2 _____
    Preparations _____

    _____

    Phone # _____
    Contract signed _____
    (Introduce performers before and thank them after performance.)

FIVE

Shower Protocol

H ere's a little easy-to-take explanation of shower etiquette that can make the difference between a shower that's ho-hum and one that makes everyone shine and remember it for years to come.

FOR THE SHOWER HOSTESS

As the party giver, you'll naturally want to make your guests as comfortable as possible. Most often all you need to do is be sure there's a way each person can meet others. You can do this either through personal introduction, name tags, or get-acquainted games and activities. If you also mention each guest's relationship to the bride- or groom-to-be, you'll give your guests a conversation starter they'll appreciate.

Take the guests of honor under your wing and let them know exactly what you've planned. Many young couples are in need of help, especially if it's their first shower.

Arrange a gift-opening area and let them know when they should begin opening presents. Ask two helpers (usually members of the bridal party) to sit on either side of the guest of honor: one to keep gift and gift card together after opening, and to pass it around for guests to take a closer look; the other to gather the wrappings and to make a keepsake ribbon bouquet (see our Decorations Guide, p. 130). Designate one other person to inconspicuously write each gift and giver's name on a sheet of paper. This will make thank-you-note time much easier, especially when combined with the Party-giver Gift in our Gift Guide on page 142.

In a nutshell, then, if you concentrate on making others as comfortable as possible, nothing serious can go wrong.

FOR THE INTENDED COUPLE

Your host(ess), relatives, and friends have planned a special occasion for *you* . . . a wedding shower. They've come together to rejoice in your intended wedding because they love you and want you to begin your marriage with warm and happy memories as well as material gifts. Yes, you're the honored guests, but you also have certain responsibilities. Nothing heavy . . . just a few hints.

If you're at all squeamish about the occasion, confide in your host(ess) and ask for help. He or she wants to make everything as lovely as possible for you and will willingly assist. Or perhaps your parents, parents-in-law-to-be, or a favorite relative can give you some advice. The point is, if you're not sure how to conduct yourself, many helpful people are available who would be flattered that you asked.

Probably the most important thing you can do is let each guest know in some way how much you appreciate the time, energy, and expense she or he has exerted on your behalf. All it takes is spending a few moments chatting with each person. Very easy for you, and it will mean a great deal to everyone.

Gift-opening time is when you'll have the stage all to yourself, but, again, help is near. If no spot has been prearranged, find a place to sit down where everyone will be able to see you. As you open each gift and hold it up for everyone to see, say a few words. Your remarks should be personal and directed toward each giver. Naturally you'll extend your thanks. It's also nice to mention how the gift will be used. Here are some remarks we've heard that were especially nice:

> "This fits our bedroom color scheme beautifully!"
> "We like to cook together and this will make it even
>   more fun!"
> "We really need this!"
> "This is just the right size to fit on our counter!"

Just take your time, choose your words, and do your best to acknowledge each gift and giver.

Now, suppose you've already got ten thing-a-lings and here's another one staring you in the face. We suggest you say your thanks along with other appropriate remarks, and then talk with the giver later, in private, to arrange an exchange. Perhaps your host(ess) will help you here.

Finally, as soon as possible after the shower, write thank-you notes using the same hints we gave you for gift opening: mention the gift and how it will be used, and offer your sincere thanks. And don't forget to write a special note to your hostess. Your thanks can pinpoint the lovely time you had, the effort and expense you know the shower took, the useful gifts you received, and the good start you'll have now, because of this special shower.

Do you feel ready? Good, because we really want you to shine!

THE WEDDING REGISTRY SERVICE

Long known as the bridal registry, the name seems to be gradually changing because of the current involvement of men in household matters. More and more couples are making decisions together in this important area.

At the registry, which can be set up at almost any store, trained personnel will help the wedding couple make their "wish list" become a reality, according to their combined tastes. They help them choose items that friends and relatives are most likely to purchase. They point out items the couple may not have thought of and show them brands with which they may not be familiar. In many stores, this is done on a computer and copies of the printout are available. After the list is completed, the couple or their families pass the word on to friends and relatives.

The wedding registry not only saves time but has other advantages. People can go directly to the named store to select a gift. They can even order by phone and have their gift wrapped and delivered. There is no duplication. They know the gift is something the couple wants. And as a bonus, in most cases, the list is saved and can then be consulted for birthday, anniversary, and other holiday gifts.

Encourage the wedding couple to choose a store that sells merchandise closely resembling their tastes. Most registries are in department and gift stores, but the manager of any type store will more than likely be happy to set one up.

SIX

Activities Guide

This last part of the book is going to be a veritable gold mine! You will find dramatic decorations, attention-getting invitations, uncommon favors, gift ideas galore, and more.

Here are timely guides full of ideas, methods, instructions and directions. Even if you never have a shower, you'll use them to add that extra something to any party.

IDEAS FROM SHOWER THEMES

- Make a corsage from ribbon and netting. Instead of using flowers, fasten small kitchen items to it. Ask the intended bride or bridegroom to explain how each item is used . . . as in Shower on a Shoestring (p. 26).

- Guests form a wide circle around the intended couple. Each person says a few words of congratulations to them. Then everyone swoops in for handshaking, kisses, and hugs . . . as in the Sunday-Go-to-Meeting Shower (p. 32).
- Take instant photos during the shower and slip them into an album on the spot. This makes a nice remembrance gift for the wedding couple . . . as in the Sunday-Go-to-Meeting Shower.
- Fill a suitcase with pennies (nickels, dimes, dollars?) and have guests estimate the total amount enclosed. Winning guess gets a prize and the wedding couple gets a surprise gift . . . as in Another Idea following the Pounding Party Shower (p. 32).
- Gather snapshots, home movies, high school and college yearbooks, scrapbooks, pennants, awards, trophies, etc., of the wedding couple's growing-up years . . . as in Home-from-the-Honeymoon, Meet-the-Relatives and Surprise Friendship showers.
- Record your shower on audio or video cassette and present this lasting keepsake to the wedding couple . . . as in Hollywood Stars and College Soap Opera showers.
- Housewives and househusbands—hold your shower during your favorite soap opera with other addicts . . . as in the College Soap Opera Shower (p. 38).
- To prepare the couple for rice-throwing time at their wedding, wind up your fun shower by blowing soap bubbles at them . . . as in the College Soap Opera Shower.
- Ask guests to fill 3″ × 5″ index cards with their favorite recipes. Punch two holes along the tops of all of them and tie with a pretty ribbon . . . as in the Share-a-Menu Shower (p. 62).
- Distribute 3″ × 5″ cards to your guests and ask them to jot down one or two handy household hints for

the couple . . . as in the Handy Andy/Hardware Hannah Shower (p. 44).

* If your shower's held at a pool, lake, or beach, get the adrenaline flowing with some balloon antics . . . as in the Apartment/Condo Pool Shower (p. 45).
* Show home movies of the bride- and groom-to-be in their growing-up years . . . as in the Meet-the-Relatives Shower (p. 52).
* Supply your guests with white plastic garbage bags and have them make their own congratulatory aprons . . . as in the Wok-on-the-Wild-Side Shower, or their vests . . . as in the No Sweat Shower (see our Decorations Guide, p. 71).
* How many flower and plant names can your guests think of that relate to love and marriage? Every time someone comes up with a good one during the shower, give a small prize . . . as in the Greenhouse Shower (p. 78).
* Make a Laugh-Ah Meter to gauge your guests' re-action to any activity that calls for impromptu re-marks . . . as in the Pounding Party Shower (p. 33).
* Supply each guest with a square of Pellon (found in fabric stores) and a marking pen. Ask them to print the one word they think is most important in a mar-riage. Then glue all the squares together and you've made a keepsake wall hanging for the couple . . . as in the Tie-a-Quilt Shower (p. 57).
* Throw a foreign-food shower. There's a whole sec-tion centered on delightful eating . . . as in Shower-wise Sprinkles (p. 83).
* Fill a twenty-four-inch-square container with wet plaster of Paris. Have guests leave a thumb print and sign their names in it. When dry, it's a re-membrance plaque for the couple . . . as in the Hol-lywood Stars Shower (p. 68).
* Take a large posterboard and write *Marriage Advice from Your Family and Friends* across the top. Dur-

ing your shower, ask guests to jot down a few words . . . as in the Home-from-the-Honeymoon Shower (p. 37).

• Use a bright lamp beam to project an image of each guest on a wall. Trace on a piece of paper. Then make a guessing game of which silhouette belongs to each guest and give a small prize to the winner, as in a Surprise Friendship Shower.

• Have a craft, napkin folding, cake decorating, or some other kind of demonstration and let your guests take part . . . as in the Show Me Shower (p. 25). Following are the directions for four popular napkin folds.

FOLDING TABLE NAPKINS
(For demonstration or decoration)

Cactus Fold

Fold napkin into four parts.
Fold square into triangle.
Pleat from A to B.
Pull down the four leaves.

Simply follow these diagrams.

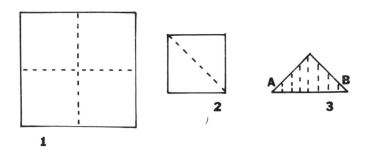

Palm Leaf Fold

Fold square napkins into four parts.

Fold diagonally across but make the fold a little off-center so as to form the base of the napkin fold.

Pleat evenly and place the base of the napkin into the napkin ring.

Set the napkin and ring upright on the plate.

Simply follow these diagrams.

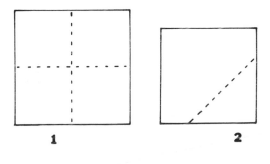

1   2

Cascade Fold

Fold napkin in four parts.

Bring back free corner H to opposite corner D; finger press.

Fold back next free corner G to C.

Fold corner F to point B and corner E to point A, finger pressing each fold.

Fold corner E back to base line of napkin.

Fold edges X and Y back until the edges overlap behind the napkin.

Tuck a red carnation in the top fold of napkin.

Simply follow these diagrams.

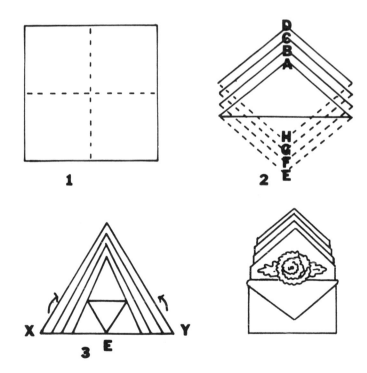

Rose Fold

Fold points A of square napkin to center B.
Repeat with new corners C that were just made. (Design will get smaller each time although diagrams are full size for convenience.)
Turn napkin over and bring corners E to center F.
Holding down center with a straight-edge cup or glass, reach under at points G and lift each doubled corner up and over to center.
Finally, pull out at points I for remaining petals.

Simply follow these diagrams.

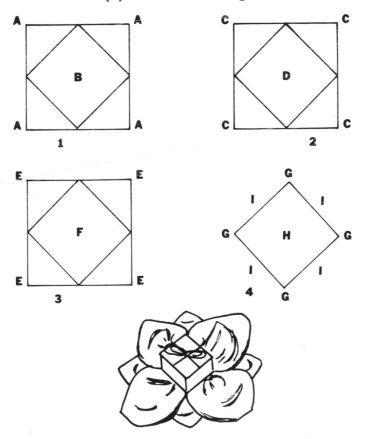

SEVEN

Invitations
Guide

I f you use one of our printer-ready invitations (pp. 115–120), simply cut inside the broken line and have your local print shop reproduce as many copies as you need. You may purchase standard-size envelopes there or wherever stationery is sold. A good-quality copy machine may also be used to reproduce our invitations.

Another idea is to personalize each invitation. Just copy our verse on attractive store-bought cards with a fine-point pen.

IDEAS FROM SHOWER THEMES

- For any shower held poolside, at the beach or lake, or on a boat, write your invitation on an inflatable children's life preserver . . . as in the Apartment/ Condo Pool Shower (p. 45).

- Balloon-a-Grams, flower bouquets, and singing tele-grams are all invitations with flair . . . as in The Elegant and Formal Pool showers (pp. 53 and 34).
- Pin invitations to T-shirts with appropriate designs (wedding bells, hearts) and ask guests to wear them to your shower, where they'll become part of your decorations . . . as in the No Sweat Shower (p. 72).
- For an informal shower, write your invitation on a pullover vest made from white plastic garbage bags. Tell guests to wear them to your shower where they'll become part of your decorations . . . as in the No Sweat Shower (see our Decorations Guide, p. 131).
- Want to get your prospective guests' attention? Write your invitation on a fan! . . . as in the Wok-on-the-Wild-Side Shower (p. 76).
- An attention-getting invitation makes you the clever one! Do yours up on plastic wineglasses . . . as in the Wine- and Cheese-Tasting Shower (p. 28).
- Write your invitation on the reverse side of chil-dren's Valentine cards . . . as in the Be My Valen-tine Shower (p. 50).

Other Ideas

- Print on tennis balls, paper dishes, or any unusual surface for eye-catching invitations.
- Frost your invitation on large cookies or lollipops. Confectioner's icing will do the job.
- Tuck an invitation into a balloon with directions to pop it on arrival.
- Cut and paste words, phrases, and pictures from magazines and newspapers to get your message across.
- Buy cards with an appropriate photo or illustration on the cover and blank on the inside. Just script in our verse (see printer-ready invitations) or your own.

Iris Fold Invitation
(See Show Me Shower, p. 24)

Fold napkin in half, A to B, to form a triangle.

Take C and fold to AB. Do the same with D to make a diamond shape.

Every diamond has four points. In this case only one of the points has completely folded edges. Use this point as F and fold not quite to E to form a kind of triangle again. Fold F down to I.

Turn napkin over; tuck one point into the other behind the triangle.

Turn the napkin again and drape the two top points to each side to form petals. Leave the remaining point upright.

Pen invitation on napkin as shown.

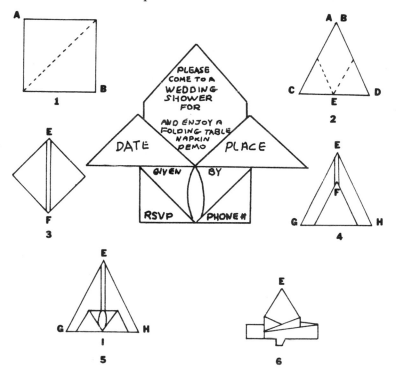

PRINTER-READY INVITATIONS

"MEET-THE-RELATIVES" SHOWER

Please come to a family shower....
Won't you join us, please
We're about to unite
Two family trees!

FOR: _____

DATE: _____

TIME: _____

PLACE: _____

GIVEN BY: _____

R.S.V.P. _____

Simply cut inside the broken line.

"BE-MY-VALENTINE" SHOWER

You're invited . . .
Cupid brought them together
And soon they'll be one,
Come to this Valentine shower
And join in the fun!

FOR: _____

DATE: _____

TIME: _____

PLACE: _____

KIND: _____

WEDDING REGISTRY AT: _____

GIVEN BY: _____

R.S.V.P. _____

Simply cut inside the broken line.

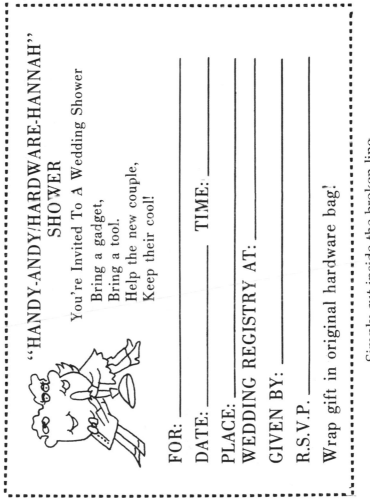

"HANDY-ANDY/HARDWARE-HANNAH"
SHOWER

You're Invited To A Wedding Shower

Bring a gadget,
Bring a tool.
Help the new couple,
Keep their cool!

FOR: _____

DATE: _____ TIME: _____

PLACE: _____

WEDDING REGISTRY AT: _____

GIVEN BY: _____

R.S.V.P. _____

Wrap gift in original hardware bag!

Simply cut inside the broken line.

"POUNDING-PARTY" SHOWER

You're invited to a Wedding Shower!

Come "Pound" the couple to give them a start....

a pound of coffee with a coffeemaker

a pound of nuts with a nut dish

a pound of nails with a hammer set

a pound of paper with a pen set

Are all gifts from the heart!

FOR: _____

DATE: _____

TIME: _____

PLACE: _____

WEDDING REGISTRY AT: _____

GIVEN BY: _____ R.S.V.P. _____

Simply cut inside the broken line.

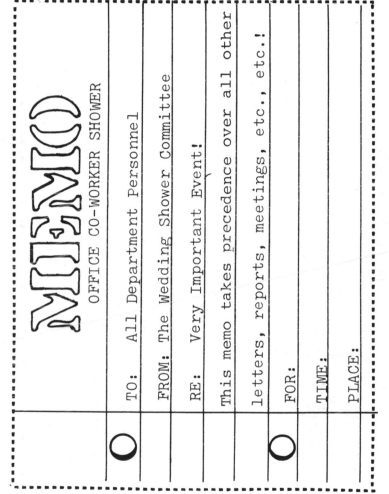

MEMO

OFFICE CO-WORKER SHOWER

TO: All Department Personnel

FROM: The Wedding Shower Committee

RE: Very Important Event!

This memo takes precedence over all other

letters, reports, meetings, etc., etc.!

FOR:

TIME:

PLACE:

Simply cut inside the broken line.

"GIFTS-AROUND-THE-CLOCK" SHOWER

You're invited . . . .
The couple's all aglow
With rings and bells and flowers.
Our gifts will show them what to do
With their happy marriage hours.

Please bring a shower gift the couple can use
between _____ and _____.

FOR: _____

DATE: _____

TIME: _____

PLACE: _____

WEDDING REGISTRY AT: _____

GIVEN BY: _____

R.S.V.P. _____

Simply cut inside the broken line.

EIGHT

Decorations
Guide

DECORATE YOUR
ROOM OR SPACE

IDEAS FROM SHOWER THEMES

- Spray almost any household throwaway with gold or silver paint to create a decorative item: jars; cut-off plastic bottles; egg cartons, etc. . . . as in the Handy Andy/Hardware Hannah Shower (p. 44).
- For our Wok-on-the-Wild-Side Shower (p. 75), we visited an Oriental gift shop and found a gold mine of ideas.

- Personalize colored balloons and other decorations by using a permanent marking pen to write the intended couple's names, the wedding date, or the words *Wedding Shower*—or all three . . . as in the Apartment/Condo Pool Shower (p. 45).
- Check with bookstores, travel agencies, gift stores, etc., for posters they receive for display but don't use. Anything that relates to your theme or to wedding showers will help you . . . as in the Romantic Novel Shower (p. 73).
- Having a shower poolside? Decorate your swimming pool with a large styrofoam heart . . . as in the Formal Pool Shower (p. 34).
- Fun posters and homemade signs that relate to love and marriage can fill in the bare spots and create a bit of fun . . . as in the Roast-the-Manager and Home-from-the-Honeymoon showers (pp. 47 and 37).
- Obtain copies of the bride's and groom's family trees. Have an artist or calligrapher reproduce and frame them. Hang in a prominent place and present them to the couple as a special gift . . . as in the Meet-the-Relatives Shower (p. 52).
- Enlarge a photo of the bride and groom, paste it on a posterboard, and print a fun caption on it, such as *Who's Boss?* . . . as in the Roast-the-Manager Shower (p. 48).
- Have blow-ups made of the couple's baby pictures (on a fur rug?) and display them in a prominent place . . . as in the Meet-the-Relatives Shower (p. 52).

Other Ideas

- wedding bells (paper, foil, satin, plastic)
- small silver "jingle" bells
- chubby cupids with bows and arrows

- red, silver, or gold hearts
- colorful flowers (fresh, silk, paper, plastic)
- ornate paper slippers filled with colored rice
- bright-colored watering can with silver or gold ribbons streaming from the spout
- opened parasols or umbrellas (paper, plastic, fabric) decorated with bows, streamers, flowers
- lavish flower garlands or baskets (fresh, silk, paper, or plastic flowers)
- plump balloons (all sizes and shapes)
- silver- or gold-tone wedding rings of all sizes
- large tied knots (paper, ribbon, foil)
- multicolor string confetti and crepe paper streamers
- sparkly foil, tinsel, sequin material, bead strings
- champagne fountain

DECORATE YOUR TABLE

Plan your table settings by allowing the shower theme, wedding colors, time of season, background colors, and use of formal or informal tableware to guide you.

For buffet or sit-down dinners, an ecru or white organza cutwork tablecloth over a light blue liner can be smashing. Carry out the color scheme with blue folded napkins, and use a spray of blue carnations for the centerpiece.

For informal parties with stoneware dishes, use a heavy, solid-color linen-type cloth (Mardi Gras cloth) with earth tones. Pull in other colors with fabric napkins and a handsome centerpiece.

For theme showers, use the colors and subject matter of the theme. For instance, at a Texas-type cowboy barbecue shower, use red-and-white-checked tablecloth and napkins, straw baskets for bread sticks and serving dishes, and a ceramic cowboy boot for a hefty centerpiece. Make red papier-mâché napkin rings (or paint wooden ones) with the couple's names on them (e.g., Liz and Ken).

For casual parties, take your choice of the beautifully patterned paper products on the market today. Some of the larger greeting card companies have done the work for you. They've put out whole lines of attractive paper tableware. At most gift stores, you'll find wedding bells, umbrellas, watering cans, and other shower motif center-pieces to start you out. Then the tablecloth, napkins, and plates are design- and color-coordinated for a "total" look.

IDEAS FROM SHOWER THEMES

- Watch your table decorate itself! Set a wine rack on it and ask each guest to bring a gift-wrapped bottle of wine or liquor to stock the couple's bar . . . as in the Wine- and Cheese-Tasting Shower (p. 28).
- Mirrored Reflection is the name of an elegant cen-terpiece that can be used when you want a little sparkle . . . as in the Dollar-Disco-Dance Shower (p. 56).

Dollar-Disco-Dance Mirrored Reflection

1. Use a mirror tile square of reflective silver as a base.
2. Arrange votive lights (candles) and glass or crystal can-dle holders of varying heights on it. Then tuck in a small spray of flowers.
3. Print the Dollar-Disco-Dance card and place it in center, as shown.

- Fun-wrapped smaller gifts can be attractive center-

DOLLAR DISCO DANCE SHOWER

for
JANE DOE
and
JOHN SMITH

You have 5 chances to win a prize!
- $1 per dance -
PLUS
Bankroll DANCE - $5

If you're dancing with the
bride and groom when the music
suddenly stops—You WIN!

(Listen for M.C.'s instructions)

---

pieces if you have more than one table. As the couple opens each one, the time spent provides an opportunity to chat with guests who are sitting nearby . . . as in the Co-Hostess Shower (p. 70).

- Ice sculptures (umbrella, watering can, wedding bells) make a dramatic centerpiece for a bountiful buffet . . . as in The Elegant and Second-Time-Around showers (pp. 54 and 40).
- Unusual items that tie in with your theme can be used to create a fascinating centerpiece . . . as in the Handy Andy/Hardware Hannah and Greenhouse showers (pp. 43 and 78).
- Decorate a cake the usual way but add your guests' names to it . . . as in the Home-from-the-Honeymoon Shower (p. 37).

Other Ideas

- Paste a round of cardboard on the back of an embroidery hoop. Fill with colored rice and set your casserole or other hot dish on it as you would use a hot pad or trivet.
- Personalize napkins, plates, glasses, and cups with pens that will write on paper, plastic, or metal.
- Fill a wide-mouth glass with colored rice and push a fat candle down the center.

DECORATE YOUR GIFT-OPENING AREA

IDEAS FROM SHOWER THEMES

- Spray wire fencing with gold, silver, or any color paint to make a nice enclosure for gifts. Do the same with a medium-size barrel, and the couple has a nifty take-home container that can later be used as a clothes hamper or turned upside down to make a cozy table for two . . . as in the Handy Andy/Hardware Hannah Shower (p. 43).
- Twist two colors of crepe paper streamers together to rope off an area for gifts . . . as in the Apartment/Condo Pool Shower (p. 45).
- Combine the color and texture of fresh or silk flower garlands and white satin ribbon for a very classy gift spot . . . as in The Elegant Shower (p. 54).
- Use a folding screen to make a V-type enclosure for gifts . . . as in the Romantic Novel Shower (p. 74).

Romantic Novel Backdrop

1. Paint replica of novel front and back covers on poster-boards (fig. 1).
2. Attach posters to two sides of folding screen (1 and 2) and use third side (3) to steady screen (fig. 2). Pile gifts in the V space (arrow).

fig. 1

fig. 2 ↑

Other Ideas

- Decorate a large wicker basket with bows. This holds shower gifts at your party and serves as a take-home container for the couple.
- Make and paint a large wishing-well replica to hold shower gifts.

The Chair(s) of Honor

- Decorate a special chair with ribbons, balloons, bows, plastic flowers, confetti, and/or crepe paper streamers for the guest of honor to sit in while opening presents . . . as in the No Sweat Shower (p. 71).
- Decorate two director's chairs and seat the intended couple at a 45-degree angle to each other. Pile gifts between them and have them take turns "directing" the action . . . as in the Hollywood Stars Shower (p. 68).

The Honored Couple

- Make a mock top hat and bridal veil for the couple to get them ready for the real thing . . . as in the College Soap Opera Shower (p. 38).

Mock Top Hat and Veil
Veil Directions

1. Using a 1-yard square of netting, sew a basting stitch and gather along dotted line. Fold corner A under gathers (fig. 1).
2. Fasten gathered netting over headband with slipstitch (fig. 2).
3. Secure a string of artificial flowers to headband and netting (fig. 3).

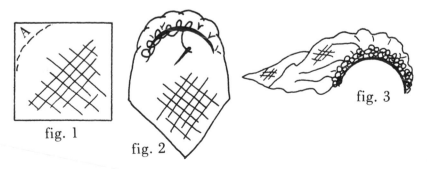

fig. 3

fig. 1

fig. 2

Top Hat

1. Cut black posterboard to fit around head as shown—
A. Cut B and C in proportion (fig. 1).

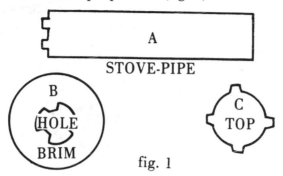

fig. 1

2. Form a cylinder by rolling A until ends meet. Tape tabs
to inside (fig. 2).
3. Insert cylinder into B, taping tabs to inside of cylinder
(fig. 3).

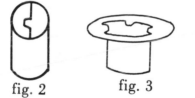

fig. 2   fig. 3

4. Tape tabs of C into top of hat
as shown (fig. 4).

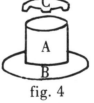

fig. 4

- For an all-in-fun shower, adorn the couple with crazy
  hats, bow ties, and more . . . as in the Roast-the-
  Manager Shower (p. 47).
- Make a ribbon bouquet keepsake for the intended
  bride out of all the ribbon ties from packages, after
  gifts have been opened . . . as in the chapter on
  Shower Protocol (p. 102).

Ribbon Bouquet

1. Cut X through center of paper plate. Draw ribbons of bows thru X.
2. Stick self-adhesive bows around outer edge of plate. When entire plate is covered with bows, it resembles a bride's bouquet.

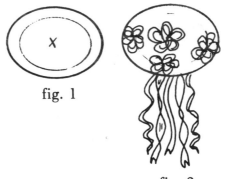

fig. 1

fig. 2

DECORATE YOUR GUESTS

IDEAS FROM SHOWER THEMES

- Across-the-chest banners can easily be made for or by your guests. Distribute marking pens and strips of paper. Ask them to write a bit of married-life advice especially for the couple . . . as in the Calorie Counter Shower (p. 66).

- Make congratulatory aprons or vests for guests . . . or have them make their own . . . as in the Wok-on-the-Wild-Side and No Sweat showers (pp. 75 and 72).

Wok-on-the-Wild-Side Apron and No Sweat Vest

Apron

Lay out a large white plastic kitchen garbage bag. In sealed end, cut along curved lines to make head and arm holes, as indicated (fig. 1). Do not cut open end.

Vest

Follow apron directions, but cut off the lower half of the bag, as indicated (fig. 2).

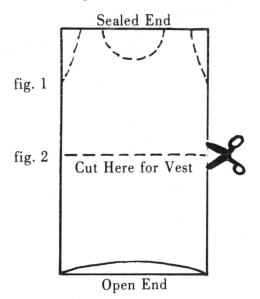

NINE

Food Table Set-up Guide

BUFFET BLUEPRINT

Serve two entrees—fish and beef—one vegetable, one potato or rice dish, condiments, buttered rolls, beverage, and dessert. Arrange a paper umbrella with ribbon and flowers for a centerpiece.

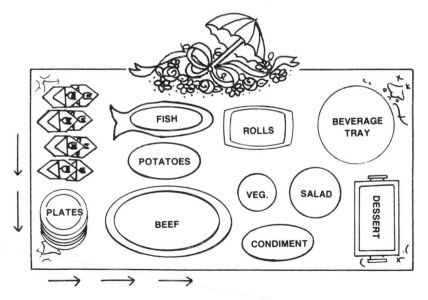

SIT-DOWN DINNER BLUEPRINT

Serve an appetizer, one entree, one vegetable, one pasta, potato or rice, one tossed salad, dinner rolls, beverage, and dessert. Decorate each table with wedding bells, one white candle, and ribbons.

DESSERT-ONLY BLUEPRINT

Serve a decorated wedding shower cake, bars, bundt cake, coffee, tea, nuts, and mints. Choose flowers closely matching the colors of the wedding party for your centerpiece.

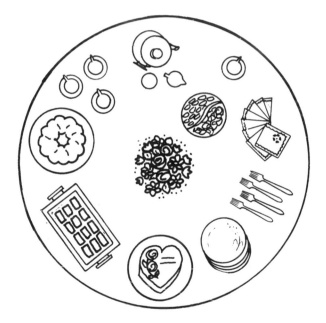

TEN

Favors, Name Tag, and Place Card Guide

The favor, name tag, and place card can be made in any size and shape. The place card is usually folded to give it a stand. Unfolded, it can be set on the plate or in a napkin fold, or it can be propped against a favor or glass.

IDEAS FROM SHOWER THEMES

- Almost any favor, name tag, or place card can be numbered in back or underneath as the basis for a door prize drawing . . . as in Another Idea following the Be My Valentine Shower (p. 51).
- Fill a small square of white netting with colored rice

and tie it all up with a pretty ribbon. Pin it to a card and it becomes a name tag. Fold the card and it becomes a place card . . . as in Another Idea following the Dollar-Disco-Dance Shower (p. 57).

- Snap instant photos of each guest with the guest of honor, or take several group shots for lasting keepsakes . . . as in the Surprise Friendship Shower (p. 65).
- Refrigerator magnets found in drug and gift stores come with a variety of clever one-liners. Or make your own . . . as in the Calorie Counter Shower (p. 66).
- Dazzle your guests with a fresh flower, presented in a spectacular napkin fold . . . as in the Be My Valentine Shower (p. 50).
- Place a small music box or miniature flower basket at each place setting for a unique favor and/or place card . . . as in The Elegant Shower (p. 54).
- Fill a heart- or bell-shape cookie cutter with candy or nuts. Tie the whole package together with netting and a plump bow for a favor/place card . . . as in the Share-a-Menu Shower (p. 63).

- Have your guests print their name in the upper left hand corner of the apron/vest favor mentioned in Decorate Your Guests (p. 130), and you've created a name tag, too . . . as in the Wok-on-the-Wild-Side Shower.
- Fill a small rectangular pocket with nylon batting and edge it with lace. Press a shiny address label to it and you've got Pillow Puff (directions follow), a very pretty name tag/favor . . . as in the Meet-the-Relatives Shower.

Pillow Puff Name Tag/Favor

1. Cut two 4″ × 3″ satin rectangles. With right sides together, sew along dotted line (fig. 1).
2. Turn right side out and fill with nylon batting. Turn unfinished edge inside and sew all around, attaching pre-shirred lace as you go. Sew small bow made from thin satin ribbon to center top (fig. 2).

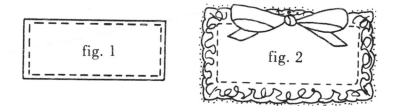

fig. 1

fig. 2

3. Press a white address label (the permanent, self-adhesive kind) to front (fig. 3).

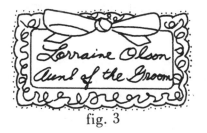

fig. 3

- Easily make a name tag or place card that features a fresh or silk flower. Ours is called Rosebud . . . as in the Open-Door Shower (p. 88).

Open-Door Rosebud Name Tag

Cut card to 1½″ × 3½″ size. Make two holes with paper punch at arrows. Push flower through holes, stem first, as shown.

Other Ideas

- Add drawings, borders, stickers, glitter, shells, sequins, etc., to a white card, construction paper, or adhesive-backed label for tailor-made name tags or place cards.
- Cut egg cups out of a plastic or paper egg carton. Spray them silver or gold. Link two together with ribbon, along with a card for a simple place card. (Directions follow.)

Bells

1. Punch holes in tops of egg carton cups "bells" and in corner of card.
2. Knot one end of each ribbon. Thread a ribbon from inside of each bell until knot rests on underside. Lace the other end of one ribbon through card and tie ribbons in bow.

- Paste or draw wedding shower accessories (umbrella, love birds, watering can, wedding bells, flowers) on name tag or place card.

- Cut a wedding bell from white paper and glue lace around the outline for a simple name tag.
- Tie ribbon around small boxes of white almond candy. Some confectioners have wedding accessory candy and boxes already made up.
- Stretch material over a small embroidery hoop and trim with lace. Appliqué a heart with the wedding date in the center.
- Take a plastic or wooden curtain ring and paste a round of posterboard behind it. Draw a heart and write the wedding date in the center. Tie a bow through the eye for a pin-on name tag.
- Place the goblet or wineglass upside-down at each place setting. Center a small white or silver doilie on top of it. Display a fresh or silk carnation (with flower pin through stem) on the doilie for a dinnertime favor. Each guest pins one on.

ELEVEN

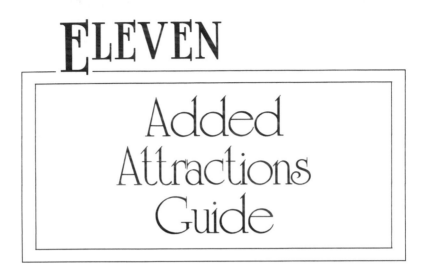

Added Attractions Guide

IDEAS FROM SHOWER THEMES

- Live background music can do more for your shower atmosphere than an umbrella! The piano, harp, violin, guitar, and accordion all lend themselves nicely . . . as in the Be My Valentine and Second-Time-Around showers (p. 50 and 40).
- Have the guest of honor picked up and delivered to your shower by limousine . . . as in The Elegant Shower (p. 54).

Other Ideas

Background stereo music, magician, clown, juggler, videotape of shower, audio recording of shower, handwriting analyst, on-the-spot computer bio-rhythm printout, craft and cooking demonstrations, synchronized swim program, horse and carriage ride, hay wagon ride, hot-air balloon ride.

TWELVE

Gift Guide

PARTY-GIVER GIFT

Here's a great party-giver gift! Purchase thank-you notes. Address an envelope to each guest and apply postage. Present these to the honored guest and tell him or her that each gift card and thank-you note will be tucked into the appropriate gift. When it's time to write thank-yous, half the work will be done. This gesture is especially appreciated because of the many details the couple is faced with before the wedding . . . as in Chapter 5, Shower Protocol (p. 103).

IDEAS FROM SHOWER THEMES

* When you're holding a kitchen shower, ask guests to include a favorite recipe with their gift . . . as in the Cookie Sampler Shower (p. 42).
* To direct gift-giving, the obvious solution is the wedding registry . . . as in the Wedding Registry Shower (p. 77) and Shower Protocol (p. 102).
* Want to hand down heirlooms at your shower? Make it meaningful . . . as in the Cherished Gift Shower (p. 79).
* Is the wedding couple getting married in another state? You can be there . . . as in the Postal Shower (p. 79).
* Every shower doesn't have to call for material gifts. Some people would rather give of themselves by offering their services . . . as in the Lend-a-Hand Shower (p. 80).

Other Ideas

* Home furnishings: towels, bathroom scale, pillows, bedspread, curtains, extension cords (regular and heavy duty), plants, hamper, flashlight, one box of miscellaneous household needs (scissor, twine, clear tape, masking tape, paper clips, index cards, hammer, screwdriver, screws, nails, tacks, picture hangers), cleaning supplies and rags, large box of rolls of toilet tissue, paper towels, or any paper product.
* Personal gifts for her: negligee, half-slip, camisole, costume jewelry, belt set, perfume, cosmetics, slippers, hostess robe, clothing storage bag, blow dryer, small clutch bag, travel alarm clock.
* Personal gifts for him: monogrammed pajamas, robe, slippers, travel alarm clock, shaving equipment, cuff

links, traveling toilet case, tie rack, comb-and-brush set, clothing storage bags, blow dryer, wallet.

- Gift from the group: toaster oven, blender, food processor, microwave oven, television set, wok set, toaster, portable vacuum cleaner, clock radio, lamp, card table and folding chairs, room divider, stack stools, stack tables, electric griddle, picnic basket with accessories, electric broom, shop vacuum, fireplace tools with canvas log tote, one-time general housecleaning service, well-stocked toolbox, drill, camping equipment, luggage, any substantial personal or personalized gift, barbecue set, dinner-for-two gift certificate, season tickets to opera, theater, symphony or sports event.
- Personalized gifts: engraved door knocker, paperweight, luggage tags, sterling bookmark, brass business card case or holder, silver bread and butter dishes, napkin rings, silverplated photo case, address labels, checkbook cover with stamped name, engraved key chain, personalized stationery, two inscribed champagne glasses, framed wedding invitation, initialed money clip, monogrammed sheets, pillow cases or towels.
- Miscellaneous: handmade articles (quilts, afghans, lingerie), brass or pewter items, health products (vitamins, herb teas, snacks), road atlas or travel books, auto plate holder.

THIRTEEN

Gift-wrap
Guide

IDEAS FROM SHOWER THEMES

- Tie in shower gifts for business associates with a wrap that matches their profession or department . . . as in the Office Co-Worker Shower (p. 60).
- When the wedding couple is apt to know what each gift package contains because of size or shape, turn the tables on them. Ask guests to use odd-size boxes or to wrap in unusual ways. Then make a guessing game of it with everyone participating . . . as in the Wedding Registry Shower (p. 77).

Other Ideas

- Buy personalized wrapping with the individual's name printed in stripes across the paper.

- Wrap large gifts in a paper tablecloth, either plain or with a wedding design.
- Use newspapers: *Wall Street Journal* for the executive; comics for a fun gift; grocery store ads for food gifts; hardware store ads for tools.
- Use wallpaper samples for a sturdy wrap, or shelf-lining paper for quick last-minute wrapping.
- Purchase gift bags or make fabric drawstring bags in the wedding party colors.
- Buy white boxes from a bakery and decorate with fancy ribbon or design them with colored marking pens.
- Make kitchen towel cakes, kitchen place mat cakes, or bath cakes. Roll up clothes to resemble a layer cake. Or ask for The Cloth Bakery cakes at your gift store. Much too pretty to wrap!
- Use large gifts as decorative wrapping for several smaller gifts: hamper with bathroom supplies; wicker basket with spices; laundry basket with grocery items.

FOURTEEN

Prizes Guide

KITCHEN GADGET SUGGESTIONS

Pie server, oval roast rack, double melon baller, plastic ladle, kitchen shears, pizza cutter, butter warmer, peg rack, measuring cup set, food server, hors d'oeuvres spreader, nylon scrubbers, vegetable peeler, cocktail forks, egg fry rings, two-way bottle caps, pastry blender, spaghetti tongs, napkin rings, magnetic hooks, apple divider, measuring spoon set, tomato slicer, acrylic honey twist, strawberry huller, whisk set, four-sided grater, garlic press, egg slicer, three-wheel pie crimper, scrapers, spatulas, funnel, plate hanger, Swedish meatballer, salad scissors, pastry brush, grapefuit spoons, ketchup saver, cookie spatula, set of scoops, can covers, cheese slicer, tea infuser, straw trivet, cake rack, soap octopus, hot pads.

PRIZE SUGGESTIONS FOR
MEN-ONLY SHOWERS

Small tools, key chain, batteries, razor blades, flashlight, sweat bands, combs, playing cards, nail clipper, pens.

PRIZE SUGGESTIONS FOR
WOMEN-ONLY SHOWERS

Scarf, perfume, combs, brush, teacup, headbands, purse organizer, herb teas, nail polish, sachet, box of all-occasion cards.

PRIZE SUGGESTIONS FOR
A COUPLE'S SHOWER

Tennis or golf balls, small sports supplies (tees, sweat bands), mug, mirror, soap balls, change holder, bookmark, sweat socks, shoelaces, tape measure, how-to books, carafe, coat hangers, jumbo clothes hook, feather duster, stationery supplies.

FIFTEEN

Unusual
Locations
Guide

Most showers are held in the home or in VFW
or similar club halls. Here are other places
for your consideration.

IDEAS FROM SHOWER THEMES

- Country club or golf club . . . as in The Elegant
  Shower (p. 53).
- Supper club, patio restaurant, or hotel/motel meeting rooms . . . as in the Second-Time-Around Shower
  (p. 40).
- Office conference room, company lunchroom or cafeteria . . . as in the Office Co-Worker Shower (p.
  60).
- Classroom or locker room . . . as in the No Sweat
  and Calorie Counter showers (pp. 71 and 65).

Other Ideas

- Enjoy the sunshine at a beach, lake, or pool.
- Park yourself in a park or picnic area with clean-up facilities.
- Rent a yacht, paddleboat, or houseboat.
- Rent a mansion, theater lobby, or public cafeteria.
- "Borrow" a greenhouse or flower garden.

Shower Theme Index

General Index